BUT NOT FORMIDABLE

A CLINT WOLF NOVEL
(BOOK 8)

BY

BJ BOURG

WWW.BJBOURG.COM

TITLES BY BJ BOURG

BUT NOT FORMIDABLE
A Clint Wolf Novel by BJ Bourg

This book is a work of fiction.
All names, characters, locations, and incidents are products of the author's imagination, or have been used fictitiously.
Any resemblance to actual persons living or dead, locales, or events is entirely coincidental.

Cover design by Christine Savoie of Bayou Cover Designs

PUBLISHED IN THE UNITED STATES OF AMERICA

CHAPTER 1

Tuesday, September 19
Mechant Loup Police Department

"Do we have a headcount of who will remain in town?" I asked my wife Susan Wilson Wolf, who was the chief of police for the small town of Mechant Loup, Louisiana. "From all accounts, this'll be a bad one—probably the worse this town has ever seen."

We had issued a mandatory evacuation order thanks to Hurricane Samson, a formidable Category 4 storm that was barreling down on us. Originally scheduled to hit the Florida panhandle as a Cat 3, the storm had taken an unexpected jog to the west yesterday and intensified overnight. We were squarely in its sights and landfall was scheduled for tomorrow afternoon. Based on the number of cars I'd seen on my drive to the station, about half of the townspeople had packed up and high-tailed it out of town.

"I don't know, Clint." Susan frowned somberly. "Only two or three families would admit to staying, but I have a feeling there will be more. You'd think people around here would've learned a thing or two from Hurricane Katrina, but there are still some who believe it'll never happen to them."

I knew she was right. We had made a pass through town earlier to knock on every door and warn our residents to evacuate, and a handful had told me they were staying put. I'd tried to talk them out of it, but they hadn't been moved by my pleas and horror stories. We couldn't forcibly drag them out of town, so our hands were tied for the most part. I'd be lying if I said I wasn't worried for them. From what I'd been told by a few old timers, Mechant Loup had never taken a direct hit from a Cat 4 hurricane, so it was anybody's guess how this place would hold up to the relentless pounding that was sure to come. If the citizens who stayed behind got into trouble during the height of the storm, they would be on their own—and I didn't like it.

I sighed as I listened to the rumbling overhead. Hurricane Samson was such an enormous storm—the largest of this very active hurricane season thus far—that the outer bands were already reaching town. I knew we had to convince as many people as possible to get out of here, but the longer they waited, the more dangerous it would be out on the highway. And if they didn't leave soon, it would be too late and they'd be force to sit tight and take their beating.

We had originally planned on making another round through town in a couple of hours to try and push more people out, but Susan decided we should head out earlier due to the latest track we'd seen on the Weather Channel.

"Are you ready?" she asked, standing and hitching up her gun belt. She wore green BDUs and her khaki polyester uniform shirt, and they fit her snugly. I just sat there grinning up at her for a moment. She cocked her head to the side. "What is it?"

"A uniform never looked so good."

It was her turn to grin. "You know, I never get tired of hearing you say that."

I stood to follow her out and Achilles, our black German shepherd, was instantly alert. I walked to where he had been relaxing in the corner and scratched his head, right between his large ears. "Sorry, big man, but I love you too much to let you go out in this weather," I said. "I'll see you when I get back."

I was almost certain I saw him frown.

"What about me?" Susan asked, feigning offense. "You mustn't love me if you're letting me go out in this weather."

"Oh, no, I love you lots—I just know you wouldn't listen to me."

"That's true."

I followed Susan down the hall and we stopped in front of my office, where Officer Melvin Saltzman's wife and daughter were setting up air mattresses. Melvin had tried to convince Claire to pack up Delilah and head north to a hotel, but Claire had refused. "I want to be where you are," she'd said stubbornly. "If you're going to ride this thing out, then I want to ride it out with you."

Afraid for their safety, Melvin had asked Susan if they could ride out the storm with us in the police department, which was built just for such occasions, and she'd allowed it. After our old police department building had burned to the ground about two years ago, the town council had acquired a spacious piece of property along Washington Avenue in the downtown district and built this new station. While it was only one-story, it was twelve feet off the ground. It was no secret we lived in hurricane country, and the council wanted to construct a building that would withstand even the most powerful of storms while also being flood-proof. I'd often joked that Samson himself couldn't knock this building to the ground, but when I heard the name of this hurricane I wasn't so sure anymore. I'd begun to pray I hadn't jinxed us.

"Hi, Mr. Clint," Delilah said, looking up at me with her large eyes. "You have a gun like Daddy."

"Yep, I have a gun like your daddy." I glanced down at the Beretta 9mm semi-automatic pistol in my pancake holster, which was different from Melvin's Glock 22 .40 caliber pistol. Like me, Melvin owned a number of reliable pistols and we used different ones for different jobs, but I hadn't carried my Glock 22 in a couple of years. I'd traded it for the Beretta 92FS after I'd used it to kill a man. While I'd had to kill more than one man in the line of duty, that one had been different—so different that I'd felt it best to retire the old Glock. It bore bad memories and possibly bad karma. Not that I was superstitious, but I figured I didn't need any help in the bad luck department.

Claire asked Susan if she thought we'd get lucky with the storm track, but Susan frowned. "The forecast gets more and more reliable the closer a hurricane gets to landfall, and they've got this one coming right through our front door."

"It's gonna come through the front door?" Delilah's little eyes were wide. "What if we lock it?"

Susan laughed. "No, no, it's just a figure of speech, honey."

"It's a fig leaf?" Delilah seemed more confused. "Mommy says we have a fig tree in our yard, but I didn't see no hurricanes."

Claire began explaining the expression to Delilah and Susan took that opportunity to make our escape. She glanced at me as we walked into the dispatcher's station. "Can you imagine me with kids? I'll have them all kinds of scared and confused."

"You'll be a great mother," I said warmly.

"You think?"

I nodded, then quickly looked away when I realized Melvin and Lindsey were staring at us. I nodded in their direction. "How's it going?"

Melvin pushed a New Orleans Saints ball cap high on his shaved head. "About as good as it can be with a monster storm breathing down our backside."

Lindsey's hands were pressed against her face and her fingernails looked to be bleeding from her chewing them off. "Do you think we'll make it out of here alive?"

"We'll be fine," Susan said. "This building can withstand a missile attack."

Lindsey didn't look convinced.

Susan turned to Melvin. "Do you have a twenty (location) on Takecia, Amy, and Baylor?"

Takecia Gayle and Baylor Rice usually worked the day shift, while Amy Cooke and Melvin worked nights. During emergency situations, it was all hands on deck and we slept in rotations, when and where we could.

"Baylor's helping Takecia board up the last of the windows at her house," Melvin explained, "and Amy's stocking the lunch room with bread and water."

Susan was just starting to speak again when a rumbling noise sounded from outside. She clamped her mouth shut and we all stared up at the ceiling, where the fan shook. The building quivered. The lights blinked.

"What the hell was that?" I started making my way to the exit. The earth trembled some more and I quickened my pace.

All of a sudden, the phone began ringing like crazy and the lines lit up like Celebration in the Oaks, a popular New Orleans Christmas tradition. Lindsey snatched up the handset and smashed one of the buttons. "Mechant Loup Police—wait, what?"

I was just entering the lobby when I heard her suck in her breath behind me. I sucked in mine, too, when I saw how dark it was outside. I tried to push the door open, but it seemed stuck. Rain was whipping against the glass and it seemed to be swirling. I swallowed and my ears popped.

This ain't good! Realization hit me just as Lindsey began screaming from her work station.

"Susan! Clint! It's a tornado!" There was real panic in her voice. "A tornado just touched down near the middle school and they said it's still moving!"

I forced the door open and was nearly swept off of the landing at the top of the concrete stairs.

"Where are you going, Clint?" Susan hollered from behind me. "You could be killed!"

"The tornado's heading away from us," I said, watching as an object swirled in the distant sky. It looked like an animal. A dog perhaps? "I need to head that way in case people are injured."

"Not without me!" Susan nearly ran me over as I was making my way down the stairs, clutching the railing as I made my descent. I heard Melvin chomping on our heels.

Once we hit the landing at the bottom of the stairs, Melvin headed for his F-250 pickup truck and Susan followed me to my unmarked Tahoe. I fired it up and sped out of the parking area, keeping my eyes on the sky as I drove. At any moment, that wicked finger stretching from the clouds to the ground could change direction and whip around toward us. I wasn't afraid to die, but I could think of more attractive ways to go rather than being hurled through space on the violent winds of a tornado.

When I reached the end of Washington Avenue, I headed south on Back Street toward the Mechant Loup Middle School, which was about four blocks away. While school had been cancelled for the week, there were a lot of houses in the area and I knew at least a few families said they were staying behind. I was hoping they were okay.

"I bet they wish they'd left now," I said out loud, gripping the steering wheel anxiously. I couldn't see the tornado anymore. The sky had gone completely dark and the temperature had fallen sharply. Strong gusts of wind bullied my SUV, rocking it from side to side as I drove.

"There!" Susan pointed to the left as we reached the old service station that was located at the corner of Back Street and Library Way. "The tornado crossed the road right there."

She was correct. A wide path of destruction had been carved out of the trees along the bayou side. I turned right onto Library Way, half expecting all of the houses to be gone, but they weren't. Slightly to the left of us, I could see the roof of the school and it seemed to be damaged. A small car had been rolled up on its side. A white house with green shutters had been hit hard. The front porch had been ripped from the house and it rested in a heap in the middle of Library Way.

The rest of the neighborhood seemed to have been spared, except for a dozen mailboxes, several cars, and even more fence posts. Thankfully, the tornado had taken the path of least resistance and followed the center of the street.

"I hope no one was on that porch when it hit," Susan said, shoving her door open when I coaxed the Tahoe to a stop. As she rushed forward to check the pile of debris that used to be the porch, I got on my radio and asked all of our units to call in with their status.

"I'm Code Four (all is well), on the east side," Amy called. "The tornado traveled across Bayou Tail, jumped East Main, tore through a patch of cane fields, and crossed Cypress Highway. It cut a wide swath through the fields to the east, but it's gone now. It's no longer a threat to anyone."

"We're Code Four," Takecia said in her thick Jamaican accent. "No damage on the north side."

Melvin had just driven through a ditch on the south side of Library Way to avoid the porch in the middle of the street. Once he was past it, he hollered out of his window that he was going check on the school.

"It's closed," Susan hollered back.

"But I saw a car parked out back earlier." Melvin waved and shot off, heading to the back of the school property.

I groaned when we approached the rubble. "I don't hear any noise, so it's either empty or the people inside are dead."

Susan dropped to her knees and scooted under the edge of the awning. "It's clear," she called, "no casualties—well, except for a stuffed bear."

Next, we headed toward the damaged house and made our way through a hole in the south wall. We checked every room and closet. There was no one inside. We stepped back out into the rain and wind and began making our way on foot, checking every house down the street. A dozen or so townspeople were starting to step gingerly from their homes, all of them looking skyward.

"It sounded like a train," one elderly woman said when we stopped to check on her and four other family members. "I...I thought we were all going to die. I thought I heard a woman screaming, but my husband told me it was just the wind. Dear Lord, it was so scary."

I pursed my lips, wanting to ask her why in hell's name hadn't they evacuated, but I kept my mouth shut and let Susan handle her business. I was the town's chief of detectives, which meant I was chief of myself, and this wasn't a criminal matter, so it was none of my business.

"There's still time to get you and your family to a shelter," Susan was saying as I walked away. "I can get a bus here from ..."

Susan's voice faded as the distance between us grew. I'd noticed something out of place in the football field to the south of us, and I was slowly gravitating in that direction.

I wiped rain water from my face and shivered as a cold drop found its way under my collar, slid down the nape of my neck, and then down the center of my back. My radio scratched to life and Melvin's voice boomed through the speaker.

"The school's clear, the car's gone, and no one's inside." There was a pause, and then he said, "We're lucky class wasn't in session. This could've gone bad."

I nodded idly, my gaze fixed on the object as I drew closer. It was red, but that was all I could tell from twenty yards away. *Is it a toy? Did it fly all the way over here from the house?*

Tornados had a way of snatching things high up in the air and then depositing them far away. They were evil like that. I was within a few feet of the object when it came into perfect view. I stopped dead in my tracks and a cold finger of dread traced its way down my spine. It was a woman's red shoe with a flat sole, and it hadn't been there long. I knelt beside it so I could visually examine it—

The ringing of my phone distracted me and I pulled it from the back pocket of my slacks. "Go," I said.

"What're you doing on the fifty-yard line?" It was Susan.

I glanced over my shoulder to see her staring at me from the shoulder of the road.

"I didn't realize middle school football meant so much to you," she continued. "When you're done praying to the football Gods, maybe we can get back to work."

"Well, that lady heard a woman scream and I just found a woman's shoe in the middle of the field—and there's no body attached to it."

CHAPTER 2

Thirty minutes later…

"Over here!" Amy called over the radio. "I found the other shoe."

I whipped my head around from where I'd been searching along Oak Lane. I couldn't see Amy, but I knew she had been searching the area between the school and the football field. I made my way east through The Tunnel, acorns crunching under my boots as I strode along.

The Tunnel was a narrow street that extended from the football field east to Main Street. It was given the name by the townspeople, thanks to the giant oak trees that lined either side of the street. Over the years, the branches had extended upward and outward and had come together to form a thick canopy overhead, forever casting the paved lane in thick shadows, making it look like a tunnel. It was even darker and more eerie now, as dark clouds continued to move in from the Gulf and thunder grumbled loudly above the canopy.

I wondered what on earth a pair of shoes would be doing out there in that weather, and I was scared for the woman who owned them.

Susan called my phone and asked if I'd heard the transmission.

"I did," I said. "I'm heading there now."

"One shoe might be discarded trash, but two shoes could mean someone was out here." Susan paused, and I knew what she was thinking. "We might be dealing with a missing person."

The branches overhead creaked as the force of the wind shoved them roughly around. I took a cautious glance upward. "Have we received any calls?"

"Lindsey said she received a dozen complaints about the tornado, but, other than that, all's quiet in town."

I had reached the end of The Tunnel and saw Amy standing near the outdoor basketball court. "Did you get the latest forecast?"

"Yeah," Susan said. "The storm sped up. I don't think it's safe for anyone to get on the road now, so whoever's left in town will be forced to ride it out."

I agreed with her and hung up when I reached Amy. She pointed to a shoe that lay sideways at the edge of the wet court. Although it had stopped raining, the wind was still blowing something fierce and the shoe was rocking slightly from side to side. It was easy to see that the shoe was the exact same type and color as the one from the football field, but I checked my phone, comparing the picture I'd taken of the first one to the one on the ground. Sure enough, it was the same shoe, except the one I'd found was a left and Amy's one was a right—a perfect pair.

"What size is it?" I asked.

"A seven."

"Same size." I rubbed my chin, scanning our surroundings. "Did you check the school?"

Amy pushed a lock of blonde hair out of her face, but the wind blew it right back where it was. "All the doors and windows are locked, but there's a hole in the roof that was obviously caused by the tornado. I talked to Melvin and he said there was a car parked in back of the school earlier, but it's gone now."

"What kind was it?"

"He said it was an older model Lexus, dark blue."

I wondered if the person wearing the shoe had come from the school or the neighborhood. I pulled my radio from the clip on my belt and contacted Lindsey, asked her to find a number for the principal. Within seconds, she was patching me through to his cell phone.

"His name is Kevin Shelton," Lindsey said as the phone rang. "He was old when I attended middle school, so I can't believe he's still alive."

I detected a hint of humor in her voice, and thanked her for connecting me to the man. I introduced myself when Kevin answered, and told him the school had been hit by a tornado.

"I'm sorry," Kevin said, "I can't hear you over the wind on your side."

I scanned my surroundings and noticed two outbuildings a few dozen yards from the basketball court. I hurried in that direction and squeezed between them, shielding myself from the strong winds that were whipping all around us.

"Can you hear me now?"

"Yeah, that's better."

I repeated the news that a tornado had hit the school. "There appears to be some roof damage, but for the most part, the building seems to be okay. I'm calling because we found a woman's shoe in the middle of the football field and another one on the outdoor basketball court."

"A woman's shoe?"

"Yeah, do you know if any employees from the school would be out here today?"

"Oh, no. We released the students and faculty yesterday morning and advised everyone to evacuate. No one should've been there today."

"Do you have a key to the place?" I asked. "We'd like to check it out just to be sure."

"I do, and I'd love to help, but we're in Arkansas. I packed up my wife and we left yesterday at noon. We decided to take advantage of the days off and came to Hot Springs to visit my daughter."

"Does anyone else have access to the school?"

"I mean, each teacher has a key, but they should all be heading out of town."

I pushed a hand against the nearest wall as a gust of wind found its way between the buildings and rocked me. The clouds overhead were active and I kept looking for another funnel cloud. "Do you have contact information for the teachers? Something you can forward to my phone?"

"I do." There was a pause and I heard him mumbling in the background. When he came back on the phone, he said he had accessed his contacts and could send an attachment. "Can I send the employee list to this number?"

"Yes, sir. I appreciate it."

"I don't know how much good it'll do, because they should all be on the road by now."

"I understand." After talking for a few more seconds, I ended the call and rejoined Amy, who had recovered the shoe and secured it in an evidence bag.

"If we don't find the rightful owner, I want them," she said. "They're my size."

I grinned idly, wondering if Susan was okay. Last I heard she and Melvin were making the rounds through town, searching for any more damage and possible casualties.

"Have you heard from Susan?" I asked Amy as we walked toward our vehicles.

"I heard her on the radio when you were talking to the principal. She's going door-to-door locking down the town. Cig's was still open, so she had to shut the place down and send the owner home."

Cig's Gas Station was the only gas station/convenience store combination in town, and it was located off of Main Street near the Mechant Loup Bridge.

"Did they jack up the price of gasoline?"

"Nah, I don't think so. If they had, she'd be heading to the station with a prisoner."

Amy was right. Susan wouldn't tolerate price gouging from anyone. While waiting to receive the employee list from the principal, I walked to the back of my SUV and grabbed a length of chain. Amy helped me secure one end to the remnants of the porch that rested in the middle of Library Way, and the other end to my back bumper.

I gave the chain one last tug to make sure it wouldn't come free, glanced up at Amy. "Ready?"

She nodded eagerly and waited while I slipped into the driver's seat. I dropped the gearshift in *neutral*, turned the toggle switch to four-wheel-drive. I then slowly applied pressure to the accelerator and kept an eye on my side mirror, where I could see Amy. She nodded as my SUV moved forward, letting me know all was well. I felt the chain jerk as the links shook out and the full weight of the twisted mess of lumber came to bear.

"It's moving," Amy called out, "so keep it going. You're doing great!"

I did, and angled my Tahoe toward the northern shoulder of the street. The wind was so strong it rocked my vehicle as I inched toward Back Street. I glanced in my side mirror again and saw Amy's hair being thrown violently about her face. I looked toward the sky, half expecting to see another tornado bearing down on us. The clouds were dark and ominous and they seemed to be getting worse, but I didn't detect another tornado.

"We need to get this out of the way and get our asses to the police department," I hollered out of the window. "It's getting more and more dangerous."

Amy nodded her agreement.

I continued dragging the heap down the street until I reached the old service station parking lot. I backed up to allow some slack in the chain so we could disconnect it. I dismounted and was struggling with the end that was wrapped around the porch when my phone rang in my pocket. I didn't want to stop what I was doing, but I knew the call had to be important.

"I've got it," Amy said, rushing to take over. The muscles in her slender arms rippled as she jerked on the loose end of the chain. "It's probably Susan."

"Hey, this is Clint," I said when I saw it was the police department. I had to press the phone tightly to my ear. "What's going on?"

"We just received a call about a missing person," Lindsey said. "A man called to say his daughter told his wife she was going to work this morning and they haven't heard from her yet. He heard there was a tornado in town and he wanted to know if anyone got hurt. I told him there were no casualties or injuries and that seemed to calm his fears."

I used my hand to shield the mouthpiece of my phone from the wind. Every now and then, droplets of rain sprayed over me.

"Where does his daughter work?"

"He didn't say. He got real agitated when I asked for more information. He said I was wasting time and I needed to get someone out to his house right away. He said she was in danger and I needed to stop jacking him around. When I tried to explain that the information would assist the responding officers, he hung up the phone."

"Where does he live?"

"I was going to dispatch Takecia, but Susan's got them doing house checks."

"It's okay. What's the address?"

Lindsey gave me the man's address and the name of his missing daughter. I jotted the information in the notes section of my cell phone. I then quickly tucked it away and helped Amy as she tossed the rest of the chain into the back of my vehicle.

"I've got to go," I told her when we were done. "Someone's gone missing."

"Who?"

"A girl named Elizabeth Bankston. She supposedly went to work this morning and never returned."

"But every business in town is closed."

"That's what I thought, too."

Amy told me she was going find Susan, and I jumped into my Tahoe, sped away. The clouds seemed lower and the wind gusts were growing in intensity. I flipped on the radio to get an update on the storm and it wasn't hard to find one. Every station was covering it nonstop. Just as the radio announcer began giving the latest coordinates, the Emergency Broadcast System was activated, announcing that we were under a tornado warning until eleven tonight. I'd heard enough to know that the projected path of the hurricane still took it right through our back door, it had sped up a little, and it would make landfall a little before noon.

I glanced at the dash clock. Almost three o'clock. I needed to get moving. Once darkness fell, it would be too dangerous to be outdoors—not just for the missing woman, but for all of us—and in this weather, darkness would come long before eight o'clock.

CHAPTER 3

"Elizabeth said she was going to the school to save the books," said Charlie Detiveaux. He was a tall man and he had some meat on his bones, but he walked gingerly, like he suffered from back problems. When I'd first arrived at his house, he had introduced himself as Beaver Detiveaux's first cousin. He hadn't seemed bothered by the fact that I had once replaced Beaver as chief of police, back before I'd resigned. Either that or he didn't realize who I was.

"She's a teacher and part-time librarian at the middle school and those books are her life," Charlie continued. "I tried to stop her—to convince her it wasn't safe—but she said she had to move all the books on the bottom shelf to the top shelf. She's an adult now, and she doesn't really listen to us anymore."

"The school flooded several years ago," said Cynthia Detiveaux, who sat at the kitchen table wringing her hands. "The school lost every book on the bottom shelf; hundreds of them. Lizzie wasn't working there at the time, but she'd heard about it and she swore it would never happen while she worked there."

I copied what they said onto my notepad. "Does she live here?"

"Oh, no," Charlie said. "She lives in the apartments on the east side. She called this morning to see if we were evacuating and she told me she was heading to the school."

"Were y'all planning to evacuate?" I asked.

The man rubbed his face with a hand that shook. "I can't sit for too long, so a car ride is out of the question. Plus, we really can't afford it."

"Besides, we rode out Katrina in New Orleans," Cynthia said, "and that was a Category 5, so we're not really worried. Well, we weren't worried until we heard about the tornado. Are you sure there were no injuries? I thought the tornado passed by the school, and that's where Lizzie went."

I nodded, wondering what kind of shoes Elizabeth might've been wearing when she left her house. "We checked the entire street and one of our officers followed the path of the tornado, but we weren't able to find any casualties."

"Maybe she took cover in the school and she's waiting for someone to come along and check on her," Cynthia suggested, but she was shot down by her husband.

"Not my girl," Charlie said, shaking his head. "She doesn't wait for anyone. If something needs to be done, she goes and does it."

As the wind howled outside and an occasional gust rattled the shutters, Cynthia continued wringing her hands and fretting. "Well, maybe she got stuck inside the school. Did y'all search it?"

"We couldn't get inside because everything was locked up tight, but there was a car there earlier. What does Elizabeth drive?"

"It's blue, but I'm not sure what kind it is—it's something fancy. All I know is she bought it secondhand and, although it's an older model, she loves that car." Charlie fished his cell phone from his pocket and messed with it for a minute. When he found what he was looking for, he turned it so I could see. "This is a picture of her the day she bought it."

I took the phone and studied the image. It was a Facebook post from an Elizabeth Bankston, and it was dated two years ago. She was posing with a saleswoman near the driver's side door of a blue Lexus. "This car was at the school earlier today," I said. "The good news is that it's gone, so she must've left in it."

Charlie exhaled in relief. "Thank God. I was really starting to worry."

"But why isn't she answering our calls?" Cynthia asked, addressing the question to her husband.

Charlie just sighed, not having an answer for her.

I didn't have an answer either, so I asked if Elizabeth had been planning on evacuating.

Charlie nodded. "She said they're heading north to her in-laws just as soon as her husband gets home from work."

"Where does he work?"

"Offshore. They're flying his crew inland because of the storm." Charlie glanced at his wife, who was fidgeting in her chair. He turned back in my direction. "They originally thought the storm was heading for Florida, so he was going to stay on the rig. Everything just happened so quick, it caught all of us off guard."

I nodded knowingly. We'd all been caught off guard when the storm made its sudden turn to the west.

"What's her husband's name?" I asked, wondering if he might've made it home and they were spending some alone time together before hitting the road. Elizabeth could've turned off her phone for some privacy. I certainly didn't like my phone ringing when I was making love to Susan.

"Steve…Steve Bankston."

"Have you tried calling him?" I asked.

Cynthia nodded. "It goes straight to voicemail."

Charlie waved his hand dismissively. "He won't have service while he's out in the Gulf. When I worked on the rigs, I couldn't make a call until we were over land."

I asked more standard questions, including what Elizabeth was wearing when she left home. Since Elizabeth didn't live with them anymore, they hadn't seen her when she left for the school. Once I had everything I needed, I collected contact information for Elizabeth, Steve, and the Detiveauxs, then stood to leave.

"Is that it?" Cynthia's mouth was open in dismay. "You're just going to leave? What about Elizabeth?"

I shot my thumb over my shoulder, in the direction of the front door, where the rain had started falling again. The rain bands were becoming more frequent and increasing in intensity. "I'm going out there to find your daughter—storm or no storm."

"Oh, thank God! Thank you so much!"

I paused with my hand on the door, thinking about the shoe. *Should I…?*

I pursed my lips and turned back to face the couple, reaching for my phone. "I want to show y'all something."

They both jumped to their feet, Cynthia asking, "Is it something to do with Elizabeth?"

"I don't know if it means anything," I warned. "We just found a pair of shoes out by the football field and I wanted—"

"What size?" Cynthia asked quickly.

"Seven."

She threw a hand to her mouth, glanced at Charlie. "Oh, God, that's her size."

"Lots of people wear a size seven," Charlie said, but his face had turned a shade lighter.

"It could mean nothing." I tried to sound reassuring as I scrolled to the image. I decided to leave out the minor detail about the woman screaming. "Like I said, it's just a pair of shoes on the ground—there was no evidence of foul play or anything."

Cynthia stood there ringing her hands and nodding in anticipation.

I studied her for a second, then turned the phone so she could view the image. Her scream was so loud it pierced my ears like a gunshot. She lunged forward and began pounding my chest with her fists, screaming, "No! No! Not my baby girl!"

Charlie moved as fast as he could in slow motion and tried to pull her off of me. I reassured him it was okay, and I just stood there letting Cynthia beat on me.

Well, those are definitely Elizabeth's shoes, I thought wryly. *The only question is: Where the hell is Elizabeth?*

CHAPTER 4

I had almost reached the east side of town when Susan called to ask where I was.

"We're all at the station," she said, "and you need to get your ass down here, too. The weather's getting worse by the minute. It's not safe out there."

That was no joke. It wasn't even four o'clock yet and it was already dark as night. The rain pelting my windshield was so voluminous that my wipers couldn't keep up. All I saw in front of me was a blurred mess of blacktop and buildings. My headlights were no match for the elements and looked about as effective as the flashlight feature on my cell phone. I almost missed the turn for the bridge that connected the west side with the east side, but saw it just in time.

"I've got to find this woman," I said. "If she's out here alone, she's in grave danger."

"Clint, it's too dangerous." Susan's voice was pleading. "We're under a tornado warning and a hurricane watch."

"I have to check out her apartment and then I'll come in."

"Promise?"

"I love you."

"But do you promise—?"

I ended the call, squinted as I reached the other side of the bridge and looked both ways. I couldn't really tell if any cars were coming, but I knew there shouldn't be any, so I quickly pulled onto East Main Street, heading right. When I reached the intersection with East Coconut, I turned left and drove to Cypress Highway, where I headed north.

The Bayou View Apartments were a mile down the highway, but

I began to wonder if I would make it. The trees on the eastern shoulder of Cypress Highway were being whipped around like sugarcane in a strong wind. My head was on a swivel, trying to spot any trees that had the potential to come down. I'd heard of more than a few people being crushed to death in their vehicles by falling trees, and some of them had been police officers.

I relaxed my grip on the steering wheel when the entrance to Bayou View Lane came into view. I was happy to put some distance between me and those trees. Glancing at my notebook on the seat beside me, I turned onto the wide and winding street. Large apartment buildings with three units each lined both sides of the street. According to Elizabeth's mom, she lived in the last building on the right, and her apartment was the middle one.

I cruised down the center of the complex, searching the buildings as I drove. A few porch lights were on and several cars were parked in front of some of the units, but, other than that, there were no signs of life. I had to swerve around a large garbage can that had been blown into the street, and continued toward the back. When I arrived at the last building, I let out a long sigh of relief. An older model blue Lexus was parked in the space in front of the middle unit.

She's probably taking a long hot bath and turned her phone off, I thought. *This is almost over.*

I parked behind the car and snatched my raincoat from the back seat. After I'd shrugged into it, I stepped out into the downpour. I didn't bother hurrying, and actually slowed near the Lexus to look inside. Everything seemed intact. I continued to the front door and knocked. It was a hollow core door and the knock was louder than I'd meant, but then I figured it was probably necessary over the sounds of the grumbling thunder and hammering rain.

I waited about a minute and then knocked again, this time harder. I was as far under the overhang as I could get, but the rain was still able to reach me. My pant legs were drenched and I cursed myself for not getting my rain bottoms from the police department. I made a mental note to load them in my Tahoe when I got back.

A third knock met with the same results—nothing. I scratched my head. Had she evacuated already? If so, why was her car still here? I hurried back to my Tahoe and jumped inside, slamming the door quickly. Water dripped freely from my raincoat. Careful not to wet the pages of my notebook, I leaned over, located the cell number for Steve Bankston, and called it.

"Damn it!" It had gone straight to voicemail. Next, I called Charlie Detiveaux and told him what I'd found.

"Go inside and see if she's there, for God's sake." His voice was laced with panic. "She's got to be inside. Maybe she's in trouble."

"Absent an emergency situation, I need permission to break into someone's home without a warrant."

"This *is* an emergency—she's missing!"

"I understand what you're saying, but I still need permission to enter."

"Well, damn it, I give you my permission."

I hesitated. Elizabeth was an adult who lived in her own place with her husband, so her father couldn't give me permission to break into her apartment. If he chose to do it, that was one thing, but I wasn't allowed to ask him to break in. Hell, even if I could, I certainly didn't want him out in this weather. An idea suddenly came to me.

"I'll call you back, Mr. Detiveaux." Without waiting for his response, I ended the call and got on the line with Lindsey.

"Thank God you're okay," she said. "We've all been worried sick about you."

I didn't acknowledge her statement. Instead, I gave her the name of the company for whom Steve Bankston worked and asked her to contact their dispatch center. "Ask them to contact the pilot of the chopper he's in and relay a message to him. First, find out if he's heard from Elizabeth. If not, I need his permission to search his apartment, because her parents are concerned for her safety. Let him know they're probably just being paranoid, but we want to check it out just to be on the safe side."

Lindsey mumbled to herself for a moment, then said, "Got it. I'll call you right back."

I shoved my phone in my pocket and stepped out of my Tahoe again. I went to the apartment unit on the left first, knocked for several minutes. No one came to the door. I then went to the apartment on the right, but met with the same results. I couldn't be upset, because we had issued a stern warning for all of our citizens to leave town. At least most of them had heeded that warning.

Pulling my hood down low over my face, I stepped off of the concrete and made my way through the sloppy ground, heading for the back of the building. When I reached the back patio of the center unit, I jumped a little metal fence and approached the back sliding door. There were vertical blinds hanging inside the doorway, but they were slightly open.

Although there was a roof on the patio, it didn't keep the whipping rain from reaching the window. I wiped the glass as best I could and cupped both hands over a portion of the glass to keep it clear. Pressing my face into my cupped hands, I peered inside. Thanks to the low light conditions outside, it was coal black on the inside.

"She can't be home," I said aloud. "If so, there'd be at least a little light glowing from the inside."

I made my way back to the front and climbed into my Tahoe to wait for Lindsey. Water dripped from my raincoat and spilled all over the interior of my vehicle.

Before Lindsey could call back, I received a text message from Susan begging me to come in out of the weather. I texted back to say I would turn in just as soon as I found out if Elizabeth was inside. She responded with a picture of Achilles, who looked despondent, and she sent a message saying he missed me. I smiled, texted back that she was not fighting fair.

I was still smiling and looking at the picture when Lindsey called.

"I got in touch with him and he said you can go in." She took a breath. "It wasn't easy getting through to him, but I finally did. It seems the helicopter he's on was diverted to Lake Charles because of the rain bands moving in, so that's why he hasn't made it home yet."

I processed that information quickly. "If he's being diverted to Lake Charles, he won't be coming home until the storm blows over."

"Yeah." She sighed. "He's really upset about that. I told him what you said about her parents probably being paranoid, but he's freaking out."

"I guess that means he hasn't heard from her."

"I asked, but he doesn't have cell service yet. They're still out over the western Gulf of Mexico. He said he'll try calling as soon as they reach land."

I thanked her and quickly stepped from my SUV—pry bar in one hand and flashlight in the other—and headed for the front door.

CHAPTER 5

Before causing any damage, I searched for a hidden key. Either she didn't have one, or I wasn't a good enough burglar. When I thought I'd spent too much time searching, I moved to the front window and popped the screen off. I slid the blade of the pry bar under the lower edge of the window and applied pressure. To my surprise, the window slid open easily. I shrugged, moved the tail of my raincoat and shoved the pry bar in my back pocket.

Reaching through the window, I pushed the blinds aside and shined my light into the room. I kept my right hand near my pistol just in case. When everything appeared safe, I slid through the window hands first and pulled my feet under me on the other side. I found myself in a simple living room. There was a cloth-covered sofa, matching loveseat and chair, a glass coffee table, and a flat screen television that was propped up on an old entertainment center.

Not wanting to surprise Elizabeth if she was home, I called out, announcing my presence and my authority. I received no response. I walked straight forward where the living room extended into a small dining room, cut the corner and found myself in an even tinier kitchen. I checked the sink and found a bowl, spoon, cup, and butter knife inside. A loaf of bread was on the counter near the toaster, and I figured she must have had breakfast before heading out.

Using my flashlight to illuminate the house, I continued on, moving down a narrow hallway next. There was a bathroom to the right, and a quick check revealed it was empty. When I reached the end of the hall, I stopped near the front door and cocked my head to the side. There was a wooden key rack on the wall to the left of the door, and from one of the hooks hung a set of keys with a Lexus emblem. I reached over and pressed the panic button on the keyless remote and frowned when the horn on the blue Lexus began blowing. I quickly shut it off.

"So, Elizabeth Bankston, you made it home after all." I turned the corner, where a flight of carpeted steps led from the door to the second level. I moved upstairs next and checked all three bedrooms, the bathroom, and four closets. There was no sign of Elizabeth.

I scowled, wondering where she could've gone. Her toothbrush was still on the counter in the bathroom and there were no dirty clothes in the hamper. I checked all of her shoes and none of them were wet. I did notice that they were all size sevens, except for a pair of cowgirl boots that were an eight.

I called Susan and told her Elizabeth wasn't home.

"But I thought you said her car was there?"

"It is and the keys are even hanging on a hook near the door, but she's not here."

"Do you think someone came by and picked her up?"

"If they did, she didn't plan on staying the night, because her toothbrush is still here."

"Maybe she has a night bag with a travel toothbrush."

Leave it to Susan to think of that. "I guess that's possible."

"It could even be a spare key on the hook."

Another possibility, but I didn't admit it out loud.

"What about her purse?" she asked.

"What about it?"

"Did you find it?"

"No."

"Well, that's a good sign."

"You think?"

"Oh, yeah. If you find a woman's purse but don't find her, that's almost a sure sign of foul play. If her purse isn't around, then it must be with her...wherever she is."

"I'm going to check the car."

"And then you're getting your ass into this hurricane-proof building—right?"

"Sure," I said idly, puzzled over Elizabeth's whereabouts. I dropped my phone into my pocket and hurried down the stairs. After snatching up the keys, I stepped outside and lowered my head against the driving rain. The hood on my raincoat did little to keep the rain off of my face and hair. Once I hit the *unlock* button, I forced the back passenger door open—the wind fought hard to keep it closed—and slid inside. I didn't want to enter through the driver door in case something had happened to Elizabeth.

I was so used to riding in trucks and SUVs that it felt like I was sitting on the ground. It was uncomfortable, but I managed to lean forward and study the front seat without disturbing any evidence that might have been there. As it turned out, nothing was there—at least not that I could see with my naked eyes—no purse, no keys, nothing.

After I'd scanned every inch of the front passenger area with my flashlight, I plopped against the back seat. I sat there for a few minutes, listening as the rain pounded the roof. The Lexus swayed roughly in the wind and I allowed my eyes to slide shut as I considered all the possibilities.

The most likely scenario was that she'd left with a friend to seek higher ground. If so, why hadn't she called her parents or her husband? And why wasn't she answering her phone? Of course, I had to acknowledge a second possibility—that she was two-timing Steve. If that's what was going on, then she could've run off to safety with her lover. Hell, she might be using the storm to cover her tracks. It wouldn't be the first time a man came home to find the house empty and his wife gone, and I'm sure it wouldn't be the last. That might also explain why she hadn't called her husband. But why wouldn't she call her parents?

I opened my eyes and stared straight ahead, wanting to believe she was either with a friend or a boyfriend, because the third option was bad. In the third scenario that played out in my mind, someone had chased her around the school grounds, killed her, and then stole her car. But why drive it to her house and just leave it? And why put the keys back on the hook? If theft was the motive, the thieves would've had the apartment to themselves and could've emptied it out.

I suddenly sat upright. Whoever brought the car back either had a ride or lived in the complex. If they did live in the complex, they could be scoping me out right now. I tried to peer out the back and side windows, but they were fogged up. After taking one last look to make sure there was no blood in the front seat, I exited and locked it up tight. I then locked the apartment, but took the keys with me. If the third scenario was the correct one, I didn't want the killers coming back to take the car. I was tempted to have the car towed to a secure location, but two things stopped me—first, I wouldn't be able to get a tow truck out here until the storm passed, and second, I didn't have probable cause to confiscate it.

I was backing out of the parking spot when I glanced back at the car. I stopped and quickly jumped out, went straight for the back of the car. My heart had begun pounding in my chest the very second the thought of finding Elizabeth in her trunk occurred to me, and it got worse the closer I got to the car.

Before I reached the back of the car, I hit the *trunk release* button and it popped free. My heart fell when I shoved it all the way open. While there was no body in the trunk, there *was* a woman's purse, a raincoat, an umbrella, and a school ID card.

"Damn it! This woman's dead."

CHAPTER 6

I pulled out my cell phone to take pictures of the contents of the trunk, but water dripped down my hands and shoulders and leaked into the trunk. I quickly shut it, stared around. There were no overhangs under which to drive the car and no tow trucks would come out in this weather. I could tow it with my Tahoe, but that would require a second driver, and I didn't want to risk anyone else's life.

Left with no other choices, I retrieved a tarp from the back of my Tahoe and set about draping it over the trunk so I could record the evidence as best I could before recovering it. As I held on to one end of the tarp, the opposite end flapped in the wind like a runaway flag. It whipped violently around and I nearly lost my grip on it.

Cursing loudly, I continued fighting to secure it, but I finally realized it wasn't going to happen. Frustrated, I rolled the wet tarp into a ball and tossed it into the back of my Tahoe. An idea came to me and I left the gate up on my SUV and jumped into the driver's seat. I drove out of the parking spot and turned my SUV around until the back of my vehicle was lined up with the back of Elizabeth's. Watching the reverse display carefully, I began backing slowly toward the Lexus. The back-up alarm beeped once, but I kept going. It beeped again and again as I drew closer and closer. Finally, it started screaming at me to stop. When it appeared that my bumper was about to brush against the bumper of the Lexus, I pressed the brake and shoved the gearshift in *Park*.

I was just squeezing through the crack in the front seats when my radio scratched to life. It was Susan and she was asking for my location. I arched my back and reached for the radio on my center console.

"I'm a bit twisted at the moment," I called. "I'll ring your cell in a minute."

She didn't answer and I knew she was probably worried silly about me. I hated disappointing her, but I had to find Elizabeth before the hurricane made landfall. Even at this moment we were in danger of losing any evidence that might be out here, but it would be worse once the hurricane blew through the area.

I dropped the radio and turned back around, lunged over the second row of seats in my Tahoe. I scrambled on my hands and knees to the edge of the cargo area, pushing my way through crime scene boxes and rifle cases. The gate provided a little cover from the rain, but not much. I'd have to work fast.

I grabbed my camera from the crime scene box and held it high against the open gate, where there was little exposure to the rain. I then hit the *Unlock* button on the keyless remote and snapped a few pictures as the trunk opened. When I had enough photos to document the exact location of the purse and other items within the trunk, I pulled on a pair of latex gloves and quickly retrieved the items. I leaned out and slammed the trunk shut and then retreated into the cargo area of my Tahoe, pulling the gate shut behind me.

Balancing on my knees, I dug out some evidence bags and secured the purse, raincoat, umbrella, and school ID card. When I was done, I smashed the *Lock* button on the keyless remote and scurried back to the driver's seat. I sat there for a moment studying the keys in my hand. There was a large gold key on the ring that looked official. *This has to be the key to the school.*

I gritted my teeth as I stared out the dark windshield. I couldn't see much of anything, so I turned the high beams on. It didn't do much good. They were like fireflies in a dark cave—not much help at all. The street lights and porch lights were almost invisible in the sheets of driving rain. Still, I had to find Elizabeth and I needed to find her ASAP. As dangerous as it was for me to go traipsing around town in this storm, it was even more dangerous for Elizabeth—*if* she was still alive.

I thought about Susan and wondered what would become of her if something bad happened to me. We had just gotten married and I knew she'd be pissed if I went and got myself killed, but I knew she'd eventually understand—

A strong gust of wind suddenly crashed into my Tahoe and rocked it back and forth. I grabbed onto the steering wheel instinctively and held on tight, as though I thought we were about to go airborne. The rain sounded like an automatic carwash as it beat a relentless tune against the side of my vehicle. Another gust, this one just as strong, blew through and I noticed a bright flash of blue lights to my right, at the end of Bayou View Lane. I glanced in that direction and realized it was a transformer. As suddenly as the flash had appeared, it was gone, and the entire complex was left in utter darkness.

I quickly drove out of the parking lot, heading up Bayou View Lane. I didn't want to remain in one place as things started to fall down around me.

I hadn't yet reached Cypress Highway when the Emergency Broadcast System screamed from my speakers. I hated to admit it, but I jumped like I'd been shot. I turned the volume down and listened as they announced we were under a tornado warning.

"...at 5:48 PM, National Weather Service Doppler Radar indicated a severe thunderstorm capable of producing a tornado. This dangerous storm was located five miles south of Mechant Loup in Southern Chateau Parish and is moving north, northeast at thirty-five miles per hour. Those in the affected areas should take shelter immediately."

I glanced at my dash clock. It was five-fifty. I smashed the accelerator and headed south on Cypress Highway. Keeping a wary eye on the dark sky in a futile attempt to scope out any danger that might appear, I maneuvered my way back to the west side of town and headed straight for the school. My phone began ringing just as I hit Back Street, and it didn't stop. I quickly swerved to the left when I realized the porch we'd dragged off of Library Way was now scattered across Back Street.

I couldn't pull far enough off the road and I winced as I approached a pile of lumber directly in my path. I tried to slow down as much as I could, but my Tahoe jostled violently and my teeth rattled in my head as I cruised right over the wood. Once I'd cleared the debris field, I held my breath as I continued on. I let out a deep sigh when I realized my tires were still intact.

The streetlights were flickering on along the highway and I raised an eyebrow. While that was a good thing, I didn't know for how long. One of the first things to go in southeast Louisiana during a storm was electricity. Knowing this, the town had equipped our new police department with a natural gas generator. Sure, we would be fine, but it would do little for the rest of the townspeople, who could be without power for days, and even weeks.

I drove through the front yard of the school and headed for the main building. Once there, I hopped up onto the sidewalk and drove my Tahoe south along the building until I reached the second building. I had seen a little cove-type area earlier where the buildings joined together to form an L, and it was in this cove that I parked my Tahoe.

Finally shielded from the wind, I snatched my phone from the seat beside me and glanced at the twelve missed calls. They were all from Susan. I called her back as I stepped out of my vehicle with Elizabeth's keys.

"Where the hell are you, Clint Wolf? You've got me worried sick over here!"

"I think she's dead, Sue."

There was a long pause on the other end. Finally, she spoke again, but her voice was softer. "Damn—are you sure?"

"I'm not positive, but I found her purse and school credentials in the trunk of her car."

"Yeah, that's not good." She was silent again for a short moment, then asked if I was heading back to the police department.

"I think I found her keys to the school, so I came by to check out the building."

"You're at the school?" Her tone was incredulous. "Why would you go there now? We're under a tornado warning."

"I just have to check and see if she's inside," I explained. "If I were to find out later that she was hurt inside this building the whole time and I could've saved her, but didn't…" I let my voice trail off. I knew Susan understood, because she told me to be safe. I was surprised she wasn't trying to rush out here to help, but I didn't want to give her any ideas, so I kept my mouth shut.

"I'll call you as soon as I'm clear," I said, and swiped my thumb across the screen. I dropped from my Tahoe and made my way to the door, scanning my surroundings as I did so. I didn't think any sane person would be out in this weather, but I wasn't taking any chances. When I reached the side door to the main building, I pulled out the gold key on Elizabeth's key chain and inserted it into the lock. It fit. The locking mechanism hesitated when I tried to turn the key, but I shoved the door with my boot and the key finally turned, freeing the lock. I took a deep breath before I stepped through the door, preparing myself for whatever I might find inside.

CHAPTER 7

It was cold inside the school—and dark. The wet clothes under my raincoat clung to my body, causing me to shiver slightly. I yearned for a hot shower and dry clothes, but I knew it was a fantasy that would not be fulfilled anytime soon—probably not until long after Hurricane Samson had come and gone.

The main building was a long corridor of classrooms and offices, and it ran north to south. There was a door at the northern end, which was where the school gym was located, a door at the southern end, where I entered, and then the main entrance at the front of the building. The main entrance was positioned on the eastern side of the school and, if I remembered right from prior visits to the place, was across the hall from the library.

I moved stealthily from one side of the hallway to the other, clearing each classroom as I made my way toward the library. I cupped my hand over my flashlight each time I turned it on, so the light wouldn't give away my position.

I had just exited the last classroom and was slinking toward the office when I saw a faint glow emitting from under the office door. I cocked my head to the side, trying to figure out if I would've seen it from the entrance. *Has it been on this whole time, or did someone just turn it on?*

All of the other computers had been turned off and covered with plastic bags, and I figured it was all due to the impending storm. *Why would they leave a computer turned on in the office*, I wondered, *when all the others were off?*

I carefully reached for my pistol and slowly slid it from my holster. With it firmly in my hand, I inched closer and closer to the office door. There was paper covering the wire glass window on the door, so I wasn't able to quick-peek inside. I sighed. I'd have to open the door and take my chances.

Crouching low on the doorknob side, I reached out with my left hand while keeping my pistol pointed forward. Slow and steady wouldn't do the trick this time. I'd have to be dynamic about my approach and use the element of surprise to my advantage. Taking a deep breath, I turned the knob and lunged off of the ground in one smooth motion, darting across the doorway and into the office.

I was able to take in most of the office in one glance. There was a large counter directly in front of me, about ten feet away. To the right there was a time clock and a bank of pigeon holes mounted to the wall. To the left and opposite the counter was a copier, shelves, and a large flat-screen television that was emitting the light. Directly to my left was another door, and this is where I headed next, moving at lightning speed.

As soon as I reached it, I grabbed the knob and twisted, but nothing happened. When the door didn't open, my shoulder smashed against it and I heard the wood creak. I winced, hoping I hadn't caused much damage. I didn't have permission to be in the school and, while I could always ask for forgiveness later, I didn't want to buy a door I couldn't keep.

I relaxed and dropped my pistol in my holster, took a closer look around me. The television was setting off a bluish glow, but it was bright enough to see that the room was empty and there were no dead bodies lying around. I glanced up at the screen and cheered inwardly—it was a monitor for the school's security system.

Making a mental note to return for the footage, I went back to clearing the classrooms, moving through them as fast as I safely could.

When I reached the library, I hesitated for a second, saying a silent prayer that Elizabeth would not be dead inside. If she was inside, I was hoping she would be safe and dry, but I knew that was not within the realm of possibilities, especially considering I already had her purse and her keys. I pushed through the door and made a quick search of the floor space. Other than furniture and books, there was nothing inside.

I shined my light around the room and noticed most of the bottom shelves had been cleared, and those books had been stacked on tables and chairs. I grinned, appreciating Elizabeth's passion for books, but my grin faded when I noticed a pile of books on the floor behind one of the shelves. "What the hell?"

I stepped closer and glanced down at the books. They were scattered about as though they'd been dropped, and one of them had fallen open in a manner that the pages had been crumbled. *Damn, that's not good,* I thought. Considering how much she cared for her books, I doubted she would willingly exit this room and leave a book in that condition.

As the rain continued pounding the roof above me, I scoured the floors, searching every inch with my light, but I didn't find anything that might indicate what had happened to her. No droplets of blood, no scuff marks, nothing.

Once I was done in the library, I continued clearing the rest of the school, but I came up empty. I did find the room that had been damaged by the earlier tornado. It was a supply room behind the stage in the auditorium, and it was where most of the drama equipment was located. There were at least three inches of water on the floor and rain was steadily pouring through a hole in the roof. Thankfully, the water seemed to be flowing outside through a crack in the wall and wasn't spreading to the rest of the auditorium.

There was nothing I could do at the moment to plug the hole and, with nowhere else to turn, I went back to the office, hurried around the counter, and approached the surveillance monitor. There were sixteen cameras displayed in the split screen and I knew they were live, because I could see the driving rain in the night vision of the outdoor cameras.

All of the hallways were under surveillance, as were the outdoor parking lots and recreation areas. I located the camera that overlooked the hallway in front of the library—it was camera 11. My hands shook with excitement as I reached for the keyboard and mouse that were attached to the surveillance system. Now that I knew Elizabeth wasn't currently in the school, I had to find out what had happened to her. I needed a clue—some jump off point from which to begin the search.

Questions abounded for me as I clicked on the control panel: *What had distracted her from securing the books? Had she left the school on her own? Was she lured away? Had someone kidnapped her? Was a sexual predator operating in our area? Was it an ex lover? Did she interrupt a burglary in progress? Was she alive? Had she faked her own disappearance?*

I navigated to the *Playback* icon and selected it, but groaned when a loud beep sounded and a dialogue box appeared asking me for the password. I reached for the wall and flipped a light switch, began searching for a password.

"Where are you hiding, you little devil?" I asked out loud, pulling drawer after drawer out and digging through the paperwork. I used to keep all of my passwords scribbled on an index card in my desk drawer, and I figured others might do the same. No such luck.

I drummed my fingers on the countertop, wondering how I could access the system. An idea came to me and I glanced at the time on the camera. It was ten o'clock. Kind of late, but this was an emergency and I was certain the principal knew the password—and I knew his number. Fishing my cell phone from my pocket, I started to scroll through my recent calls when I saw five messages from Susan. The last one read, *"Please...just let me know you're okay."*

Sorry, I was searching the school, I wrote back. *I'm Code 4.*

Next, I located the principal's number and pressed the phone icon and waited as it rang. It continued ringing for what seemed like five minutes, but there was no answer. I left a message asking him to contact me with the password as soon as possible, and I let him know what I'd discovered so far. I was about to end the call when something in the camera caught my attention.

I leaned close and tried to process what I was seeing. The rain was still falling, but there was something different about it. Earlier, it was falling at a sharp angle—almost sideways—but it was now falling closer to ninety degrees. When I swallowed, my ears popped and I suddenly heard it. It was a rumbling sound, sort of like a locomotive rumbling through town, only there were no trains that passed through here. It was then that I realized why the rain was falling straight down. It wasn't rain at all, but hail—and that was a tornado coming!

The windows in the room rattled and hard objects peppered the glass, busting one of them out. Wind gushed into the room and sent papers flying into the air. I saw a flash of blue light somewhere out in the distance and the surveillance system suddenly went black. I whirled around and sprinted for the doorway. I remembered searching a broom closet earlier that was located down the hall. It had no windows and was constructed of solid concrete, and I headed straight for it. Given the circumstances and the fact that teleportation wasn't real, that closet was my safest bet.

The rumbling grew louder and I could feel the pressure building in my ears again. The building seemed to quiver around me and I heard more glass breaking from somewhere down the hall. I couldn't see where I was going, so I was rubbing my hand against the wall as I ran, trying to remember how far it was down the hall. It seemed as though I'd already run a mile, but I hadn't felt a solid door yet. *What if I'd passed it up?*

If I had passed it up, I was running toward the side doors to the main building and right into danger. The rumbling outside was deafening and I was starting to think I should just drop to the ground and cover my head when I felt my fingers slide across a smooth door with no window. I skidded to a stop—nearly slipping to the ground as I did so—and lunged to retrace my steps. I clutched at the doorknob and threw myself into the closet, kicking the door shut behind me. I felt around in the dark, searching for something to put over my head to protect it. The only thing I found was a metal mop bucket. Thankful it was dark and there were no witnesses, I shoved the bucket over my head and rolled into a ball in the farthest corner, saying a silent prayer that I'd get to see Susan again.

CHAPTER 8

As fast as the rumbling and violence had arrived, it was gone. I hurried out of the closet and glanced up and down the hall. It was so dark I didn't know if my eyes were open or closed. I quickly pulled out my cell phone and used the light from it to begin searching the floor in the hall and then the closet. Somewhere along the way I'd lost my flashlight and I needed to find it pronto. That was one of my most important tools at the moment.

"Clint, are you okay?" Susan called over the radio, sounding even worse than she had earlier.

"Ten-four," I responded after pulling my radio from my back pocket. "I'll call you in a minute."

I pushed a large box of toilet paper away from where it was positioned against the wall under a wooden shelf, and held my phone over the area. I gave a little cheer when I saw my flashlight in the corner. Apparently, I'd flung it through the air when I made my crazy dash into the closet and it had ended up behind the box. Hoping the surveillance cameras hadn't captured that moment of embarrassment, I scooted under the shelf and snatched up my light. When I straightened, I hit the switch to make sure it worked. It did.

I was about to turn away when I noticed a dark circle on the wall. I cocked my head to the side and leaned close, aiming my light directly at the blotch. "What the hell?"

I pressed my index finger up against the wall and it disappeared into the darkness. It was some kind of hole. I put my eye to the hole while simultaneously trying to shine the light through it, but it was no use. I couldn't see anything. I shrugged and gave up.

As I walked down the hall, flashlight in hand, I called Susan.

"How are y'all? Did the tornado make it to Washington Avenue?"

"I don't think so. I just looked at the radar and there's a break in the rain squalls. We're heading out now to assess the damage. I think we'll have about thirty minutes to work. Melvin and Amy are heading to the south end, Baylor and Takecia are checking out the east side, and I'm heading north. I told them to immediately head back to the station if it starts storming again."

"Gotcha. I'll be in the area of the school." I smashed the push bar on the door and stepped out into the night, still holding the phone to my ear. While the rain had stopped, the wind was still blowing with a vengeance. "I've got to find that teacher, Sue. She's out here somewhere. I can feel it."

"Come on, Clint, you know we can't save everyone—especially if it'll endanger all of our lives."

"Not all of us—just mine."

"And what do you think will happen if you get into trouble? We'll all have to come looking for you and we'll all perish in this damn hurricane. Please be smart about this. We can find her when the storm blows over."

I wanted to tell her it would be too late by then, but decided to change the conversation a little. "Can you have Lindsey call Elizabeth's husband and see if he's heard anything from her? Maybe call her parents—"

"Wait, he called for you—didn't she put him through?"

I remembered all the missed calls and messages I'd received from Susan, realized it could've been lost in the mix. "It's possible…"

Without waiting for her to say goodbye, I ended the call and quickly scrolled through my voicemails. I found one message that wasn't from Susan's number. My iPhone had transcribed the message and, although the transcription was choppy, I could tell it was from Steve Bankston. I quickly called him back, knowing he wouldn't care about the time.

"Hello? Detective? Did you find her?" The man's voice was laced with panic. "Please tell me you found her and she's okay."

"I'm sorry, but we don't know any more than we did earlier." The wind howled all around me and it was hard to hear what he was saying, so I moved closer to the exterior wall of the main building. "I've searched the school and your apartment, but she's nowhere to be found."

"Did you hear me?" Steve asked. "I'm afraid something bad has happened to her."

"Why do you think that?"

The man was silent for a long moment.

"Well, I received a voicemail from her. It came in at one-thirty this afternoon. It sounds like she's in some kind of trouble."

"What did she say?"

"She…um, she's begging me to pick up—" Steve stopped abruptly and I thought I heard him sobbing quietly. When he started talking again, his voice was hoarse. "After begging me to pick up, she just says she saw something she shouldn't have seen and that she's sorry and she loves me."

"Is that it?"

"She…I heard her scream and then the call goes dead right after that."

"Can you hear any noise in the background?"

"I mean, it sounds like the wind is blowing, so I think she's outside, but that was it."

I mulled over what he'd said, shining my light along the sidewalk where I stood. There was no blood, no scuff marks, no evidence of anything at all. I shined my light against the double doors that I'd come through, which might have been the same doors through which she had entered and exited, but everything looked normal. No pry marks or damage to the doors.

"Detective, are you still there? What do you think it all means?"

"Does she have any friends who might know where she is or what happened?" I asked. "Someone else she might've called if she were in trouble?"

"I've called all of her friends, but none of them heard from her all day. All of her friends evacuated and, at first, I thought she might've left with one of them, but I checked and she didn't."

I was trying to decide if I should tell him about the purse when he interrupted my thoughts.

"My mother-in-law says you found her shoes outside the school. Is that true?"

"I did."

"What were they doing outside? Why would she leave them in the yard?"

"That's what we're trying to figure out."

There was a long silence in the background, and I began to think he knew more than he was saying.

"Mr. Bankston, is there something you think I should know?"

"I…I don't know how much I should say."

"At this point, I think you should say it all. I need to know everything I can about your wife in order to increase my chances of finding her. If she's delinquent on a loan, I need to know about it. If she cut someone off in traffic last week, I need to know about it. I need to know everything you know, and I need to know it now."

"It's not easy being the wife of a man who works offshore, if you know what I mean," Steve said slowly. "I spend more time on the water than I do at home, and it can get lonely cooped up in an apartment all by yourself."

I groaned inwardly as I started to get the picture, but I kept my thoughts to myself. I didn't want to jump to conclusions out loud, just in case he was talking about something else.

"We had been married barely a year when I found out she was going to the bars while I was at work. One of my friends saw her sitting on a guy's lap at the Bayou View Pub one night. When my friend approached them, the guy copped an attitude and my friend busted his ass. Elizabeth called me crying that night, apologizing and begging me not to leave her."

"What'd you do?"

"Well, I was mad as hell, that's for sure. When I got home I broke up with her and we stayed broken up for the two weeks I was in. I'm not proud of this, but I did mess around a bit during those two weeks. You know, to pay her back."

"Did she know about the affairs?" A sudden gust of wind blew through the little cove by the double doors, whipped the hood of my raincoat into my face. I pushed it away. "Did you tell her?"

"No. It happened while we were broken up, so it was none of her business."

"Then how was that paying her back?"

"I…I guess it worked out in my mind. Anyway, when I returned home from my next hitch we got back together. We've been together ever since." He sighed audibly. "Do I think she would do that again? No, I don't think so. Am I positive? Not at all. I didn't think she would do it the first time."

"Is there anyone you might suspect—someone who might be a little too close to her?"

"No, sir."

"Is there any way she found out about the affairs you had while y'all were separated and left because of it?"

"Nah, that was three years ago. That's old news. Besides, the girls I slept with were mostly from out of town. I met them when I'd go party in New Orleans. I'd give them a false name and a fake number so they could never come back into my life and cause trouble."

We talked for ten more minutes—me asking probing questions and him being surprisingly candid—and then I told him I'd do everything I could to find his wife.

"Please bring her back home. I…I don't know what I'd do without her." He began sobbing again. "She's my whole world."

I frowned when I ended the call. I didn't want to admit it to him, but things were not looking good for his wife. If she was presently alive, she probably wouldn't last much longer under these conditions. More tornados were likely and flooding a real possibility. She was in grave danger.

I stepped out from the cover of the buildings, walked to the passenger side of my Tahoe. A large tree branch had fallen from a nearby oak tree and was leaning against the front passenger door.

"That'll leave a mark," I said, grabbing the thickest part of the branch and giving it a shove. The tiny fingers that extended out from the branch made a screeching noise as they slid across the paint job. I winced, wondering how bad the damage would be.

Once the branch had fallen free, I jumped inside and fired up the engine. The automatic headlights splashed against the wall in front of me, and I squinted against the sudden and unexpected brilliance. Being careful not to rub up against the fallen branch, I backed away from the building. I whistled when my headlights splashed against the front of the school. Nearly all of the windows in the classrooms lining the eastern side of the main building had been blown out.

I knew the rain had to have been pouring freely into those rooms, destroying everything inside. While it had stopped for now, this event was far from over. I wanted to do something to shield the place from what was coming, but there was nothing I could do. I didn't have the lumber or the time to secure the windows. Even if I did, it would be hell trying to carry a sheet of plywood in this wind.

I turned my steering wheel to the left so I could head north once I finished backing up, but I smashed the brakes and lurched to a stop when I saw it. At first, I thought it was part of the tree branch, but I immediately dismissed that idea, because oak leaves and branches aren't blue. I pulled forward to get more light on the object and leaned closer to the windshield. I grunted. It looked like a piece of loose fabric and it was blowing in the wind like a tiny flag. *What the hell is that doing here?*

Curiosity getting the best of me, I stepped out of my Tahoe and approached the tree with my flashlight in hand. When I got close to the branch, I reached out and brushed my fingers against the fabric. It was soft. I tugged gently and it pulled free. I turned and held it where the headlights could illuminate it. A cold sliver of dread began to creep up my spine when I realized it was a piece of clothing—most likely a woman's dress.

I pulled my flashlight slowly from my back pocket and turned it on, aiming it upward. "Well, that sucks!"

CHAPTER 9

I held my light steady with one hand while calling Susan with the other. "I found Elizabeth," I said when she answered, "and it's not good."

"Are you at the school?"

"I'm in the front yard. She's up in a tree. I'll need an extension ladder and a chainsaw." I rubbed my wet face. "She's not moving. I think she's gone."

"I'm on my way." I could hear the urgency in her voice. "I'll call Melvin and have him meet us there with the equipment."

I shook droplets of rain from my face and stared up at the mangled mess above me, trying to map out a route to the body. From my vantage point, I could see patches of blue and white fabric wrapped up in the leaves and tree limbs. Parts of the blue fabric—it looked like the edges of a skirt—whipped in the wind. I moved the beam of light over the white fabric, and I could make out the feminine features of an adult woman underneath what looked like a tube top. One arm dangled free, protruding out from a clump of leaves like it was part of the tree, and I saw a bare foot a few inches from the arm. It wasn't supposed to be in that position, so I knew her body had been twisted in a bad way.

When I had the route to her body memorized, I shoved my flashlight in my back pocket and began climbing the tree. I worked my way up the tree by feeling with my hands and feet. It was impossible to see anything. While there would normally be a helpful glow from the moon and stars, the cloud cover was too thick. I let go with my right hand and was stretching toward where the next branch was located—or where I thought I remembered it to be—and a violent gust of wind suddenly ripped through the area, catching me by surprise.

The force of the wind spun me backward and my left foot slipped from the wet knot that I'd been standing on. Cursing silently, I held on for dear life with my left hand and worked my feet like claws, trying to gain a foothold. I didn't know what was directly beneath me and I didn't want to find out. More wind blew through and I felt my fingers slipping from the wet bark above me.

"Come on!" I threw my right arm forward and tried to wrap the tree in a bear hug, but it was too big. I did manage to shove the fingertips of my right hand between pieces of bark and it helped meld me to the tree for a few crucial seconds. Feeling somewhat secure, I carefully felt around with my left foot and was able to locate the original knot I'd been standing on.

Holding my breath, I gently began transferring my weight to the knot. It held. Relieved, I let go of the finger hold with my right hand and felt around for another branch. Once I found one that felt strong enough to support my 185 pounds, I pulled myself higher into the tree. I continued my ascent, but I moved slower and more methodically.

After several long minutes of careful climbing, I reached up and felt something cold, clammy, and prickly. Once I'd anchored myself in place, I removed my flashlight from my back pocket and confirmed my suspicions—it was a woman's shaved leg. I scooted over on the branch that held me and searched for the woman's hand. When I located it, I pushed my index and middle fingers between the bone and tendon over her radial artery. My mouth was slightly open as I concentrated. Nothing.

I frowned. I wasn't expecting much, but I was certainly hoping for more. Now, I'd have to figure out how to get her down from the tree without causing more damage to her body. Sure, she was already dead, but I didn't want to inflict any unnecessary punishment.

I was studying her position when tires screeched from somewhere below me. A moment later, a light was shining up in my direction.

"Why didn't you wait for the ladder?" Susan demanded. "A gust of wind could blow you—oh, my God!"

I figured she must've just seen the body. "You could say that again."

Sirens blared from across town and I figured Melvin was on his way. I idly wondered why he was running sirens when there were no other cars on the road, but I figured it was habit.

"How on earth will we get her down?" Susan asked, raising her voice to be heard. "It looks like she's wrapped up tight."

I had maneuvered to a position slightly above Elizabeth—or whom I thought was Elizabeth—and was trying to inspect her for injuries. So far, I'd only observed a badly mangled foot and an arm that was bent ninety degrees in the wrong direction. I called down to Susan as I discovered each injury.

"We'll be here all night if you're going to count every bump on her body," Susan said. "I just hope she died quickly. I'd hate to think she was trapped up there waiting for help to arrive…"

Her voice trailed off and I knew she was thinking the same thing I was thinking. We had scoured the area behind the school earlier in the day—searching for the owner of the shoes—and never thought to search the trees in the front yard. I never would've guessed a tornado had snatched her off the ground and punted her over the building. I stopped and scowled as I considered that possibility. The path of the tornado didn't extend to where her shoes had been located, and her car had been parked on the other side of the school, so how'd she cross its path?

"Melvin's here with the ladder and chainsaw," Susan called from below. Her voice sounded distant over the howling wind, but I understood what she'd said.

I nodded to myself, continued searching Elizabeth for injuries. Thus far, I hadn't been able to reach her head. I would have to work my way around the trunk to see her upper body—either that, or just remove her from the mess of gnarled branches and examine her on the ground, which seemed like the safest option.

"Heads up!" Melvin called from below. He had aimed the lights of his F-250 at the base of the tree and it helped to illuminate the area.

I scooted farther along the branch I was balancing on so he could lean the extension ladder against the trunk. Once it was secured, he disappeared from my view and Susan stepped to the ladder with a rope in her hand.

"Ready?" she asked, dangling the coiled rope in one hand and squatting slightly, ready to throw it up to me. Her brown eyes sparkled in the light from Melvin's truck and her nose flared a little. I could tell she was worried about me. I was moved by that fact, but also bothered by it. I didn't like people worrying about me.

I leaned forward and extended my hand. "I'm ready…"

She straightened from her crouched position and, swinging her right arm violently upward, launched the rope high into the tree. I quickly backed away as it shot in front of my body and easily snatched it from the air with one hand.

"Move over, Drew Brees," I hollered down at her.

She grinned, then stepped away when Melvin appeared with a chainsaw. I tied one end of the rope to a stout branch and dropped the other end, which Melvin secured to the chainsaw. Once I'd hoisted it to me, I cranked it to life and set about clearing branches and twigs from around Elizabeth's body. One branch had been bent at a weird angle and it had Elizabeth's torso pinned against the trunk of the tree. If I could cut that one away I knew I could free her body, but I needed to balance with one foot on the ladder while leaning far to my right to reach it.

"What're you doing?" Susan called from the ground, ever watchful. "You're going to fall."

"I've got it," I said forcefully, stretched to the limit. The muscles in my right arm burned as I worked to move the chainsaw over the precise spot. When the chain rested against the branch I expelled a lungful of air, allowed the muscles in my arm to relax for a second.

"Clint, please be careful…"

"Geronimo!" I called as I smashed the trigger and the small engine roared. The chain zipped easily through the wood, spitting sawdust in the air. The wind swirled in all directions and blew the tiny shavings into my face and eyes. I blinked and my right eye smarted from a speck of dust that lodged there. Try as I might, I couldn't get my eyelid to stay open. When I did force it open a little, all I saw was a blur of darkness. I was flying blind and the chainsaw was going wild.

I was about to let my finger off the trigger when I heard a thunderous snap. I turned my head so I could see what was going on with my left eye, but it was too late. The chain had cut through the branch and it recoiled like a trap, flying directly toward my face.

With no time to react, I instinctively lowered my head and the branch smashed into my forehead. I heard a scream from below and I flailed backward. I don't know how I managed it, but I hooked my left arm around a large branch and managed to stop my fall. I quickly brought my right arm around to meet my left one and clung to the branch for dear life.

"Hold on, I'm coming!" Melvin hollered.

I did as I was told and heard his boots clambering up the aluminum ladder. My left foot was twisted in the crook of a branch and it hurt something fierce. I wanted to let go with my arms to relieve the pain in my ankle, but dared not. I could still hear the chainsaw motor, but it was no longer in my hands. *Where'd it go?*

Oh, God, did it hit Susan?

I twisted around, trying to see toward the ground.

"Don't move," Melvin said. "I'm almost there."

"Susan…the chainsaw…is she okay?"

"I'm fine, you big lug." Susan's voice was strained. "Just hold on."

When Melvin reached me, he worked on my left boot, freed it from where it was trapped. "There's a giant branch just below you," he said, lowering my leg slowly. "You can reach it from where you are."

Still clutching onto the branch, I allowed my left leg to drop and I felt my foot brush against something solid. I brought my right leg beside it and stood gingerly, releasing my death grip when I was on solid footing. I smacked, could taste blood in my throat. "What the hell happened?"

Melvin pointed toward the recent cut I'd made in the tree. "You freed the dead girl, but you nearly joined her."

"Don't say that, Melvin!" Susan barked.

"I'm okay." Although I felt a little woozy, I tried to sound reassuring.

Melvin mumbled an apology to Susan for his crude joke, fished a small light from his pocket. He shined it in my face. "Lower your head."

I did as ordered.

"Push your hair back."

I complied.

"Damn, are you sure you're okay? You've got a knot the size of Alaska on your forehead."

"Well, I guess it's a good thing I've got hair." I grinned as I imagined what Melvin would look like with a giant knot on his bare head.

"Yeah, and it probably helped cushion the blow." Melvin turned toward Elizabeth's body and his full face seemed hollow in the dim light beaming up from his truck. "Well, you think we'll be able to get her down now?"

"I think that did it." I moved back into a position to remove Elizabeth from where her body had come to rest. I tugged on one of her arms, trying to roll her in my direction, but she seemed to be snagged on something. I reached across her back and felt a rough object. I stood on my tiptoes to see better, shined my light on her back. Her tube top was pulled up and a jagged twig protruded up through her smooth flesh. "Oh, wow, she's stuck on a twig—it ran through and through her body."

"Do you need the chainsaw?" Melvin asked from where he was crouched on a large tree limb to my right. "It fell to the ground, but I can drop the rope to Susan—"

"Something's wrong with this picture," I said, interrupting him. There was no blood in the wound, which meant she had to have been dead when she was impaled. I ignored Melvin's inquiry as I worked my way higher on the tree. Putting my hand on her back to steady myself, I found a foothold that allowed me to hover over her body. I was able to inch toward her upper body and examined the back of her head. She had flowing brown hair, but it was matted and appeared sticky. It had to be blood. I leaned over to look down at Melvin. "Hey, do you have a latex glove?"

He nodded and reached for a pouch on the back of his gun belt. He handed me a pair and I slipped them on.

"What's up?" he asked.

"I'm not sure yet." I donned the gloves and moved back to my original position. Cradling Elizabeth's head in my right hand, I eased it up and around to where my light could shine on her face. I groaned out loud. It was Elizabeth Bankston alright, but this was not what I'd expected to find. "Damn, Melvin…this ain't good."

CHAPTER 10

It took us nearly an hour to get Elizabeth's body down from the tree. We had to stop twice and take cover because of rain bands blowing through the area. Each one seemed to grow in intensity and I knew we were running out of time.

When she was finally on the ground and lying on top of an open body bag, Melvin and I moved her to the covered sidewalk—near where I had entered the main building earlier—and rested her there.

"She was shot in the head," I explained to Susan, pointing out the obvious bullet hole at the center of her forehead. I shined my light on the bullet hole to highlight the star-shaped tattooing around the wound, which was indicative of a contact shot. "And she was looking into the eyes of her killer when she died."

"She was executed." Susan shook her head. "But why? What's going on?"

"And why would she just stare up at her killer?" Melvin asked, rubbing his smooth head. "Why not fight back?"

"She was most likely begging for her life." I took some pictures with my camera while Melvin and Susan struggled to hold open the flaps on the body bag. The wind gusts were getting stronger and morning was quickly approaching, which meant Hurricane Samson was breathing down our necks. "Can y'all turn her head so I can get some shots of where the bullet exited?"

They did, and I took some photos of her blood-caked hair. We'd have to wait until the autopsy when the coroner could shave the back of her head to examine the exit wound. I was hoping that could be done tomorrow evening sometime, but I was probably being overly optimistic. I had spoken with Doctor Louise Wong not long after I first found Elizabeth's body, and she told me she was in a hotel in Beaumont, Texas.

"I'll come back when they declare it safe to do so," she had said. "I won't place my family's lives in jeopardy for my job."

"I understand," I'd said, "but what am I supposed to do with the body? She won't fit in my freezer."

She told me the pass code to the coroner's office and asked if I could make it to Central Chateau to put the body in a freezer. "We've got a generator that'll automatically come on if the power goes out," she said, "so her body will keep until I get back. But I guess the question is whether or not you can make it there."

"I'll make it," I had assured her—but that was earlier. Things had deteriorated since then.

"Where do you think she was shot?" Susan asked.

"In the head," Melvin said quickly, grinning.

I was zipping the body bag when Melvin made his joke and I laughed. Susan shot Melvin a hard stare and his smile disappeared.

"No," I said when I straightened, "I've got no clue where she was when she got shot. I guess the best I can do is come out during daylight and follow the path of the first tornado, see if there's any evidence of the murder along the way. I know the killer didn't throw her up in that tree and I know the tornado didn't shoot her, so they must've been working in cahoots."

Susan shot a thumb over her shoulder, indicating the storm-force winds and driving rain that had begun to fall again. "Good luck with that. Your crime scene—wherever it might be—is being washed away as we sit here."

I cursed silently. Even if I did develop a suspect and recover a weapon, it would be next to impossible to link it to Elizabeth's murder without a projectile or a shell casing for comparison, and that's where the crime scene came in. A crime scene was the place where it all began and it's where everything usually came together for detectives. Sure, we could solve a case without a crime scene, but it made things more challenging.

Pulling the zipper high on my raincoat, I motioned for Melvin to get the other side of the body bag. Once we'd lifted her from the ground, Susan hurried ahead and opened the back of my Tahoe. We loaded Elizabeth into the cargo area and quickly shut the gate.

"Want me to come with you?" Susan had to raise her voice to be heard over the wind and rain.

I shook my head. "No need risking more than one of us."

"Someone needs to help you carry the body inside," she

countered.

"I'll do it, Chief," Melvin said hurriedly. "I'm already wet anyway."

Susan frowned, but finally nodded her resignation. "I'll notify Mr. and Mrs. Detiveaux on my way back to the office. They need to know what happened."

I filled her in on everything I'd learned from Steve Bankston, then thanked her and asked that she be careful.

She kissed me softly on the lips and hurried to her own Tahoe that was parked nearby. "Let me know when you get there," she called over her shoulder.

We drove in a small caravan—Melvin first, followed by Susan, with me bringing up the rear—making our way carefully through town. Our headlights did little to illuminate our way. The rain was falling in thick sheets and visibility was less than nothing. I didn't know how Melvin was able to stay on the highway. My only guide was Susan's brake lights. That is, until she peeled off and turned down Mr. and Mrs. Detiveaux's street.

When Melvin and I finally made it to the police department, we parked under the building and I waited for him to jump in with me. He shed his raincoat and shook it off before slipping into the passenger seat.

"What do you think happened to that poor woman?" he asked when we were backing out of the parking lot.

I shook my head. I'd been wondering the same thing for hours, but couldn't come up with anything that seemed logical. People committed murder for all kinds of reasons, but most of our citizens had been too busy packing up and heading out of town. They didn't have time to stop and execute someone.

"On the other hand," I said aloud, considering my earlier thoughts about the crime scene, "this would be a great time to murder someone—especially outdoors. After this storm blows through, there won't be a scintilla of evidence left for us to process."

"I bet the killer didn't count on you searching for Elizabeth in this weather," Melvin offered. "Most departments usually put out the word that the citizens who refuse to evacuate are on their own until the storm blows through, and everyone knows that. Maybe the killer knew that, too."

I nodded to myself, glanced sideways at Melvin as I turned north onto Main Street. His face was covered in a greenish glow from my dash lights. He seemed older, a little less jovial. He had only been back to work for about three weeks since the stabbing, and it looked like that incident had taken something out of him. It had certainly had a profound impact on all of us—reminded us of the importance of body armor—and I shuddered when I remembered how desperate I felt that night.

I shook my head to clear it of those horrific memories and tried to concentrate on the task at hand. It was normally a twenty or thirty minute drive to the coroner's office—depending on who was driving and how fast they elected to go—but it would probably take us an hour to get there. The wind howled angrily outside, pushing my Tahoe around like a schoolyard bully, and I couldn't see the road in front of us. All I could really see was the white line on the shoulder of the road, so I used it as my guide.

We had been driving for over forty minutes and were rolling into the central part of Chateau Parish when Susan called to say the Lake Charles Police Department had made contact with Steve Bankston at his hotel room and notified him that his wife had been murdered. I was surprised I hadn't heard from him yet, and said so.

"Well, there's a good reason for that," she said softly. "They arrested him."

"*What?*" I could feel my mouth hanging open. "Why?"

"He went crazy, started tearing up everything. He tried to run out onto the interstate near his hotel. They took him into custody for his own safety. I can't say that I blame him. If something happened to you, I'd…" She paused for a long moment. "Hell, I don't know what I'd do, but it wouldn't be good."

I frowned, knowing that feeling of loss all too well. "What about Elizabeth's parents? Did you get to notify them?"

"Yeah…they didn't take it well at all. Of course, I didn't expect them to. How could they?"

I drove in silence for a few seconds, listening to the sound of her steady breathing in my ear. Lightning flashed ahead of my vehicle and lit up the roadway for a brief moment. It was only then that I realized exactly where we were along the route. We were almost there.

"Did you get to question the Detiveauxs to see if anyone had a reason to want Elizabeth dead?"

"I did, but they said she didn't know a stranger and everyone loved her. Her mom gave me the names and contact information for her closest friends. I'll forward those to you."

"What about ex lovers?"

"They said she's been with Steve since she was a teenager. I asked them about the incident at the Bayou View Pub, but they hadn't heard about it. As far as they knew, Elizabeth and Steve have never had any problems."

"What about work problems? Did she ever complain about anyone at school? Fellow teachers? Or students, even?"

"No. They said she loved her job and the people she worked with. She looked forward to going to work every day." Susan sighed heavily. "They're completely stunned—not just by her death, but by the fact that she was murdered. They just can't believe anyone would do that to her. They think it has to be a stranger, someone who didn't know her."

"We need to check with the motel and every bed and breakfast in town, see if any tourists stayed here for the storm." I slowed to turn onto the street of the coroner's office. "We're pulling up to the morgue. I'll see you back at the police department within the hour."

CHAPTER 11

Wednesday, September 20
Mechant Loup Police Department

I was up at the first hint of light. After returning from the morgue, I had taken a shower in the department locker room and slipped into warm clothes for the first time all day. After eating sandwiches with Susan, we'd retired to our cots in her office and were asleep instantly. Baylor and Takecia kept watch during the night, and I found them in the front lobby when I padded through the office in my bare feet.

"Any excitement while I was out?" I asked.

Takecia, who wore dark BDU pants and a T-shirt that read, *Jamaican me crazy*, twisted around from where she was standing near the glass door. Her dark features were calm, and she faked a yawn. "You call this a hurricane? Where I'm from, this is morning."

I grinned and headed for the employee break room. We had stocked up on water, bread, and canned goods. I made a peanut butter and jelly sandwich and brought it back to Susan's office. While I ate, I searched our database for anything related to Elizabeth Bankston. Her name was in our system three times. Two years ago, she'd been involved in a fender bender in the school parking lot. As she was pulling into her parking spot one morning, a parent of a student had been in a hurry and backed into her car. The damage was minor and they had decided to handle it amongst themselves. A report was filed for insurance purposes.

The second incident involved a student who had become unruly during last school year and flipped over a desk in the library where

Elizabeth taught computer skills. The kid's name was Liam Wells. He was a seventh grader who, as it turned out, had a long history of problems in town. I made a note to pay him a visit later.

The third incident was two months ago, during the summer. She was home alone when she had been awakened at three in the morning by loud noises coming from the apartment next door. She'd called 911 and Amy had responded to find a woman passed out on the sofa in the neighboring apartment. There were drugs scattered all over the apartment. When Amy had initially knocked on the door, the husband, a fellow named Jude Lathrop, had opened it and freaked out when he saw Amy's uniform. He'd pushed her and run through the house, making his escape through the back door.

"Ah, I remember this little bastard."

"What bastard?" asked Susan, her voice muffled.

I turned to see her sitting up in her cot, rubbing her eyes. Her T-shirt was loose-fitting, but it did little to hide her curves. I wondered for a brief moment if we could make love on that cot without breaking it, but then caught her staring at me with disapproval.

"Not in this office, Clint Wolf," she said. "Not with the whole department out there. Now, tell me what bastard we're talking about."

I groaned, wanted to tell her that's why God created locks, but I knew I wouldn't win this battle. "Jude Lathrop…remember him?"

We had located Jude two days later at his mother's home and— just as we'd anticipated—he'd made a run for it again when Amy knocked on the front door. Susan and I had covered the rear and Jude took Susan's forearm to his throat when he crashed through the back door. He hadn't put up a fight after that, but he'd lodged some threats later, saying he would kill whoever turned him in.

"Oh, yeah, I do." Susan yawned. "Why? What's up with him?"

"Elizabeth Bankston was the neighbor who reported him."

"Shut up!" She was suddenly wide awake. "When are we going after him?"

I backed out of the computer screen I was in and started a new search, looking for anything I could find on Jude. He had bonded out of jail two weeks after the arrest, only to find that his wife was no longer living in the apartment. Following the arrest, the manager at the complex had begun eviction proceedings for breach of contract regarding their criminal activity, but Jude's wife, Esther, wasn't waiting around. She had bonded out of jail two days after her arrest and had apparently packed up everything and high-tailed it out of town. Jude had caused a disturbance at the manager's office, but he'd left before Takecia could arrive. That was the last record we had on him.

I glanced toward the window in Susan's office, forgetting we'd closed the shutters in anticipation of the storm. Only a sliver of dark light bled through the crack. "I'll have to wait until the storm blows through, I guess."

Susan followed my gaze. "Yeah, that's best."

With nothing left to search on the computer, and it being as bright as it would get outside, I stood and changed into jeans and a T-shirt. I shoved my holster into my belt and secured my Beretta inside. Susan followed my lead and was dressed within a minute.

"Where're we going?"

"I'm going to search for a crime scene." I looked down at her, frowned. "Wouldn't it be best if I went alone? You've got a police department to run. They need you here."

She didn't like it, but she knew I was right. "You need to be careful. You have to promise me that."

I cocked my head to the side and stepped closer to her, pressing my hands against her face. "What's wrong, Sue? You haven't been yourself lately. You seem overly worried about me."

She frowned and it pushed the dimple on her left cheek deeper into her flesh. She lowered her head. "I…I mean, I guess everything that happened with Melvin kind of made me realize how vulnerable we really are—all of us." She looked up and snapped her fingers. "It could all end in a second, for any of us."

I brushed the brown hair out of her face. "You've always known that, Sue. You were almost killed, too. It's the nature of the job."

"I guess I haven't fully let go of that night yet." She took a deep breath and exhaled, forced a smile. "I'll be okay. Just don't go getting yourself killed. I need you in my life."

I promised I'd stay north of six feet and set off to find the crime scene. I spent most of the morning braving the rain and wind, searching every inch of Library Way along which the tornado had passed. There was an inch of water on the street and even more water on the surrounding properties. The ditches had been transformed into raging mini rivers. Twigs and leaves littered the landscape for as far as the eye could see.

It was almost ten o'clock and, according to the latest coordinates from the National Hurricane Center, Samson would make landfall within the hour. That put the eye of the storm two hours from downtown Mechant Loup, and it meant I wasn't going to locate the crime scene today—if ever. The only ray of sunshine in the news report was that the hurricane had been downgraded to a Cat 3 storm.

I hadn't seen a soul in the area of the school. Before heading to the police department, I drove home to check on our place. We'd lost a few shingles from the roof and a tree had fallen through a section of the back fence. I held my breath as I drove toward the end of the street where the women's shelter was located, but smiled in relief when I saw that it was virtually untouched.

I took one last look around the place, hoping everything would still be standing by this time tomorrow, and headed back to town with my blue lights flashing. I drove slowly, searching for anyone who might be in trouble or in need of help before the worst of the storm came ashore.

After driving through town for thirty minutes or so and finding no one out and about, I turned onto East Main and headed toward Washington Avenue. A weather alert blared across my car radio again, warning that we were experiencing winds of sixty-five to seventy miles per hour, with gusts of up to ninety miles per hour. Their advice was for anyone outdoors to seek shelter immediately, preferably in a strong building. I sighed. It was time to crawl in our hole and hide. I didn't like the idea, but I knew it wasn't safe out here anymore.

The force of the relentless wind nearly pushed my Tahoe off the road, and I had to hold tight to the steering wheel. Having lived in Louisiana my entire life, I'd weathered my share of hurricanes, but I'd never experienced one since rolling into Mechant Loup. This place was farther south than La Mort and would be closer to the action. I wasn't sure what to expect.

A strong gust rocked my vehicle and I saw blue lights flashing from a power pole as another transformer blew. Leaves and branches littered the streets. Every tree I saw was bent and some had even blown completely over. Street signs were twisting violently back and forth. The power lines overhead were being stretched to the point of breaking.

"And the storm hasn't even hit yet," I muttered.

I was still about a mile from Washington Avenue when I saw something flipping end over end to my left, heading straight for the driver side of my vehicle. I smashed the accelerator and my vehicle lurched forward, barely clearing the object. I looked in my rearview mirror just in time to see that it was a trampoline hurling through the air and it crashed into the side of a parked truck.

"Damn, that was close!"

Farther down the road, I saw a red barn-style shed flipped onto its side. In the same yard, a tree had fallen onto a pickup truck. I suddenly glanced overhead, looking for anything that might come crashing down on me, but the sheets of rain made it impossible to see much of anything.

I was actually relieved when I turned onto Washington Avenue, but that was short lived. A gust of wind snatched a metal garbage can from its perch outside of a jewelry shop and sent it right into the front passenger window of my Tahoe, causing it to explode. Shards of wet glass peppered the right side of my face and the can lodged within the window frame.

Cursing, I twisted in my seat to kick the garbage can free with one leg, while keeping the brake pedal smashed with the other. It took several tries, but it finally broke away and fell to the ground. I then sped off in the direction of the police department, driving like a crazy man. I knew I didn't have to worry about pedestrians, because there was no one crazy enough to be out in this weather.

I made it to the end of the street in record time and whipped into the parking lot, heading straight for the underside of the building. When I was under the solid concrete umbrella, I shut off the engine and sighed.

This was not how I'd wanted my day to end, and it had nothing to do with the busted window—that was the least of my worries. My biggest worry was the formidable water monster that was heading straight for us. It would pressure wash the hell out of the crime scene—wherever it might be—and destroy every piece of evidence that might happen to still exist, which would make it extremely difficult to build a case against Elizabeth's killer.

I felt like I'd covered every inch of the area that had been hit by the first tornado, but the telltale signs of this crime scene would be subtle—a scar on the blacktop street, a single drop of blood, a tiny piece of pulverized lead—and hard enough to locate on a regular day, but nearly impossible during a storm and under an inch of water.

I stepped from my Tahoe and paused when I heard the generator humming in the background. We'd lost power and the automatic generator had kicked on. *Well, that didn't take long.*

I sighed and started removing my firearms from my cruiser. While I doubted any burglars would be searching for loot in this weather, I wasn't willing to chance it. I'd paid too much money to take my weapons for granted and I certainly didn't want them falling into the wrong hands. I tucked my Springfield Model 1911 .45 pistol in my front right pocket, my Smith and Wesson .357 revolver in my front left pocket, and cradled my twelve-gauge shotgun and AR-15 in my arms.

I could feel water dripping down my face as I walked. The clothes under my raincoat clung to my flesh. I longed for another hot shower and some warm, dry clothes.

But what's the use? I thought. *I'll just end up heading back outside for some emergency call and get wet all over again.*

More than a shower, I longed for this rain to stop. Why couldn't we have been dealt the dry side of the storm? A little wind would not have destroyed the crime scene and I would've still been able to search for Elizabeth's killer.

"Dear Lord, what happened to your face?" Lindsey asked when I stepped into the dispatcher's station, struggling to open doors while holding my weapons.

"I bumped my head on a log last night."

"Not your head"—she shoved a finger in my direction—"your *face!*"

"What's going on?" Susan stepped into the radio room, stopped short when she saw me. "What'd you do to your face? You're bleeding!"

I remembered the garbage can and my busted window. "They're just scratches. A metal garbage can flew through my window."

"Will you let me clean it up?" Susan reached for my shotgun. "You look like a savage."

"Maybe I'll leave it like this for when I find Elizabeth's killer." I followed Susan to her office. Before letting her tend to me, I wiped down my firearms and then secured them in her closet. It was only then that I followed her to the women's bathroom, where she doctored up my face. Once she was done, we had a meeting in the conference room with everyone else and she assigned shifts for the remainder of the day.

"We'll take turns sleeping throughout the day," she said, "so we can all be rested up for tonight. I'm sure we'll start getting emergency calls when the storm blows out of here, so we'll have to be at our best."

I stole a glance at Melvin, who sat staring down at a spot on the table. His mind seemed elsewhere. When Susan concluded her meeting, I followed him to the break room.

"Hey, buddy, you okay?"

He grabbed a bottle of water, frowned as he opened it. "Since the stabbing, Claire has been giving me a lot of grief about my job."

"She wants you to leave police work?"

"She's tried this before, attacking from the financial angle, telling me we couldn't even afford to bring Deli to Disney World. She wanted me to go back to school and get a law degree, so I can better support my family. Now, she's playing the death card, asking me things like, '*Who's going to walk Delilah down the aisle if you get killed?*'"

"What do *you* want to do?"

"I love being a cop, Clint. It's the only thing I'm good at." He scowled. "I don't want Deli growing up without a father either, but I don't plan on getting myself killed. I don't give her crap about working at a bank. She could be robbed and killed in her job just as easy as I could get killed in mine."

"Did you tell her that?"

"Nah, I don't like arguing with her. I didn't say anything."

I was thoughtful. "Would you be happy doing anything else?"

"Not at all, but I'd rather be miserable and give up my job than lose her and Deli. I'm afraid she'll leave me if I don't do what she wants. She's that set on me quitting the force."

"Maybe you should let her know how you feel before giving up something you love. Tell her you're willing to do it for her and Delilah, but it would make you miserable. She loves you, so she should understand."

Melvin just grunted. "I doubt that."

CHAPTER 12

Four hours later…

Susan stepped out onto the concrete porch of the police department, stared up in awe as the sun beamed down on the town. Although everything appeared calm at the moment, she knew they were about to get battered again. She looked up and down the street as far as she could see. Other than knocked over benches, blown down signs, and one storefront window that was broken, things looked surprisingly well.

"Are we in the eye of the storm?"

Susan turned to see Claire standing in the doorway, both arms wrapped tightly about her torso.

"Yeah, it's deceptive, isn't it?" Susan smiled. "Imagine how the first humans who ever experienced a hurricane must've felt when the eye passed over them. I bet they looked up at the sun and bright skies and thought everything was over. But then"—she slapped her hands together—"*wham!* Round two comes along and ruins their day."

"They must've freaked out." Claire took a cautious step out onto the porch and surveyed the area. "I hope our house is still standing. Our entire lives are tied up in that place—everything we've worked so hard to build."

"Well, the most important parts are right here, safe and sound." Susan scowled when Claire frowned. "What's wrong, Claire? You look sad."

Tears formed in Claire's eyes and she quickly brushed them away. "It's nothing. I'm okay."

"No, it is something, and you can talk about it." Susan stepped closer and touched Claire's arm. "What is it? What's bothering you?"

"It's Melvin." The tears flowed free now. "I think he loves this job more than he loves me and Delilah."

"Hey, come here…it's okay." Susan pulled Claire close and wrapped her arms around the dejected woman. "Let it all out and then we can talk about it."

Susan glanced over her shoulder a moment later as the sky darkened. Thick clouds were moving in and the wind began to pick up again. It was as though a wall of destruction was approaching from the south, and she said a silent prayer that they would remain safe over the next couple of hours. The wind was most dangerous at the eye wall of the hurricane, and she could see that fearsome beast heading straight for them.

Claire pushed away from Susan and wiped her eyes. "Being a cop's wife is hard, and he doesn't seem to realize that or even care about it. Every damn time he leaves the house for work I wonder if I'll ever see him again. Every time he kisses me goodbye I wonder if that'll be the last time our lips ever touch."

Susan frowned, and nodded her understanding.

"But things got worse—like, *really* bad—after Delilah was born. Sometimes, when the phone rings while he's gone, I start having a panic attack, because I think it's someone calling to say he's been killed." Claire stopped to wipe her eyes. "And when that all happened this summer…God, it nearly killed me. It was like all of my fears were coming true. I tried to talk to him about it, but he won't say anything. He just stands there with this blank expression on his face."

Susan rubbed Claire's shoulder and nodded, giving her time to let out all of her frustration. After a moment of silence, Susan asked Claire if she thought Melvin would be happy doing some other job.

"I mean, I think he could learn to like something else."

"I've worked with Melvin for a long time and I know that being a cop is all he's ever wanted to do." Susan paused to study Claire's reaction. She was listening, but had crossed her arms in front of her chest. "This job isn't for everyone, that's for sure. It has its low points and it can certainly take a toll on people, but if they're built for it—as I know Melvin is—it's one of the most rewarding professions around.

"We're not just out here putting people in jail; we're impacting people's lives in a positive way every single day. *Melvin* is impacting people's lives in a positive way every day. I know it sucks that you feel like you have to share him with the rest of the community, but

I'm here to tell you that this town loves Melvin, they respect him, and they *need* him—and I think he needs them."

"Yeah, well, sometimes I think he puts his job before his family."

"Oh, trust me…I know it can feel that way. If I didn't work in law enforcement along with Clint, I'd think the very same thing of him, but I can tell you with certainty that Melvin loves you and Delilah more than anything in the world. He'd give up his job for y'all—that's how much he loves y'all."

Claire scoffed. "That'll be the day. I could be standing at the door with a suitcase in one hand and Delilah in the other and he'd just watch us leave. No, he loves his job more than anything else in this whole screwed up world."

"Just between us girls, he told Clint earlier that he was going to quit his job to make you happy."

Claire's eyes lit up. "Really? He said that?"

Susan licked her lips. "He did."

"Wow, I didn't think he'd ever do that." Claire was beaming now. "I mean, that's great news!"

"Is it?" Susan winced inwardly when she realized how stern her voice sounded, but continued. "Would you really feel good about making the man you love quit a job he loves just to make you happy?"

"It's…it's not about that. It's for his own good—for his own safety. Plus, I can't raise a child without a father. I have friends whose husbands left them early on in their children's lives and I see what they go through." She shook her head. "I just don't know how they do it. Those poor children—"

"I'm one of those poor children," Susan said, interrupting. "My mom lost my dad when I was young and I saw how she struggled, so I certainly know what you mean. But I think you need to take a step back and realize that you're not them and Melvin's not dead. Try to focus on living in the present—in the here and now. If you spend your time worrying about what the future holds and trying to force him to give up something he loves, you'll waste the precious moments y'all have together. Besides, Melvin would be miserable doing another job, and I'm sure you want him to be happy."

"It's better to be miserable and alive than happy and dead," Claire retorted, jutting out her chin.

"Is it?"

"At least he'll be there when Delilah graduates from high school and college. He'll be able to walk her down the aisle when she gets married. To me, that's all worth him quitting his job."

"Claire, there's no guarantee he won't be killed doing another job. He could get killed cutting the grass, or crossing the street, or even eating a hot dog. Just because he changes jobs doesn't mean he'll be around to walk—"

"No, but his life expectancy will increase dramatically." Claire unfolded her arms and straightened. "Look, I'm sorry I brought it up. I don't expect you to understand, since you've never had children. Please, just don't tell Melvin we had this discussion."

Susan chewed on her bottom lip, hesitating. Claire turned to walk off, but Susan stopped her. "What if I do understand what you're going through?"

Claire was suddenly curious as she turned to face Susan again. "What do you mean?"

"Look, I haven't been myself for the past week or so. And lately, I've found myself fretting over Clint more than usual." Susan shuffled her feet. "I've been busy preparing for this hurricane and…"

After a moment of silence, Claire stepped closer. "And…?"

"My boobs are swollen and tender, I've been an emotional wreck lately worrying about Clint's safety, I threw up this morning, and—"

"Oh, my God! You're pregnant!"

"I don't know." Susan shot a glance over her shoulder to make sure no one had heard. The wind was howling again, whipping their hair all around their faces, so even if anyone had been standing inside the door, there was no way they heard anything. She turned back to Claire, who was holding the rail for support, and continued, "I'm so regular, Rolex Corporation calls me to set their watches by my cycle—and I'm two weeks late. That's never happened before. I was one week late once in my life and took a pregnancy test, but it was negative."

"Did you take a pregnancy test this time?" The women were yelling now, trying to be heard over the approaching storm.

"I want to but all the damn stores are closed!" Susan huffed. "I swear, if this storm doesn't hurry and pass, I'm going to start looting the pharmacy."

Claire laughed, but then Susan saw her expression change. She pointed with mouth agape. "What the hell is that?"

Susan turned to see swirling clouds hovering over them to the south. They were rotating in a menacing manner and a long thin finger of a cloud reached out to the east, moving like a snake in the air. Another one moved below that one. It was such a strange formation. Susan squinted through the wind, trying to determine what it was. She'd never seen anything like it before. Her eyes suddenly widened when one of the fingers dipped toward the ground. "They're funnel clouds!" she hollered. "Get inside—*now!*"

CHAPTER 13

I was awakened by Susan yelling at me to get into the women's bathroom as fast as I could.

"Hurry, Clint!" she said. "We've got multiple funnel clouds overhead!"

I rolled from my cot, rubbed my eyes. "What's going on?"

"Get your ass in the bathroom now!"

Achilles, who had fallen asleep next to my cot, didn't need a second invitation. He was gone before I could spring off the cot. I sprinted through the doorway, staying right on their heels. The women's bathroom was the safest interior room on our side of the building, and the men's bathroom was the safest room on the other side of the building.

When we raced past the dispatcher's station, I glanced through the door and saw figures dashing for the men's bathroom. I was relieved that they had also received the warning. When we reached the end of the hall, Susan crashed through the thick door and we squirted inside. I kicked the door shut with my boot, looked around.

I immediately saw Melvin, Claire, Delilah, and Amy crouched in the far corner, all of them staring up at the ceiling. We joined them just as the lights blinked and the building shook. Achilles pushed as close to me as he could, shoved his snout in my hand, and began whimpering. I'd never seen him scared before, and it made me wonder if I should be worried.

"Mommy, are we going to die?" Delilah shouted.

Melvin, who was as calm as I'd ever seen him, scooped her up in his thick arms. "No, Deli, no one's going to die. This building was made to beat hurricanes and tornados. It's the safest place in town, and probably the whole world."

That seemed to settle Delilah, and she plopped down in Melvin's lap, completely unworried. I smiled inwardly as I watched the dynamics between the two of them. Delilah had complete faith in her dad and trusted his every word. Claire was another story. Her face was twisted in fear.

"We were outside and I saw them," she was telling Melvin. "Susan and I saw them flying everywhere. There must've been a dozen of them."

"Two," Susan corrected with a smile. "There were only two of them."

Claire glanced around the room, shifting her eyes from Melvin to Susan to Amy to me, and then back to Melvin. "How can y'all be so calm in a situation like this? We could all—"

"Win free tickets to Disney World," Melvin said quickly, interrupting Claire.

"Disney World!" Delilah nearly jumped out of Melvin's lap with glee.

Melvin put a beefy arm around Claire and looked her right in the eyes. "I'm not going to let anything happen to you," he said softly. "I'll keep you safe. It's what I do. It's what I'm good at."

"He *will* keep you safe, Claire—because his blood runs blue," Susan said softly, frowning. "Do you know how I know his blood runs blue?"

Claire raised an eyebrow to Susan.

"Because I saw it."

I thought I saw a tear roll down Claire's face, and I knew she was probably feeling guilty for trying to force Melvin out of his job. I turned to Susan, who was leaning against the wall beside me, staring up into my face.

"What?" I asked. "Do I have drool on my face?"

She smiled. "No, you handsome devil, you don't have drool on your—"

Something suddenly smashed into the roof of the building, making a thunderous sound. I saw Claire jerk in her skin. "What was that?" she asked.

No one answered, because we all knew it could be anything; a tree limb, another trampoline, a car—a body, even. Pressure built up in my head and I swallowed to clear my ears. I saw everyone else swallowing and yawning to clear theirs. Delilah twisted around in Melvin's lap and looked up at him. "It sounds like I'm under the water, Daddy."

Melvin laughed and explained what was going on.

More objects slammed against the exterior walls as the wind continued its relentless attack. I could only imagine what the town would look like when this was all over, and part of me hoped Elizabeth's killer would meet with a far worse fate than she had endured.

After an hour or so of waiting for the pounding and pressure to stop, I motioned to Susan that I was heading for the door. She only nodded, and I figured she realized it would be futile to argue. Staying low, I crossed the room, stepped out into the hallway, and made my way to the other side of the building to check on the rest of our crew. Once I cleared the dispatcher's station, I rounded the corner and pushed into the men's bathroom and stopped short. I was surprised to find Takecia sitting on the floor all alone staring at her cell phone.

"I'm getting no service," she grumbled, tossing the phone to the floor beside her. "How can I flirt with my boyfriend when I have no service?"

"You have a boyfriend?"

She shrugged. "Maybe, maybe not. I am talking to a boy from New York, but I do not know yet if I like him."

I glanced around the room. "Where're the others?"

One of the stall doors slowly creaked open and I saw Lindsey's terrified face peer out from the little crack.

"Is it over?" she asked. "Is it safe to come out?"

The stall door next to hers opened and Baylor quickly stepped out, looking a bit embarrassed. "I...I wasn't sure what was happening or what we should do. I didn't know what to expect, so I took cover."

Takecia began laughing from where she sat on the floor. "They thought they were going to die. It was the funniest thing I have ever seen."

Baylor's face was red. "I'm not used to hurricanes and tornados yet, but I'll get there. Just give me a little time."

"I was raised here my whole life," Lindsey said, "and I'm still not used to them. They scare the hell out of me."

I shook my head and listened as the rumbling continued outside. The building seemed to shiver every now and then, and I kept hoping the contractors had done a solid job when they built the place. I had worked in construction for a couple of years after I lost my wife and daughter, and I'd met this one foreman who liked to cut corners. I refused to go along with his shenanigans and was eventually moved off of that job site. But there were other workers willing to do whatever they were told, and if that happened on this building, we might not live to know about it.

Once I was sure they didn't need anything, I left the bathroom and made my way around the building. I checked for broken windows, leaks in the ceiling, and cracks in the drywall, but everything looked intact. The shutters were apparently holding up, as were the concrete walls and metal roof. I nodded as I made my way back to the women's bathroom. This building might just pass its first driving test after all—and when this was over, I could get back to trying to solve Elizabeth Bankston's murder.

I frowned as I thought of Elizabeth. The poor woman had stared into the eyes of evil, and that evil had ended her life. It took a cold and hardened individual to look someone in the eyes and pull the trigger—this I knew from personal experience.

While the method used for the murder might offer some insight into the killer's mindset, it did nothing to help me identify the person. I'd worked homicides long enough to know you could never tell how evil a person was by looking on the outside. You'd have to cut them open to see the devil on the inside, and that simply wasn't legal around here.

I wiped beads of sweat from my forehead as fear enveloped me like a cold body of water. Not fear of death, but of failure. More than anything, homicide detectives feared unsolved cases, because that meant a poor victim would not see justice and a killer would still be on the loose. Since I had exactly zero evidence and no crime scene, this case would be nearly impossible to solve. I needed a miracle, and I wasn't too proud to ask God for help.

Back when I was a homicide detective in the city of La Mort, I'd amassed a 100% arrest and conviction rate on all the murder cases I'd investigated. I'd even received an award for my accomplishments, but the award didn't matter. The recognition didn't matter. The only thing that mattered was finding justice for the victims, and I couldn't take credit for all of it. While I did possess the drive and determination it took, the rest was luck and a lot of prayers from my mom. I suddenly wished I could call and ask for her prayers right now, because I was worried sick my streak was about to come to an end.

At least my suspect pool is small, I thought, pushing open the women's bathroom door and stepping inside. Thanks to the hurricane, the town was mostly empty. I would simply need to find out who had stayed behind and focus on them. *As soon as this thing passes, I'm heading back to the school. That's where I'll start. God willing, I'll find something useful.*

CHAPTER 14

Thursday, September 21
Mechant Loup Police Department

The police department was bustling with activity. Susan had hosted a meeting first thing in the morning with officials from the parish and town governments, as well as the sheriff's office, and they had organized a methodical accounting of the damage and injuries caused by the storm in the southern part of Chateau. Large trucks carrying water and other essential supplies were heading straight for town, courtesy of the Louisiana National Guard.

Although the storm had passed, dangerous winds and occasional rain bands persisted, so the power company would not be able to immediately put crews on the ground. That would delay getting the electricity back on in town. The longer it took to restore power, the worse the living conditions could get for everyone who had stayed behind.

It was seven-thirty by the time I had finished dressing for work. After pulling on my boots, I sat at Susan's desk and went over the two reports we'd printed out earlier. I held the one detailing the incident with seventh-grader Liam Wells in one hand and the drug complaint involving Jude Lathrop in the other.

"Which one to interrogate first?" I asked out loud. I turned to Achilles, who was lying patiently in the corner of the office watching me with drooped ears. He looked sad, as though he knew I was about to leave him. "What do you think?"

He barked and it sounded more like Jude than Liam, so I decided to pay the drug dealer a visit first. According to our records, he was no longer living in the Bayou View Apartments. He had a brother living on the east side of town and another living in Central Chateau. I decided to try the east side first. The address was on Locust Lane and it was in the more seedy side of Mechant Loup, not far from the apartments. We made regular drug busts there and residents were always making complaints about shots being fired in the area. Luckily, no one back there could shoot very well, and rarely did a bullet find a human target.

I shoved my pistol into my holster and stood to leave, hesitated before walking out. Achilles had sat up and was licking his chops eagerly. *What the hell?* I thought. *The storm is over and he could use some fresh air.*

"Let's go, boy." I slapped the side of my jeans. "You can come with me."

Letting out a screech, he lunged from his bed and reached me in two bounding leaps. The pads of his paws slid across the floor as he tried to stop, but he crashed into my legs, nearly knocking me over with his large frame. I laughed and rubbed his ears. "Let's go get 'em, big man."

We stepped out into the hallway. The dispatcher's station was crowded and we had to move around a bit so I could catch Susan's eye and wave her over.

"I'm heading out," I told her. "I'll be working the murder case."

"Please call if you even think you need backup." She frowned. "I can't lose you, Clint Wolf."

"I'll try to keep you informed of my movements." I gave her a quick kiss when I didn't think anyone was looking. "You know I'm hard to kill."

She grunted. "Don't go getting all cocky on me. I've got enough to worry about without wondering if you're out there taking unnecessary risks."

"Don't worry. I've got Achilles protecting me."

"That doesn't make me feel any better." She rubbed his head. "I can only imagine the trouble you two could get into."

I waved and pushed my way through the building and out onto the porch at the front of the building, with Achilles right on my heels. Many of the business owners in town were fortunate in that their buildings had fared well, but not all of them had been so lucky. Some of the less fortunate businesses had suffered extensive roof damage or been damaged by flying debris, while a few shops had been completely demolished. The same was true for the houses in town. If you looked up one street, it appeared nothing much had happened, but then if you looked in the opposite direction it looked like a war zone.

The wind blew my hair around as I walked to my Tahoe and held the door for Achilles to enter. In one effortless leap, he went airborne and landed on the front seat. He then crossed over to the passenger side and sat proudly on the seat, staring about like a curious teenager.

When I saw the busted out window on the passenger door, I instinctively rubbed the small bandages on my face. I had forgotten about the injuries and wondered how mean I looked with my face all cut up and my head swollen. I certainly felt mean. I hadn't eaten much, hadn't gotten much sleep, and I was pissed as all hell at the bastard who killed poor Elizabeth Bankston. It didn't matter what the killer's reason was for doing what he did, that woman hadn't deserved to be executed.

As I headed to the east side of town, I could hear the steady hum of generators along Back Street. People had started trickling back into town to check on their property, and most of them had brought generators back with them. It seemed they were settling in for the long haul, as we all knew how long it could take for crews to get the electricity back on. They certainly couldn't start working until the wind subsided, and that would probably not be for another day or two.

I waved as I passed two deputies from the Chateau Parish Sheriff's Office on the bridge that connected the west side of Mechant Loup with the east side. They were helping Susan and our officers go door-to-door checking for injuries, fatalities, and survivors. Thus far, I hadn't heard of any reported deaths, but it was still early in the assessment phase. At least three people had been taken to the hospital. One elderly man had started having chest pains during the storm and was now unresponsive, a teenager had been hit by a fallen tree branch while playing in a ditch, and the roof of a house had collapsed and smashed a woman's legs.

On one hand, I felt bad for not helping, but, on the other hand, I knew I had to solve this murder. For all we knew, the killer was still in town and could strike again. "And that might be him right there," I said to Achilles, slowing my Tahoe as we approached a maroon and tan trailer on the right side of Locust Lane.

I recognized Jude immediately. He was standing on a flimsy blue and white ladder that was made for above ground swimming pools, and he was trying to connect a cable wire to the trailer. He stopped what he was doing when he heard my vehicle and craned his neck to see who it was.

I couldn't pull onto the shoulder of the street because there were five large barrels filled with trash, a large television, and some broken furniture beside the ditch. Afraid that Jude would make a run for it, I parked in the middle of the street and quickly stepped out of my cruiser.

Jude dropped the wire and reached for the rails on the ladder, but he froze when I hollered at him.

"If you even think about running"—I shot my thumb toward Achilles, who had his head hanging out of the broken window—"I'll set the dog on you."

Jude had no idea whether Achilles was a trained killer or a house pet, but he proved right then and there that he wasn't stupid, because he remained on the ladder.

"What the hell do you want with my old man?" called a shrill voice from the steps of the trailer. "Don't you think we've been through enough without you coming here and harassing him?"

I glanced in that direction and saw a woman wearing skimpy black shorts with a blue pocket, a black tank top, a yellow bra, and black sneakers. Her clothes were so tight they looked like they'd been tattooed onto her. She held a yellow broom in one hand and a dustpan in the other, and it appeared she'd been working her ass off. Sweat dripped down her face and chest, and there were smudges up and down her legs.

Jude, on the other hand, wore designer jean shorts that were three sizes too big and stretched down to his ankles. His white T-shirt was as clean as anything he'd ever worn—which meant they were streaked in stains—and so were his white sandals.

"Esther, am I right?" I asked, addressing the woman. "How are you?"

She scrunched up her face, then grunted annoyingly. "I remember you."

"It's nice to see that y'all are back together." I turned my attention once again to Jude. "I need to ask you some questions, Jude. We can do it here or down by the station, but we need to talk in private."

Jude waved for Esther to go inside.

She huffed. "Don't tell me what to do, you little asshole."

CHAPTER 15

Jude opened his mouth to respond to Esther, but she had whirled around and stormed inside the trailer.

"She's a feisty one," I muttered.

"Am I under arrest?" Jude asked from his perch above the ladder, keeping a wary eye on Achilles.

"No. I just need to talk to you." I crossed the ditch and approached the ladder, where I could reach him if he tried anything stupid. "Did y'all ride out the storm here?"

He nodded. "And it's the last time. I thought we were gonna die."

"What's with all the garbage by the road?"

"The storm ripped a hole in the roof and everything got wet. It's all ruined." He shook his head. "I'm glad it's not ours."

"Who does it belong to if it isn't yours?"

"The landlord." He shrugged. "I called and he said just throw it to the road. He said he'd only charge half the rent this month if I pulled up all the wet carpet, too."

"Well, I don't want to take up much of your time, so I'll get right to it." I paused and studied his face. He hadn't bothered asking what the questions were about, so that usually meant the suspect knew why he was being questioned. Of course, in this case, my suspect had probably committed a dozen crimes in just as many days, so he might not know exactly which crime I was here about.

"Where were you Tuesday night?" I asked bluntly.

His expression went blank, then he scowled. It was an ugly scowl, and I wanted to tell him he probably shouldn't do that again, but I didn't.

"Tuesday night..." His voice trailed off and he scratched his head. After a few long seconds, he said, "I'm not sure. I was probably home."

"You'll have to do better than that, young man," I said. "This is important."

"No, wait a minute…I'm *sure* I was home." He nodded for emphasis. "Yep, I was here all night long."

"Great. Now what about during the day?"

"Um, I don't know. I must've been home." He blinked several times. "Wait, what day are we talking about again?"

"Tuesday—two days ago."

"Oh, yeah, I was home all day and night."

"And I guess Esther will verify that fact?"

He nodded. "I can call her out here and—"

"Nah, that's okay." I started toward the front door. "I'll ask her myself."

"Wait up!" Jude started to scramble down the ladder, but I threw out my hand and yelled at him to stop. He stopped abruptly, nearly toppling the ladder over. "What? What's wrong?"

I pointed toward Achilles, who was staring intently at us. "If you get down from that ladder, it's quite possible my K-9 companion will view that as a sign of aggression and he'll attack you."

Jude gulped out loud. "What…what do I do?"

"Just stay put and I'll ask Esther if she was with you all day and night on Tuesday."

He hesitated, but didn't dare move. I walked to the door and rapped loudly on the thin metal. I was lifting my hand to knock a second time when the door abruptly opened.

"What is it?" Esther stood with a hand on her hip, tapping her foot with a bad attitude. "I'm trying to clean up in here."

"Can I come inside for a minute? I just have a quick question."

She huffed and walked into the living room area. "Whatever. Just make it fast. This house won't clean itself."

I stepped through the doorway and felt the floor give a little under my weight. I pushed a little with my foot and realized the subfloor was rotten.

"Well, what's the question?"

"If Jude told me y'all were on the west side all day Tuesday, would he be lying or telling the truth?"

"If he said that," she said slowly, after hesitating for a second, "then it's true."

"What do *you* say? Where were y'all Tuesday during the day?"

"Like Jude said, we were on the west side."

"What were y'all doing on the west side?"

She shrugged. "I don't know. Just hanging out."

"Where?"

"On the west side."

"Where on the west side?"

"At a friend's house."

"What friend?"

She turned and walked toward a sofa that was positioned against the back wall. While her back was turned to me, I scanned the room. The kitchen was to the left and a bedroom was to the right. The bedroom door was slightly ajar and I could see the bed. There—in plain sight from where I was standing—was an AR-15 rifle and a pump-action shotgun resting atop the mattress.

"Esther, whose guns are those?" I shot a thumb toward the room. "And don't make me ask twice."

She spun around. "What guns? There aren't any guns—"

"Sit on the sofa and don't move." I said it with such authority that Esther's mouth clamped shut and she sank to the stained cushion without uttering a word.

Keeping an eye on her, I pushed the door open and glanced inside the room. In addition to the guns on the bed that seemed out of place, I saw a Mac Book, a Canon camera with a big lens, two flat screen televisions, and a box of jewelry on the floor.

When I looked at Esther again, her gaze had shifted downward and she was fidgeting in her seat.

"Aren't you tired of going to jail for Jude?"

Tears welled up in her eyes and a few drops spilled to the floor. She quickly brushed them away.

"I bet you were a good girl before you hooked up with him, weren't you?" I studied her long face. "I know your life isn't going the way you planned for it to go, but it's not too late to make some adjustments. You can change your future, and I can help."

"How?" Her eyes were bloodshot when she looked up. "How could you possibly help me?"

"For starters, if you tell me where Jude got this loot, I won't arrest you. I'll recommend that the district attorney's office use you as a witness." I paused while she considered my offer. Finally, she shook her head.

"I can't. He'll kill me."

"Why do you say that?" I asked, leaning forward. My heart pounded a little faster in my chest. What did she know? "What's he done to make you think he'd murder you?"

She waved her hand. "Nothing, but if I tell on him I'm sure he'll hurt me."

"What do you know about the woman he killed?"

Her mouth dropped open and she recoiled in horror. "He killed someone?"

"You tell me."

"Tell you what?"

"Tell me what you know about the woman he killed."

"I…I didn't even know he killed someone. Who was it? When did it happen? Is this why you're asking me about Tuesday?"

Ignoring her questions, I walked to the door and checked to make sure Jude was still on the ladder. He was, and he was locked in a stare-off with Achilles. Achilles' ears were pointing straight up and his jaw was set. It looked like he was trying to decide if he should come out and eat Jude or stay in my truck. He was disciplined, so I knew he would stay put.

"Look," I said, turning toward Esther once again, "I'll find you a safe place to stay if you cooperate with me."

"But I don't know anything about a murdered lady."

"What about the loot in the bedroom? Where'd Jude get it?"

Esther shuffled her feet. "You know how I told you we were at a friend's house on the west side of town on Tuesday?"

I nodded.

"Well, that wasn't entirely true."

"I'm not surprised."

"We…well, Jude told me he wanted to go to the west side to see if any stores were open. We were out of milk." Esther's eyes shot toward the door when she heard a noise.

"Go on, it's okay. Jude hasn't moved from the ladder. If he does, my dog will take a chunk out of him."

"He's deathly afraid of dogs." Esther took a deep breath and placed a hand over her throat. "He asked me to take him to the west side to look for some milk. Everything was closed because of the storm, so he told me to drive back to the east side. Although it was still daylight, we didn't see a soul in sight."

She paused to swallow, and I wondered if she was going to lose her nerve. "He told me to park on the side of Cypress Highway, where they have those houses all close to each other. You know the place?"

I nodded, she continued.

"He then jumped out of the car and was gone for about an hour. When he got back…" Her voice trailed off and she stared at her hands. "When he got back he had those guns. He threw them in the back seat and told me not to go anywhere. He made two more trips from the houses to the car, bringing the television, computers, and other stuff with him."

I shot a thumb toward the bedroom. "Is that everything he stole?"

"I think he got some cash, but that'll be in his pockets. He never shares any money with me."

"Were you scared during this time? Scared that he might hurt you if you didn't go along with his plan?"

"Nah, I wasn't scared."

"Would he have hurt you had you refused to go along with his plan?"

She shrugged. "I never really thought about it."

"Are you scared of him now?"

"I mean, if he finds out I told on him, he'll be mad."

"Do you think he'll hurt you?"

She shrugged again. "I guess it's possible."

"Has he ever hit on you?"

"No, but I never told on him before."

"Okay, so what happened after he made the second trip?"

"Well, he had just left to make a third trip when some hail started falling. They were big chunks of ice. Next thing I know, Jude's screaming for me to start the car. He was running from the house and pointing toward the sky." She shivered. "When I looked up, I saw a tornado coming down from the sky. It was the scariest thing I'd ever seen."

"What did you do next?"

"I drove as fast as I could and we came straight here. We saw the tornado pass on the road behind us and go toward the fields."

I was thoughtful. If what she was saying was true, Jude couldn't have killed Elizabeth, because he was on the wrong side of town when the tornado hit.

"Do you know anything at all about the dead girl?"

She shook her head hurriedly from side to side. "I swear it."

I sighed, told her to stay on the sofa. "I won't tell Jude what you said, and neither should you."

CHAPTER 16

Jude was still clinging to the top of the ladder when I stepped outside carrying the two guns. "You're a felon, Jude. You're not supposed to be in possession of firearms."

His head sank and I thought he was going to fall off the ladder. "Those aren't mine."

"No kidding. They're stolen, you dimwit." I approached the ladder and looked up at him, cited the Miranda rights. "I don't have a lot of time, so I need you to be honest. I don't want to have to work for the truth, got it?"

He licked his lips and nodded slowly, glancing from me to Achilles. I knew he wanted to run, but he was too scared. He was convinced Achilles would chase after him if he did so.

"So, where'd you get the guns?"

"They were in the trailer when I got back home from visiting my friends. Someone must've broke into my house."

"When was that?"

"It was right before the storm. In fact, that's why I didn't call the law. I was waiting for the storm to pass so I could report it."

"Just so I understand what you're saying—someone broke into your trailer and left guns and other stolen items behind?"

He threw up his hands. "Now, wait a minute—I didn't know they were stolen. I just thought someone put it there for safekeeping. You know, until after the storm. But I knew I wasn't supposed to be around guns, so I stayed in the living room and was waiting for the storm to pass so I could call the law."

I took a deep breath, trying to remain patient. On a normal day, I would have been amused by his story and would've enjoyed talking him into a confession, but I didn't have time for his lies today. He wasn't my killer, so I needed to finish with him and get back to work. I could get a warrant and pick him up after the electricity was back on and things returned to normal.

"Jude, I know you broke into that house off of Cypress Highway and stole these two guns, the television, and all the other stuff in your bedroom. Just tell me why you did it and we can both go on about our business. I'll let you go for now, but I'll get a warrant for your arrest and I'll expect you to turn yourself in after the storm."

"Arrest? For what? I didn't do nothing!"

I rested the butts of the guns on each of my boots. "Jude, was Mrs. Smith dead before or after you broke into her house?"

Jude's Adam's apple shifted upward as he swallowed hard. "I already told you...I don't know nothing about no break in."

"Forget the burglary—that's small potatoes compared to what you might be facing." I shook my head slowly and frowned. "I never figured you for a killer, Jude."

"I'm not! I never killed nobody."

"Well, she didn't kill herself." I studied his face, which had turned several shades whiter. "The way it looked to me, Mrs. Smith came out the bathroom and caught you in her house. She threatened to call the cops and you panicked. You didn't mean to hurt her, but you were scared—"

"That's all bull! No one was even home."

"Are you sure?"

"Positive. If someone was killed, it was after I left."

"How'd you get inside?"

He sighed heavily, realizing he'd given himself up. "There's not a dead woman, is there?"

"I don't know, I haven't been out to the house yet." I hefted one of the guns. "So, how'd you get inside?"

"I broke a window on the back door. Everything else was boarded up, so I knew nobody was home."

I questioned him for about twenty minutes more and he laid it all out for me.

"What were you planning on doing with these?" I asked about the guns.

"I...I owe some important people some money. I needed a gun to carry with me for protection, and I needed to raise as much money as fast as I could."

I cocked my head to the side. "How were you going to carry these? Hide one up each pant leg?"

"I was looking for a handgun, but that's all I found. I know a lot of people who like AR-15s, so I thought I could trade it for a handgun. I was going to use the shotgun for home protection." He lifted a hand. "Look, I know I'm not supposed to possess a firearm, but my life's in danger—and it's the law's fault."

"The law's fault?"

"Yeah...the law and that bitch who used to live next door to me. The merchandise they took belonged to someone else, and now they're after me for their money."

The man in me wanted to jerk him off the ladder, but the cop in me knew I couldn't. "Would it surprise you to know that Elizabeth is dead?"

"Who's Elizabeth?"

"That bitch who used to live next door." My voice was cold as I repeated his words.

His face turned even paler. "No!"

"Yeah, so show her some respect." I considered what he'd just revealed. If Jude was burglarizing a house on the east side during the storm, he couldn't have killed Elizabeth, but that didn't rule out these "important" people, who were clearly drug dealers.

"I need to know whose drugs they were, and I need to know now." I stepped closer to the ladder. "There's a good chance they executed Elizabeth—and if so, they're coming for you next."

Jude shook his head violently from side to side. "No way! I'm no rat."

"They'll kill you, Jude. As sure as I'm standing here, they'll hunt you down and execute you and Esther, just like they did to Elizabeth."

"I'll have to take my chances."

"Look, I can arrest you right now and you could end up spending another large chunk of your life in prison."

Jude scoffed. "Sorry, but I'm more afraid of them than I am of you. You've got rules you have to follow—they don't. As long as I come up with the money I owe, I'll be okay. They know I'm loyal."

I chewed on this for a minute, then started hammering him with more questions. I must've interrogated him for another thirty minutes, but he wouldn't give up the names of his supplier. Next, I left him on the ladder and tried my luck with Esther, but she knew nothing.

"I know he sells drugs, but I never met the people who bring it to him." She shook her head. "And I don't want to. Jude said they're scary."

The only other thing she knew was that Jude met them somewhere in Mississippi. "When he makes a run," she said, "it usually takes him four hours."

That didn't do much good, because she didn't know how long it took to carry out the deal or if he stopped anywhere along the trip, so it would be impossible to accurately predict a location based on the time of travel.

After securing all of the stolen merchandise into the back of my Tahoe, I reminded Jude that I would be obtaining a warrant for his arrest.

"You're lucky the rest of the town is in the middle of a cleanup effort and I'm working a murder case," I said, fixing him with cold eyes. "Otherwise, I'd take you right off that ladder and haul your ass to jail this very minute."

He nodded his head, still focusing on Achilles. "As long as you promise not to bring that big dog around here no more, I'll turn myself in whenever you say the word."

Not liking that circumstance had forced me to allow him to run free, I just grunted and drove off.

As was to be expected, cell service was sketchy after the storm, so I used my satellite phone to call dispatch. When Lindsey answered, I asked if she could contact the sheriff's office and get me the number to Mallory Tuttle's SAT phone.

Mallory Tuttle was a detective with the Chateau Parish Sheriff's Office. She was one of Susan's closest friends, and she was a great law enforcement resource. When I was connected to her, I dropped Jude's name and asked if she'd ever heard of him.

"No." There were loud noises in the background and she had to raise her voice for me to hear her. "What's he into?"

"He's a low-level drug dealer from town. According to his girlfriend, his drugs are coming in from Mississippi."

"Is he the guy y'all seized the meth from a couple of months ago? I believe I heard Amy worked the case?"

"That's him."

"No, other than the newspaper article, I've never had any dealings with him—" She paused to holler at someone, then came back on the line. "I'll run his name and do some digging as soon as things get back to normal."

"Are you on a traffic point?"

"For the past ten minutes—and I'm ready to kill someone already."

CHAPTER 17

After leaving Jude's house, I pulled onto the shoulder of the road and snatched up the juvenile report on Liam Wells. There wasn't much to the report. His parents' names were listed, as was their home address. They lived a block from the school on Pine.

I scratched my head, wondering if they had remained in town for the storm. I hadn't gone down Pine Street when we were doing the door-to-door notifications, so I wouldn't know if they'd planned on staying or not. Something suddenly occurred to me and I headed down Washington Street—where business owners were moving about their shops trying to get everything up and running again—and then north on Main.

The checkpoint at the town limits had been set up much earlier in the morning, just as the back end of Hurricane Samson was making its exit. The officers working it had been instructed to only allow citizens with proper identification through.

"We don't want strangers with bad intentions rolling through town looking to take advantage of the abandoned neighborhoods and homes," Susan had told her officers at the briefing. "If they don't have some form of identification with a Mechant Loup address, they don't get in—period."

While that was the normal procedure during hurricanes and it made perfect sense to keep sightseers and potential looters away, I suddenly realized I could use it to my advantage. The re-entry logs could provide me with the names of everyone who had evacuated. Once I had this list, I could eliminate as suspects the residents whose names appeared on it, and I would then be able to focus on those who had remained in town during the storm. As far as we knew, everyone who had evacuated had done so before the tornado struck town.

I slowed my vehicle and cruised through Mechant Loup North, where there was a large concentration of bucket trucks along the shoulder of the road. The workers were waiting until the wind died down so they could start repairing the power lines. I wanted to call Claire and ask her if she'd rather Melvin work with power lines instead of law enforcement. Personally, I'd rather face a bullet than the electricity that flowed through those wires any day.

When I reached the checkpoint, I saw Baylor Rice sitting in his patrol car on one side of the barricade, and a Chateau Parish deputy was in his cruiser on the other side. The two cars were parked side-by-side and each officer was leaning out of the driver side window talking. I pulled up on the passenger side of Baylor's cruiser and slid my window down. He did the same and leaned over.

"What's up, Clint?" he asked. "Did you catch the bastard who killed Elizabeth Bankston?"

I told him I hadn't, then asked how things were going on the checkpoint.

"Slow at the moment." He ran his hand over his short cropped hair. "We haven't had a customer for at least an hour."

"Can I see the log?"

He nodded and grabbed a clipboard from the seat beside him. Stretching as far as he could, he extended his arm in my direction and I retrieved the clipboard from him. I scanned the sheet, turned it over.

"Only one page?" I asked.

He nodded. "Everyone we've met so far came in from the Lafayette area. The folks who headed north and east are probably still getting hammered."

He was right. The storm was heading northeast, right into the face of anyone thinking of returning. Samson had been downgraded to a tropical storm, but he was still a force to be reckoned with.

I went over the names one-by-one, sliding my finger across each line as I read them aloud. Achilles moved his head over my arm, staring down at the list as though he could read English.

"Do you see it, big man?" I asked. "Because I don't."

"Who're you looking for?" Baylor asked.

"I'm looking for a kid named Liam Wells. His dad's name is Smitty and his mom's name is Anne." I sighed and handed back the clipboard. "I've got no real reason to think he's involved, but I'm trying to cover all the bases."

"How'd his name come up?" Baylor hadn't been a cop long and

he was eager to learn. "I've always wondered how detectives develop their suspects."

"Well, in this case, he simply flipped over a desk in the library where she teaches computer skills. It doesn't make him a suspect, but it's someone she's had problems with in the past, so it's worth checking out."

He nodded. "That makes sense."

I thanked him and started to drive away.

"Smitty Wells, you said?" he asked, a pen hovering over his notepad.

I nodded and he told me he'd keep an eye out for them.

I thanked Baylor and drove off, heading south toward town. If Liam and his parents were home, it meant they stayed through the storm and would've been in town during the murder. The proximity of their house to the school would provide Liam opportunity, but it seemed a stretch to think that just because a student flipped a desk over in class he would want to kill his teacher.

If it *was* him, there had to be some other motive—like she got him expelled or kicked off the football team or some other thing that a current eighth grader would consider tragic at that age.

CHAPTER 18

The Wells' home was on a corner lot and I raised my eyebrow when I saw a short skinny kid straddling a large broken tree branch in the front yard. He was wearing an old T-shirt and cut-off jeans and holding an electric chainsaw in his hands.

While there hadn't been any pictures in the report, the kid appeared to be the right age and this was the right address, so it had to be Liam. The kid didn't look up, so I made the block and approached from the opposite direction.

The exterior of the home was made of orange brick and trimmed in white. The bricks were discolored and the paint on the wooden trim was peeling in most places. There were a few spots that had been weathered down to the bare wood and seemed rotten. The wooden fence that wrapped the southeastern corner of the house appeared new, so it was a shame that the fallen branch had taken out an eight-foot section when it crashed to the ground.

The driveway was just wide enough to fit one car—it was an old blue sedan—and the rear end of the vehicle was nearly hanging out into the road. I parked behind the sedan and shut off my engine. There was an old white truck backed into the yard on the western side of the house and it was cluttered with junk. A basketball goal that was cemented into the ground was bent in half and the goal was resting on the ground—just another gift from Hurricane Samson.

After telling Achilles to stay put, I walked around to the back of my Tahoe and popped open the rear gate.

"Can I help you?" asked a gruff voice from inside the wooden fence. I glanced over my shoulder and saw a balding man with a potbelly standing near the boy. He wore thick leather gloves and was holding a crowbar in his hand.

I pulled my chainsaw from the cargo area and turned to face them. "It looks like y'all could use a hand—or a tool."

The boy jumped down from the tree and shut off the electric saw. The fence was only four feet tall, and the boy's head couldn't have been more than twelve inches higher than it. "Dad, he's got a real chainsaw."

"I can see that, Liam." The man walked to a generator and hit the kill switch. He then approached me and held out his hand. "The name's Smitty."

"Clint." I nodded in Liam's direction. "Liam, am I right?"

The boy nodded. His messy brown hair was plastered to his head and sweat rolled freely down his face. It was still overcast and the wind was blowing strong, but cutting up a tree was hard work.

"Where would you like me to start?" I asked priming the pump on my chainsaw.

"It would be great if you could get that big branch off the fence." Smitty pointed to the section that had been caved in. "Until I get that thing cut away, I won't be able to patch the damn hole."

"Cool." I walked over to the limb that rested on the fence and fired up my chainsaw. The chain sliced through the wood with ease, and within seconds the limb fell free.

Smitty waved Liam over and they lifted the branch off the fence and placed it in the yard. I then set about cutting the larger branch into manageable two-foot chunks. As I worked, I kept my eye on Liam, trying to decide if he was a cold-blooded killer or not. He appeared to be any normal teenager, but I'd worked enough homicide cases to know that murderers were a lot like books—you couldn't judge them by their covers.

Once I was done, I shut off the chainsaw and set about helping Liam and his dad stack the logs in the back yard. I didn't really have time for this, but I felt like it would go a long way toward building a rapport with Smitty. If I could get him on my side, he would make his son talk.

"So, did y'all ride out the storm?" I asked as Smitty and I bent to lift one of the larger logs together.

He nodded. "It wasn't bad. A little wind, a lot of rain—typical summer day in Louisiana."

We carried the log to the back yard and dropped it. I then turned to Liam. "I bet you were going crazy locked up in the house, eh?"

Liam scoffed. "I wasn't locked up in the house."

"Oh, no?"

"I ain't afraid of no storm."

"What'd you do?"

He shrugged. "Rode my bike, did some work on my truck...stuff like that."

I shot a thumb toward the old white jalopy. "Is that your truck?"

"Yeah. Dad said if I fix it up I can have it when I get my license."

"That's cool." I continued making small talk for a few minutes and a girl came outside holding two bottles of water. She looked annoyed.

"Mom said I should bring some water." She stopped short and her attitude changed when she saw me. "Oh, I'm sorry, I only brought two. I can get another if you like."

I waved her off. "No need."

The girl returned inside and Smitty and Liam sat on the ground, leaned against the house.

"So, I'm actually here on official business," I said, squatting on my heels. I studied Liam's face for a reaction and I saw the skin around his eyes tighten.

"What kind of business?" Smitty asked, glancing sideways at Liam. "I swear boy, if you messed up again, you're not getting that truck."

"But you said I could have it if I fixed—"

"And I can change my mind, too." The man turned his scowling face in my direction. "Are you here because of Liam?"

I nodded slowly. "I am, but it might not be what you're thinking."

"How do you know what I'm thinking?" Smitty asked.

"Well, I can imagine you're probably thinking he might have done something mischievous." I paused and watched him nod his head slowly. "But that's not the case. You see, I'm working a homicide investigation."

"Wait...what?" Liam asked, nearly falling over. "Isn't that a murder?"

"Are you saying my son killed somebody?" Smitty's voice shook with anger. "Liam, did you hurt somebody?"

"Now, just hold on, Mr. Wells." I raised a hand to calm him. "No one's saying Liam killed anyone. I just have some questions for him. But before I get into that, I have to read him his rights and allow him some time alone to consult with you."

The first question most people asked when I read them their rights was if they were going to jail, but Smitty didn't. That told me he'd done this a time or two and he knew the drill—he'd get fifteen minutes alone with Liam, I'd question the kid, and if he admitted to a crime he'd be released into his dad's custody. If it was something really bad, he'd be placed in juvenile detention.

I gathered the rights form from my Tahoe, completed it, had each of them sign it, then walked back to allow Smitty and Liam about fifteen minutes alone. I hadn't told them whose murder I was investigating, because I wanted to see if he'd slip up and mention Elizabeth.

I called Susan while I waited in the driver's seat and turned to Achilles while the phone rang.

"What do you think, big man? Did the kid do it?"

Achilles cocked his head to the side, but didn't answer.

"Yeah, I hear you, boy. I've got no clue either."

"No clue about what?" Susan asked.

"Oh, I'm just talking to Achilles."

"How's he enjoying the ride?"

"He loves it so far, and so do I."

After updating me on their efforts, she asked if I'd found anything on Jude Lathrop.

"Nah, he was burglarizing a house on the east side during the murder."

"Were a couple of guns stolen? An AR and a shotgun?"

"Yep."

"Lindsey received a call about it a few minutes ago. The homeowners just returned from Alexandria and found their place broken into and a bunch of stuff missing." She sighed. "I told Lindsey to tell them we'd respond as soon as possible, but we're still assessing the damage."

I explained how I'd recovered everything and was going to get a warrant as soon as things settled down in town. "I hated to leave him running free, but I've got to run down this murderer."

"He'll be out within the hour anyway," she said with a grunt. "His parents must have money, because they always post his bail, no matter how high the amount or what he did."

Smitty was leaning close to Liam's face and, although my windows were closed and the wind was howling outside, I could hear him yelling. Liam was trying to explain something, but the man didn't seem to care. I smiled to myself. If he did commit the murder, I wouldn't have to work for this confession, because Smitty would get it out of him—one way or the other, and in ways I couldn't.

When it looked like they were done talking, I told Susan I'd have to call her back, and stepped out of my Tahoe.

CHAPTER 19

"Well?" I asked Smitty. "Are y'all willing to talk to me?"

"Sure," Smitty said. "He swears he doesn't know anything about a murder."

"I don't know a thing." Liam scratched his unkempt hair. "I've never seen a dead body in my life and I don't even know who you're talking about."

"I'm talking about Elizabeth Bankston." I paused to study his expression, but his face was blank.

"Who's that? I don't know no Elizabeth Bankston."

"Mrs. Bankston, one of your seventh grade teachers. She taught computer skills. You don't remember flipping a desk over in the library?"

His eyes widened. "You mean Miss Liz?"

I nodded. "She was found murdered."

"Oh, wow, that's crazy." He leaned back against the house and shook his head in awe. "I never did like her, but I can't believe she's dead."

"Why didn't you like her?"

"She was a bitch—"

"Liam!" shouted Smitty.

"Oops, sorry!" Liam cleared his throat. "She was mean. She was always sending me to the office saying I was disrupting her class, but I wasn't."

"What were you doing that would make her say you were disrupting class?" I asked.

"I mean, I'd clown around a little, but I did that in all my classes. The other teachers didn't mind. They even laughed at me." He shook his head. "She just didn't like me, I think. She was always comparing me to Beverly and saying what a model student she was and asking why I couldn't be more like her."

"Who's Beverly? Your girlfriend?"

Liam's face contorted into a grimace. "Uh, gross! No, she's my sister."

"Was your sister in the same grade as you?"

"She's one grade ahead of me. She had Miss Liz two years ago. She's not at the middle school anymore, because she's a *high schooler* now." He wriggled his fingers in the air when he said "high schooler".

"Have you had any classes with Miss Liz this year?" I asked.

"No. She only—"

"It's no *sir*, son!" Smitty hissed.

"Sorry—no *sir*. She only teaches computer skills in seventh grade, but she teaches in the library so I see her sometimes when I check out books."

"Did any of your buddies share your feelings for her? Any of them hated her like you do?"

"I don't *hate* her, I just don't like her. And yeah, none of them liked her. She was always getting us in trouble."

"Any of them hated her enough to want her dead?"

His eyebrows lifted high on his face. "I don't know anybody who would actually kill a person. Sure, we do it in video games, but that's just a game. I don't know anybody who would do it in real life. That's insane. I've never even known a person who was murdered."

I asked him for his whereabouts on Tuesday, between noon and three.

"I was home, I guess...maybe riding up and down the neighborhood looking at the storm. I don't really keep track of time when we don't have school." He held up his left wrist. "I don't have a watch, so I never know what time it is."

"Don't you have a cell phone?" I asked.

"I do, but I never look at the time. I just chill and have fun."

"Did you hang out with any of your friends on Tuesday?"

He shook his head. "They all evacuated. Their parents aren't cool like my dad, so they didn't get to stay and watch the storm."

"I'm not cool, son," his dad retorted. "We just couldn't afford it."

I frowned, knowing this was the case for a lot of folks. Since they didn't have the extra money to flee during disasters, their only two options were to stay put or head to one of the public shelters that were available. Considering these shelters usually consisted of large and crowded gymnasiums, rough cots for beds, and absolutely zero privacy, it was no wonder most families decided to take their chances with Mother Nature. It was sad.

I decided to try another way to nail down Liam's timeline. "Do you remember a tornado blowing through here early on Tuesday? There was one later in the day, but I'm talking about the one that blew through early on."

His eyes lit up. "Yeah! I saw it!"

"You did?"

He pointed toward the school with one hand as he dug a cell phone from his pocket with the other. "I even videoed it."

I leaned close as he slid his finger across a cracked screen and accessed his image file. He scrolled through some photos and then finally stopped on a video file. He set it to play and turned it so I could see.

I whistled as I watched the funnel cloud appear out of the darkness and snake across the sky, heading straight for earth. The tornado touched down a couple of blocks from where Liam was standing, so he hadn't been able to catch the ground action. However, his video captured the movement of the tornado and even showed debris being flung into the air and getting caught up in the rotation.

I asked him if I could hold it and, after a slight pause, he surrendered the phone. I held it closer to my face and played it again, trying to see if I could detect blue fabric up among the debris. It was no use. The tornado was too far away and the items spinning around were too small to identify by shape or color.

When I'd watched it a couple more times, I handed him the phone and asked if he could forward the video to me.

"I don't have service right now, but I can when I get it back."

I pulled a business card from my pocket and handed it to Smitty.

"Now," I said slowly, studying both Liam and Smitty, "I have to ask about guns."

"What about them?" Smitty asked.

"Do y'all have any?"

"I've got a twelve gauge shotgun," Liam offered. "It's a Mossberg."

"And I've got three rifles and two shotguns," Smitty said. "I got all of them from my grandpa right before he died, and Liam got the Mossberg from my dad."

"Any handguns?"

"I had two handguns, but one of them got stolen," Smitty said.

"Now I only have one."

That got my attention. I'd worked a couple of cases over the years where legal guns were used in robberies or murders and then the registered owner conveniently reported them lost or stolen.

"Stolen, eh?" I asked, glancing in Liam's direction as another idea came to mind. If Liam had taken his dad's gun and used it to kill Elizabeth, surely he wouldn't have put it back.

"Yeah, it was in my car and someone came in and stole it." He pointed toward the front yard. "My car was parked out near the road one night and the gun was in the glove box. When I got called out for work the next morning, I saw the glove box was open a little. That's when I noticed it was gone."

"When did this happen?"

"A couple of years ago."

My shoulders drooped. That was too long ago to be linked to Elizabeth's murder. "Did you make a report?"

"Sure did."

I made a mental note to check on the report just to cover all my bases. Next, I asked if I could see his semi-automatic pistol, and he nodded his head.

"Afterward, I'd like to search your house," I said. "It's routine in cases like this for us to try and get permission to search a suspect's residence."

"You really think Liam had something to do with this, don't you?"

"At this very moment, I don't know who did it, so I'm trying to be as thorough as possible. If I had evidence that he did it, I wouldn't ask for permission. Instead, I'd get a search warrant and just barge into your house and start searching."

"What would you be looking for?"

"I'm searching for any and all evidence that might prove a connection between a suspect and the victim," I explained. "And I'm doing this with every suspect. If Liam didn't do it, there won't be any evidence against him and I can clear him as a suspect."

Smitty stood slowly and then nodded. "Sure, you can search my house, but don't mind the mess. We moved everything up on chairs and tables in case it flooded, so it's chaotic inside."

Once we entered the house, Smitty called his wife Anne and daughter Beverly into the living room and explained what was going on.

Anne Wells was a robust woman with a quick smile and a friendly demeanor, but her face suddenly fell when she heard the word "murder".

"Is this about the teacher who was found dead near the school?" she asked. "Why would you be searching our house about that? I thought she died in a tornado. At least that's what I heard."

"They think I did it," Liam blurted. "Someone told them I hated Ms. Liz and they think I murdered her."

"She was murdered?" Beverly asked incredulously. "Dear Lord! Did you do it, Liam? Did you?"

"He didn't kill anyone," Smitty said, waving for them to calm down. "The detective is just doing his job. He's checking out everyone in town. Am I right, detective?"

"Correct." I nodded to reassure them. "I'm sure Liam had nothing to do with any of it."

That seemed to satisfy Anne and she went to talking in hushed tones with Liam while I followed Smitty to the back bedroom. He opened a closet door and pulled a box from the top shelf. He then handed me his semi-automatic pistol, which was a Ruger P85 nine millimeter.

I hadn't seen one of those in years and whistled. I dropped the magazine and locked the slide back, confirming that it was empty. I then pulled out my cell phone and turned the flashlight feature on. While holding the pistol with the muzzle pointing up, I shined the light into the barrel. Thick fouling lined the bore, which meant it hadn't been cleaned in quite some time, and that was actually a good thing for Smitty and Liam.

If this had been the gun used in Elizabeth's murder, there would've been flesh and blood blown back into the bore and up against the muzzle, unless it had been cleaned. Since there was no blowback and the bore appeared to have been dirty for some time, I was fairly confident it hadn't been used in her murder. Had it been clean, I wouldn't be able to rule them out, because it would've been possible they cleaned the pistol after killing her.

I handed the gun back to Smitty and spent the next thirty minutes searching the house. I turned up nothing of evidentiary value. Before leaving, I asked them to call if they heard anything.

I slammed my door a little harder when I got into my Tahoe. Elizabeth had only been dead for two days and I'd already run out of suspects. Usually, one interview would lead to another and then another until I found the person responsible for the crime. In this case, neither Jude nor Liam had led me to another suspect.

With nowhere else to turn, I headed toward the school. Maybe I'd get lucky and find the crime scene.

CHAPTER 20

There were more tree branches scattered about the school yard than earlier—some of them huge—and a section of gutter had been ripped from one of the sides of the main building. Other than that, the rest of the school appeared in the same condition as we'd left it.

I parked behind the main building and slid all the working windows in my Tahoe down, told Achilles to guard the truck. He whined a little, but when I gave the sharp command to *Stay*, he quieted down and settled into his job. Thick clouds still hovered over the town and the strong wind blew through my windows like a shop fan, keeping Achilles nice and cool.

After moving to the passenger side to rub his ears, I walked out to the football field and spent the next two hours scouring the surrounding area. I expanded my search from yesterday, trying desperately to find any hint of a crime scene. I stopped several times to allow Achilles to stretch his legs, drink some water, and do his business, and then I'd go right back to searching, but I had no luck.

I was walking back toward my Tahoe when I saw a car parked in the back lot, not far from a side door to the main building. It hadn't been there fifteen minutes earlier when I'd looked in that direction, so they must've just driven up.

I glanced toward Achilles, who was sitting with his head hanging out of the driver's window, his eyes half closed against the strong breeze. His tongue dangled from his mouth and he seemed to be loving life. He was happy to be outside again, and I didn't blame him. I'm sure he didn't understand why I'd locked him up in the police department for two days, and he had probably been mad at me at first, but one look at his face and I knew all was forgiven.

I hurried toward the building, stopping to feel the hood on the car on my way. It was warm. Out of force of habit, I used my right thumb to make sure the safety on my Beretta semi-automatic pistol was off.

As I walked along the back of the main building where the office was located, I heard shoes crunching glass just to the inside of where I was passing. I didn't know if the person on the inside knew I was there or not, but I wasn't taking any chances. I wanted to see them before they saw me, so I crouched low and made my way stealthily toward the southern end of the building and around to the front.

After checking to make sure everything was clear, I pulled on the door handle to the same double doors I'd entered last night. They opened, so whoever it was had a key. I relaxed a little, but still slinked carefully down the hall. I had gone about fifty feet when I heard some cursing coming from the office. I straightened fully when I recognized the principal's voice.

"What's up, Kevin?" I asked when I'd stepped into the doorway.

"Oh, shit!" Kevin Shelton spun around and threw the book he'd been holding high in the air. It bounced off the ceiling and fell to the floor to my right. "Jesus Christ, detective…you nearly gave me a heart attack."

I grunted inwardly as I took in the man. He couldn't have been more than fifty-five, sixty, yet Lindsey thought he was so old he should be dead. I was thirty-three, so fifty was suddenly young to me. Of course, I could remember thinking my mom was old when I was a kid, but she would've been my age back then.

I'd love to know how old Lindsey thinks I am, I wondered wryly.

"Sorry about scaring you, Mr. Shelton." I scanned the room, noticed there was about an inch of water on the floor near the windows. "When did you get back into town?"

"We rolled in about nine this morning." He picked up the book and tossed it onto the counter. "Luckily, my house didn't have much damage—just a few dents in the roof and a downed tree in the front yard—but the school didn't fare so well. I just hope the electricity comes on soon."

I glanced over at the surveillance system. "Do you have a generator in this place?"

"We do, but it's out of commission." Kevin continued scurrying about the room—his curly black hair looking like he'd just crawled out of bed—trying to move the electronic devices as far away from the window as possible. "I told the school board we needed to get it fixed back when the Hurricane Center named the first storm of the season, but did they listen? No! Now, here we are, getting hit by number nineteen, and it still isn't fixed."

He was right, we did have a busy hurricane season, but none of them had made landfall along the Louisiana coast. In fact, most of them didn't even enter the Gulf of Mexico. Of the five that did enter the Gulf this year, two hit Mexico, one hit Texas, one hit Florida, and we had just gotten hit by the fifth one—and it was the biggest of all five so far this season.

"I need access to your surveillance footage as soon as possible." I pointed toward the DVR resting on the shelf. "If I brought a portable generator in here, do you think we could get the surveillance system up and running?"

He pushed his fists into his hips, which made his back hunch slightly and it pushed his protruding belly farther out. My guess was that he skipped the gym on a regular basis and sat around drinking beer on most days.

"I don't see why it wouldn't." His face seemed troubled. "Since you're here, I'm guessing you didn't find Elizabeth yet."

"Actually, we did." I wiped my face, shot a thumb over my shoulder. "Her body was located in that giant oak tree at the corner of the two buildings."

Kevin's ruby face turned to ash. "Her *body*? Are you saying she's dead?"

"Worse…she was murdered."

Kevin stumbled backward and reached out with his hands. He grabbed onto the counter to steady himself. His mouth moved, but no words came out. I thought he was going to faint.

I stepped forward, grabbed a chair from the corner, and slid it in his direction. "Are you okay? You don't look so good."

He didn't resist when I guided him to the chair. When he was seated, he dropped his face into his hands. "It can't be so. Elizabeth was one of the good ones. I…who would want to do something like this?"

"At this point, we have no suspects, so it's imperative I get my hands on those surveillance videos."

"Wait—do you think it happened here? At the school?"

"I found her shoes in the back of the school. It looked like someone was chasing her and, at some point, she was taken by the tornado." I paused. "But, before that, someone shot her in the head."

Kevin clutched at his face. "Oh, God, is it safe to be in here right now? Should I leave?"

"The killer's long gone, but I do need to see that footage."

He nodded. "Certainly…absolutely. I'll do whatever I can to help. Elizabeth was like family to us."

I wanted to call Melvin and ask if he could bring a generator to the school, but I'd heard a call over the radio requesting his help to search the wreckage of a mobile home across town, so I knew he was busy.

I told Kevin I would head home to pick up my generator and then I'd be back. He promised he'd be right there when I returned.

CHAPTER 21

After I lugged the generator into the back of my cruiser, I paused to take a breath and decided to check in with Baylor. I called him on the radio and asked him to go to a private channel.

"Got any more names for me?" I asked.

"A few families came through, but not many," he said. "Ready to copy?"

"Shoot." As he called out the names, I wrote them down. When I was done, I thanked him and jumped into my Tahoe. I sped up our street and then headed north on Main, arriving at the school ten minutes later. I parked in the back parking lot and unloaded the generator, straining my back as I did so. I was glad the damn thing had wheels.

"Damn, I'm getting old," I muttered to Achilles, who was looking over the front seat at me like I was crazy. I was worried he'd try to eat Kevin, so I told him to stay. I pulled the gate closed and grabbed the handle, putting my weight into it.

It had been thirty minutes since I'd left but, true to his word, Kevin was still in the office. I tossed him one end of an extension cord and then wheeled the generator back out into the hallway. The orange cord slid like a snake behind me as I pulled the generator down the hall and toward the main entrance. I pushed open the front door and parked the generator in the doorway where there would be adequate ventilation.

I turned on the fuel valve, primed the pump, and then jerked the crank rope. After coughing for a bit, the engine roared to life, sputtered a bit, and then settled into a steady vibration.

I plugged my end of the extension cord into the generator and walked back to the office. Kevin looked up when my shadow fell across the floor. "Are we good to go?"

I nodded. "Flip the switch."

He turned on the surge protector and I saw flashing lights appear on the monitor. Within a minute, Kevin had booted up the surveillance system and the screen proudly displayed the cameras around the school. He hummed to himself while he navigated to the playback feature. I moved to the row of windows and checked on Achilles. His eyes were fixed like a laser on the back doorway to the main building, which was where he'd last seen me.

I waved an arm out the window, called to him. His eyes found me immediately and he fidgeted in his seat. I knew he wanted to jump right out of the window and come for me, but I reminded him to stay. He opened his mouth and clamped his jaw shut, as though cursing me for not letting him join us. I laughed, but stopped when I heard Kevin curse.

"I don't understand," he said, tapping on the DVR. "This thing was working perfectly when we left."

My heart sank. "What's wrong?"

"I don't know. It says it doesn't recognize the hard drive. When I run a diagnostics check, it says the hard drive can't be found and that there's zero of zero space available."

"But the live view is on, so it should be working, right?"

"It's working, but it doesn't look like it's recording."

"What?" I let out a long groan. I needed that footage! "This can't be happening."

"You can go ahead and see for yourself." Kevin stepped back and waved me in. "Maybe you can figure it out."

I stepped forward and took over the mouse. After a few minutes of working with the system—clicking on every option and scrolling through every field—I realized it was no use. The hard drive was dead, and that's all there was to it. I slid the mouse across the counter—a little rougher than I'd intended—and I heard a tiny clanking noise as something bounced off the wall and hit the floor.

"What was that?" I asked, stepping back to scan the floor. "Something fell."

"What fell? I didn't hear anything."

"It was something tiny. I heard it hit the floor." I indicated with my hand for Kevin to step away and I dropped to the floor on my belly. Pushing the good side of my face to the damp tile, I stared across the surface of the floor, looking for anything that stood out. Kevin had wiped up the water from the floor with a mop he'd retrieved from the broom closet, and everything was still shiny.

After methodically scanning every inch of the floor, I finally saw something protruding up from the smooth floor. I slid forward and smashed the pad of my index finger on top of it. When I lifted my finger, it was pressed up against my flesh. I sat up and examined it.

"This is a screw." I scowled. "What's a screw doing on the desktop? Was anything serviced recently?"

Kevin shrugged. "Not that I know about."

"And you're sure this hard drive was recording before you left?"

"Yeah. We pulled some surveillance footage just last week of a fight that took place on the basketball court."

It felt like my ears perked up. "Was Elizabeth involved in any way in that fight? Did she break it up? Did it occur between two of her students?"

"No, it was between two football players. Elizabeth was nowhere around."

I nodded, placed the screw in a paperclip container, and drummed my fingers on the countertop, studying every piece of equipment on it. Everything seemed to be in place, except…

"Has the DVR always been on the edge of the shelf?" I asked, pointing to the large square device. All of the other items on that shelf were positioned farther back, but the DVR was crooked and the front of it extended slightly over the edge of the shelf, as though it had been moved.

Kevin shrugged. "That's where the I.T. people set it up when they installed it. We've never moved it."

"Did you touch it when you were cleaning up?"

He shook his head.

Pulling some latex gloves from my back pocket, I carefully lifted the front of the DVR and looked under it. There was a dust pattern on the shelf, but it was not aligned with the current position of the DVR. It had definitely been moved. I lifted it higher and examined the underside of it. "No kidding," I said to myself.

"What?" Kevin asked from behind me. "What'd you find?"

"Do you have a screwdriver?"

"We have a tool kit somewhere around here."

"Can you bring me the smallest screwdriver you have?" When he was gone, I stared at the front left corner of the bottom of the unit intently. There were five screws—all of them identical to the screw I'd found—holding the cover in place, but there were six slots. The slot located at the front left corner was empty, which meant a screw was missing.

When Kevin returned with the screwdriver, I backed out the five remaining screws and set the DVR down. Tossing the screwdriver aside, I carefully removed the cover. I cursed out loud when I saw that the hard drive was missing.

"What is it?" Kevin was standing on his toes trying to see over my shoulder. "What happened?"

"Someone removed the hard drive." I placed the cover down and scowled. "Why would they do that? Why not just destroy the unit?"

Kevin stood there with a blank expression on his face, not even attempting to answer my questions. "That's why you're the detective and I'm just the principal."

I nodded absently, lost in thought. If the DVR had been working last week, then it meant someone removed the hard drive between then and now. I hadn't noticed the precise position of the DVR when I was in the school Tuesday night, so I couldn't be sure it was recording then.

"When did you close down the school?" I asked.

"We secured everything Monday after classes let out and then we locked it up." He scratched his sweaty head. "Apparently, someone came in here since then, because the books are all up in the library. I'm guessing that was Elizabeth and that's why she was here."

"Would anyone else have come with her? Does she have a friend at school who might have given her a hand?"

"They all evacuated. I was able to make contact with every one of them as I was heading back today, and they're all still out of town. I told them to stay put until they hear from me. I was planning on calling them as soon as the school board made a decision on when we could go back to classes." He glanced around the room and sighed. "We've got some repairs to make before that'll happen."

"Well, I'll need to limit the amount of people who come in here," I said, waving my hand around. "This whole area is a crime scene and I'll need to process it for prints, DNA, and everything else I can find."

"You think she was killed in here?" Kevin shuffled his feet. "Like, in the office?"

"No, but someone disabled the surveillance system, and I need to find out who and why."

While he sat in a chair in the corner, I retrieved my crime scene kit and dusted every smooth surface in the room, except for the DVR, which I collected as evidence. I didn't know if the crime lab was functioning, but I'd need this thing processed.

It must've taken me two hours to finish processing the office and library, and my stomach was grumbling by the time I was done. While it didn't look like Kevin missed many meals, he hadn't complained once about food. I'd heard him on the phone earlier talking to his wife about Elizabeth, and I could've sworn he was crying.

I'd been around death a lot over the years and, for me, it was just a natural way of life—another day at the office. I often forgot that most people didn't experience death on a regular basis and they found it deeply disturbing, especially when it was an act of violence that ended the life of someone they knew.

With Kevin's permission, I had allowed Achilles to hang out in the hallway while I worked in the office and library, and I called him over as I was collecting my gear. I told him to grab one of the boxes, but he didn't listen, so I had to carry everything myself. We walked out to my Tahoe and I stowed my gear in the cargo area. I was about to tell him to get in the front seat when I remembered something.

CHAPTER 22

Achilles nudged my hand with his cold nose. I guess I must've stood there for too long staring blankly at the school. I scratched his head.

"We're not done yet, boy," I said, snatching up my flashlight. "There's one more thing we have to check on."

I hurried back to the school with Achilles on my heel.

"Mr. Shelton!" I called as I hurried through the doorway and down the hall. "Mr. Shelton, where are you?"

Kevin's head popped out from the office door. "Here…I'm in here."

I stopped in the hallway and pointed toward the closet. "I need to check something in here."

"Sure." He walked over and watched as I opened the door. "It's our broom closet. It's where the janitors keep all of their cleaning supplies."

"I took shelter in here when the tornado hit Tuesday night." I propped the door open with a mop bucket and grabbed my flashlight. When the light flooded the tiny room, I pointed to the back wall. "I found that hole in the wall. Where does it lead?"

"I've never seen that before." Kevin scowled, leaned forward to examine it. "How'd you find this?"

"I moved some stuff to retrieve my flashlight from the floor and I noticed a dark spot on the wall."

He leaned close to the hole and pushed his eye up against it. "I can't see anything."

I moved to the side of him and knocked on the tile. "What's on the other side of this wall?"

He straightened and studied it for a minute, then backed out into the hallway and surveyed his surroundings. "Why, I think that's the faculty bathroom."

"What?"

"Follow me."

Kevin was shorter than me, but his legs pumped like pistons and I had to walk fast to keep up. I called over my shoulder for Achilles to lie down and stay. I knew he'd be right there when I got back. He was a smart dog and it hadn't taken long for me to teach him to stay. Once he understood the command, I would issue it and then walk away. At first he wanted to immediately jump up and run to me, but I'd stop and reset him. Eventually, I could walk all the way around my house and come up behind him, where he would still be lying motionless, staring at the last spot he saw me.

I followed Kevin to the main entryway, where we took a right into that short hall and then another right into a nurse's office. We passed through that office and then entered what looked like a lunchroom. We had come full circle. He stopped and pointed toward a door on the western wall.

"That's the faculty bathroom." He just stood there as though he were afraid to look inside. "That's got to be where the hole comes out."

I stepped forward and opened the door. There was a sink directly in front of me. To the left of the sink there was a urinal, and to the left of that a stall and toilet. I instinctively flipped the light switch up, then groaned when I remembered the electricity was out.

"I do that all the time when the electricity is out," Kevin said. "It drives my wife crazy."

I just nodded as I dug out my flashlight and examined the back wall to the bathroom. Everything above and under the sink looked intact. I checked the urinal and there were no holes in that area either. When I moved to the stall, I pushed it open with the tip of my boot and scanned the area to the left and right of the toilet. There was no hole. I frowned, studied the wall more closely.

"Aha!" There, on the wall to the right of the tank and about even with the flush knob, was a tiny chip in the tile.

"I think I found something," I called over my shoulder. I leaned closer and could detect a tiny black hole at the center of the chip. It was much smaller than the hole in the closet, but it might be big enough to allow someone to peep inside the restroom. Now that I knew what I was looking for, I rechecked the rest of the wall and found another chip near the urinal.

I stepped out of the bathroom and handed Kevin my light. "Can you aim this at the ceiling in there? I'll go back to the closet and see if I have a visual."

He seemed deep in thought as I walked off, but I didn't have time to ask him what he was thinking. I hurried to the closet and shut the door behind me. I immediately saw light bleeding through the dark hole. When I put my eye to the opening, I could see Kevin standing in the bathroom holding my light to the ceiling.

"You little peeping bastard!" I muttered, wanting to know the names of every janitor who worked at the school. I hollered through the hole that I had what I needed, and I saw the light move and then disappear.

"Can you see into the bathroom?" Kevin asked when he had rejoined me in the hallway.

"You've got a pervert in the school," I said. "I'll need the names of every janitor you have."

Kevin fell back against the wall in exasperation. "You mean to tell me someone has been watching us go to the bathroom? Someone has been peeping at us in our most vulnerable and private moments?"

I nodded. "I'll need those names."

"Well, I only have one janitor at the moment."

"And who would that be?"

"Ty Richardson."

My mouth fell open. "Is it possible someone else in the school uses this closet? I mean, it's not like it stays locked."

Kevin shook his head. "No…no one else goes in here."

I sighed heavily. I liked Ty Richardson and didn't want to believe he was a Peeping Tom.

CHAPTER 23

Ty Richardson lived at the end of Orange Way and he battled mental illness. Last I'd heard, he was winning that battle and doing well, so I found myself hoping he hadn't been watching the staff use the bathroom.

I was about to cross Main Street and head south toward Orange Way when I heard a desperate call over the radio.

"Help! I need help on Jezebel Drive!" It was Takecia and her voice was laced with panic—so much so that I could hardly understand what she was saying. "I've got a family trapped in their home! I need help!"

I whipped my Tahoe around in the middle of the highway and raced toward Jezebel. I knew the street well—it was where I lived when I first rolled into town three years ago. When I turned onto the street, I saw Takecia's marked police car parked sideways in the front yard where an RV was located. A giant tree had been uprooted and had crashed onto the very center of the RV, nearly splitting it in half.

I hollered at Achilles to stay and I rushed from my Tahoe. The entrance to the RV was smashed under the tree and there didn't seem to be a way in. Takecia was swinging her police baton at the side wall, trying to beat her way inside. I remembered my chainsaw and quickly ran to the back of my Tahoe.

My feet sloshed in the saturated mud underfoot as I ran toward the wreckage, and I nodded inwardly. I'd heard of this happening—where the roots from large trees would lose their grip on the earth after a heavy downpour—and I made a mental note to check the trees around my house.

Just as I reached Takecia, I heard sirens in the distance and I knew more help was en route. I was hoping it was the fire department and that they were bringing their jaws of life.

"It fell just now," called a young boy from a neighboring trailer when he saw me approaching Takecia. "We heard a big popping sound and the earth shook. When we looked outside we saw it crashing on top of the trailer."

"Get back," I hollered to Takecia, firing up the chainsaw. I wasn't sure how it would perform on the thin metal, but I was willing to try anything. Takecia backed away and dropped her baton. She bent over and rested her hands on her knees, trying to catch her breath.

"Hurry!" screamed a woman from the adjacent yard. "They're trapped inside! There's a small baby inside!"

The chainsaw screamed in my hand as I pushed the blade against the metal. Sparks exploded outward from the chain, peppering my arms and face. I pressed on, not caring about the flecks of burning metal that was raining down on me.

Over the roar of the chainsaw, I could hear a woman screaming from inside the rubble and I knew I had to work fast. An opening began to appear in the exterior wall and I felt a sense of triumph. *Yes! We can do this!*

The wind began picking up as I cut a square opening in the wall, and the sky seemed to grow darker. Finally, I eased off on the trigger and hit the kill switch. The square was complete, but the section of wall was still attached. I felt a presence beside me and realized it was Susan.

"Ready?" Susan asked, and I nodded.

She wore a pair of leather gloves and wriggled her fingers into the crack on the left side of the cut-out square. I dropped the chainsaw and grabbed the right side. Together, we tugged on the section of the wall, pulling as hard as we could. From the corner of my eyes, I could see the muscles in her slender arms rippling as she strained. While I had managed to cut away the metal, there were wires and other pieces of material still attached from the inside, and they were resisting our attempts to pull it free.

As the square cut-out bent outward during one of our attempts, I caught sight of a bare leg pinned under what looked like a table. There was blood on the skin and I knew it couldn't be good. In that brief moment, I also heard the screaming from inside more clearly. The sheer terror and desperation in that scream spurred Susan and me on. We began jerking in unison, counting as we went. Finally, the square cut-out gave under the pressure and we fell backward, staring up at a hole that was big enough for us to squeeze through.

Being a trained cage fighter, Susan was more nimble than I and she scrambled off the ground and was through the hole before I could right myself. But I wasn't far behind her.

I felt the gnarled metal clutching at my clothes and flesh as I forced my way through the opening. I was so close to Susan that I could smell the leather on her boots, but it quickly faded when I caught a whiff of freshly spilled blood.

Susan grunted as she forced herself into a tight spot, trying to get to the other side. "Hang on, ma'am," she called. "I'm coming."

I went left, where the bare leg was located. I had to suck in my stomach in an effort to slide under the smashed table and get to the body that was attached to the leg.

The woman's screams were loud in the tight enclosure. Although I couldn't see the woman and she was hard to understand, she kept uttering two words that were crystal clear: "My baby!"

I finally wriggled my way around the table and pushed upward against a portion of the ceiling that had caved in. I sucked in my breath when I saw what lay underneath the ceiling—it was a young man and his eyes were wide open, but he didn't appear to be breathing. I reached for his neck and felt for a pulse, but there was none.

"I'm almost to you, ma'am—just hang on!" Susan called from somewhere in the wreckage. I could see part of her boot through splintered wood and twisted metal.

"Forget me—get my baby!" The woman's voice was shrill. "Oh, God, I can't hear her!"

Susan's boot disappeared and I heard her rustling through the rubble. The pocket of space I'd crawled into was so tight I could hardly catch a deep breath. I thought I saw an opening on the other side of the smashed roof, so I began pushing my way in that direction. I had to twist sideways to slink past a tree branch that had punctured the RV.

Once I broke free of the tiny quarters, I found myself in a space large enough for me to prop up on my elbows, and that's when I saw the woman. Her blonde hair was painted red and there was a nasty gash across the left side of her face. Tears poured down her cheeks and left faint streaks through the blood that was smeared across her flesh like war paint.

Our eyes locked and I told her it was going to be okay.

"I can't hear my baby," she said in a weak voice.

I glanced around, but my field of view was limited. The RV had been smashed like a tin can and there were only tiny pockets of livable space here and there. The top half of her body was positioned in one of these spaces, but I couldn't see her hips and legs. It appeared they had been smashed, and I knew she was in grave danger.

"We'll get you out, ma'am—just hang in there."

As I tried to maneuver my way to her, I heard dozens of voices outside the RV, and I knew the fire department had arrived with their power tools. I called out to Susan, asked if she was okay.

"I can see the baby, but I'm having a hard time reaching her." Susan's voice was strained, as though she were trying to squeeze her way through a tight spot.

Noise suddenly exploded from the rear end of the RV as the fire department began attacking it with their equipment. I was scooting closer to the woman when the RV vibrated violently in place and the roof shifted downward, smashing against my back. The shift apparently caused more pressure on the woman's trapped legs, because she cried out in pain.

"Whoa, damn it! Go easy!" someone called from outside. "There are people trapped inside."

"Susan, how are you?" I grabbed the corner of a mattress and pushed it ahead of me, allowing me to see into what looked like the living room area. I figured if I could make my way into that space, I could circle around and help the woman.

When Susan didn't respond, I began to worry that the roof had crushed her.

"Sue, are you okay?" I couldn't hide the panic in my voice. "Please answer me!"

I couldn't hear much over the rumble of the rescue attempt, and I was hoping that's why she hadn't responded. Driven by fear and determination, I was able to scramble to my hands and knees once I'd squirted through the hole that the mattress had made. I was about to call out to Susan again when I heard her gasp. It was a horrific sound and my first impression was that she'd been injured.

Abandoning my approach to the woman, I began fighting my way toward the sound of her voice. A splintered chair and broken glass littered the floor in front of me. Grabbing two pieces of wood from the broken chair, I used them as platforms for the palms of my hands.

"Susan, are you okay?"

"I…I'm not hurt," was all she said.

Her voice was on the other side of a thin wall that had buckled under the weight of the tree. I grabbed the top portion of the wall and pulled with all of my strength. The particle board snapped under my weight and I was able to pull myself to my knees and see into the next room. What I saw shocked me to my boots.

Susan had crawled into a narrow hallway that had the top smashed in. There was a narrow crack in the roof and light spilled into the area, offering a clear visual of my wife lying on her back in the tight quarters. Cradled in her arms was a tiny baby wrapped in a green and yellow blanket. I saw a little hand dangling out from under the blanket and it didn't move—not even a flinch.

"Where's my baby?" cried the woman from several feet away. She might as well have been fifty yards away—thanks to the mangled rubble separating us—and I was glad she couldn't see what I was looking at. "Did you find my baby?"

I noticed that the parts of Susan's body I could see were trembling violently. Her bronze-colored arms were covered in white dust and yellow insulation. The right sleeve of her uniform shirt was ripped from her bicep up to her shoulder. Her pant leg on that side was also ripped and I saw blood leaking down her leg.

"Sue, are you okay?"

Still, she didn't answer, but her body continued to tremble. I didn't know if she was in shock or having a seizure. Panic grabbed me by the throat and threatened to squeeze the life out of me. I pushed out with my feet, trying to climb higher on the wall. Finally, I was able to shift my position enough so I could see her face, and it was then that I realized she was sobbing violently, but silently. Her eyes were squeezed shut and she was biting her lower lip, trying not to make a sound. Her face was red and puffy and I knew she was being quiet for the woman's sake.

I frowned as I watched the woman I loved lying there suffering all alone. There was nothing I could do. I couldn't even reach her to offer comfort. I wanted to cry out and tell her I was coming, that I would make everything better. But to do so would alert the mother that her baby hadn't made it, and it was clear Susan didn't want the mom dealing with that cruel revelation while she lay there fighting for her own life.

That was vintage Susan—always putting the needs of others before her own. It was one of the reasons I loved her, and also one of the reasons I worried so much about her. She would give her life for a total stranger, as would most of the cops I knew. However, I was selfish when it came to Susan. I didn't want her risking her life for anyone, but I knew that was something I'd have to live with. What I couldn't live with was sitting idly by while she suffered on her own.

CHAPTER 24

I was trying desperately to squirm my way over the smashed wall in an attempt to reach Susan, but I wasn't having much luck. The mom had stopped calling out for her daughter and I paused for a moment, listening intently.

"Ma'am, are you okay?" I asked, cocking my head to the side to better hear any sounds she might make. She said nothing. Not a peep. "Ma'am, please speak up if you can hear me."

Still nothing.

"Oh, God," Susan said in a hoarse voice, opening her eyes for the first time since I'd found her. "Is…is she gone?"

"I don't know."

I had started to worm my way out of the tight spot I'd forced myself into when a large jagged hole suddenly appeared in the wall toward the front of the RV. I saw a gloved hand pulling a section of wall back and a man wearing bunker gear stuck his head inside.

"Is everyone okay?" He made eye contact with me and I think he read my expression. "Are there any survivors?"

I frowned, gave a half shake of my head. "I don't think so."

He couldn't see Susan, so I pointed out her position. "Can you get her out of here? I'll go back and check on the mother."

While fire department personnel worked their way toward Susan and the lifeless baby, I retraced my steps and finally reached the woman again. Her eyes were half closed and what I could see of them had been glazed over. I reached for her neck and, like the man in the RV, she didn't have a pulse. I cursed profusely under my breath and then rolled onto my back and took a series of long and deep breaths. The storm had claimed the lives of an entire family.

Like the snap of a finger, their lives had all been extinguished. It just didn't seem right. It wasn't fair.

I don't know how long I lay there, but I finally rolled to my side when I heard Susan telling the firefighters to be careful with the baby. I continued backing my way out of the RV until I reached the original opening I'd carved into the wall. I squirted out of it boots first and pulled myself to my feet.

I was just in time to see Susan being helped from the wreckage. Her dusty face was streaked with tears and was still red. She lowered her head and immediately walked away from the group of first responders, heading for an old shed at the back of the property. I lumbered after her and pulled up short when I reached the corner of the shed. She was squatting with her back to the tiny building and her face was buried in her hands. She was sobbing again.

I took a few steps closer and then coughed to let her know I was there. She quickly bolted to her feet and wiped her eyes. "I'm…it's okay. I'm good."

I frowned and stepped forward, wrapping her in my arms. She sank into my chest and the dam inside her seemed to break open once more. I must've held her for five minutes as she let it all out. When she finally pulled away and rubbed her eyes, she groaned.

"God, I haven't cried like that since you were shot."

"What's going on?" I asked. "I've never seen you so emotional at a scene. I'm worried about you."

"I know. I'm usually good at holding everything in until I walk away, but…but I guess seeing the baby just got to me."

"Yeah." I nodded. "That's hard to take in."

"I'll be okay, though." She forced a smile to try and reassure me. "I promise."

I wasn't buying it, but I didn't force the issue. "Want me to get out there and buy you some time?"

"Please. I don't want anyone to see me like this."

I kissed her lips—tasting the salt from her tears—and then strode back toward the wreckage. The firemen were pulling the mother's body from the rubble when I walked up. The husband was already laid out on the ground near the baby, and both were covered with a white sheet. I glanced over at Takecia, who was sitting on a log, a look of despair on her face.

"Why the baby?" she asked when I approached her. "What could a baby do to deserve such a tragic ending?"

"I don't know, Takecia." I thought back to my own daughter, and wondered what she had ever done to deserve what happened to her.

"This is a cruel and unjust world—that much is clear."

Melvin drove up a short time later and he had Amy in his truck with him.

"Is it true a baby was—?" Melvin stopped talking when he saw the blanket covering the tiny figure on the ground. "Damn, that's horrible! Who found the child?"

I didn't want to bring any unnecessary attention to Susan, so I ignored the question while we were in front of everyone and grabbed my chainsaw off the ground, returned it to my Tahoe. Melvin noticed my expression and followed me to my vehicle. When we were out of earshot of the rest of the first responders and onlookers, I told him what had happened.

"Oh, man." He wiped sweat from his shaved head. "Will she be okay?"

"Yeah, you know Susan. She's as tough as they come." Although I tried to sound sure of myself, I was worried about her. She'd seen dead children before and, while it was always heart-wrenching, she'd been able to maintain her composure in the public eye.

We watched the action at the scene and I wondered if the coroner's office would be able to get a hearse out to our location. I hadn't heard how the rest of the parish had fared, so I asked Melvin.

"From what I hear, they got lucky. There's a lot of damage and quite a few injuries, but no fatalities so far."

Darkness was overtaking us and I knew it would hamper the assessment efforts. Save for the glow from the fire department vehicles, there wasn't a light on for as far as the eye could see. The breeze was strong enough to toss my hair around, but it had definitely calmed down from earlier. I stomped the ground and water sprayed into the air. I hoped no more trees would come crashing down on top of our unsuspecting citizens. It was a horrible way to go.

"How's the search in town coming?" I asked. "Any other casualties?"

"Just one—an elderly man. We found him on his living room floor, but it looked like he had a heart attack." Melvin turned away from the wreckage and looked out into the darkness behind us. "I wonder what else we'll find once we peel back all the layers of debris littered about this town."

"Is Baylor still at the checkpoint?"

"Yeah. He said it's been slow. Dispatch has been getting calls all day from citizens wanting to know if the power is out, so I guess they'll stay away until the electricity comes back on." He grunted.

"We've even had about a dozen people call and ask if an officer could go out to their homes and let them know if there's any damage. Some even wanted pictures texted to them."

"What'd y'all do?"

"Sent the pictures as we had the time."

I smiled, but it was only on the outside. On the inside, I was worried about Susan and I was hoping everyone who lived in the worst-hit areas had evacuated.

As we stood there, I began to realize how tired I was, but I knew it would be a long time before I got any sleep. Melvin asked how the investigation was going, and I told him.

"Damn, you really think Ty Richardson is a Peeping Tom?"

"I hope not."

I straightened and became fully alert when I saw Susan emerge from the shadows along the outer edges of the glow from the lights. She was calling out instructions to the surrounding responders and she seemed to be in full control of her emotions. After a minute or so, she peeled from the group and approached Melvin and me.

"The coroner's got a wagon en route for the victims," she said. "According to the driver licenses we found, they're from out of town—South Carolina—so I've got some calls to make. Oh, and Doctor Wong said she performed the autopsy on Elizabeth Bankston. Other than the single gunshot wound to the head and some scrapes on her knees, all of her injuries were post mortem."

I wasn't surprised to learn that most of her injuries had occurred after she died, because I'd been certain the tornado had nothing to do with her death.

"We can't do much more in the dark," Susan continued, "so we'll shut it down after we clean up this mess."

I told her I was heading to Ty Richardson's house and she frowned. "Are you sure it's safe to do so? Can't you wait until the morning?"

I considered it for a second, then shook my head. "No, I'd like to find out what he knows as soon as possible so I can game plan. I keep coming up empty and it's starting to worry me."

"Well, if you'll wait a second, I'll take a ride with you." She tossed her keys to Melvin. "Can Amy drive my ride back to the station?"

"Sure." Melvin caught the keys in midair. He turned toward me when Susan ambled off to finish up. "I talked to Claire."

"Oh, yeah? How'd that go?"

"Better than expected, actually." He sighed. "She said she's still going to worry and give me hell about my job, but she told me she respects what I do and is willing to accept it. She promised not to ask me to give it up anymore."

"What changed her mind?" I wanted to know.

"She talked to Susan." Melvin shook his head. "I don't know what Susan said, but I'm glad Claire talked to her. It's much easier to do this job when you have your family's support."

He wasn't kidding.

CHAPTER 25

After meeting with Baylor Rice and getting an updated list of the town's re-entrants, I checked it carefully to see if Ty Richardson's name was on it. It wasn't, and neither was his mother's name. If I located him at his home, that meant he didn't evacuate. If he admitted to going to the school on Tuesday, he would end up on my list of prime suspects.

When I pulled into the driveway of Ty's mother's small gray house, I heard the steady humming of a generator and saw flickering lights through the windows of the camper trailer next to the house. Last I remembered, Ty lived in the camper and his mother lived in the house. Not wanting to disturb his mother at nine o'clock in the evening, I went directly to the camper and rapped loudly on the door.

I had to blink twice when I saw the man who answered the door. When I'd first met Ty some time ago, his eyes were wild, his beard was thick and unkempt, and he smelled of stale sweat and armpit juice. This man was calm and his beard neatly trimmed. His hair had been cut and it appeared clean.

"I'm Clint Wolf, detective for the Mechant Loup—"

"I remember you, Detective Clint." Ty stuck out his hand and I shook it. "You gave me that toy car."

"Ah, that's right, it was—" Before I could continue speaking, he cut me off.

"I still don't know why you gave me a toy car. I mean, I'm a grown man for Christ's sake." Ty suddenly scowled and looked at his wrist watch. "It's late. Did you need something?"

"I wanted to talk to you about your job down at the school."

His face lit up. "I'm the janitor there. They let me do all kinds of stuff. I sweep the floors, I cut the grass, and I fix the plumbing when it breaks. I get to do just about everything."

"When was the last time you went to work?"

"Let's see…" He scrunched his face and stared up at the dark sky. "It was the day before the hurricane. Tuesday, I think."

My shoulders drooped. "Tuesday? Are you sure?"

"Yep, I'm positive."

"Was anyone else at school that day?"

"Well, I know I was there for sure, but I can't really remember who else was there."

"Why were you there that day?"

"I had to get all of my stuff picked up. I had to put the mop bucket and caution signs in the closet and I had to close up the locker room under the football stadium."

"What time were you there?"

"I got there at my normal time, seven-twenty-five."

"What time did you leave?"

"Um, I don't remember the exact time, but I know there was a tornado and I got scared and left right away."

"Did you see anyone at the school that day?"

"Yeah, I saw Miss Liz."

"Elizabeth Bankston?"

He shrugged. "I don't know who that is. I saw Miss Liz. She was putting books on the top shelves to keep them out of the water if it flooded."

"Did you talk to her?"

"I told her hello."

"Was she still there when you left?"

"I don't know."

"Did anything out of the ordinary happen?"

"What do you mean?" Ty's brow was furrowed. "You mean, like did something bad happened?"

I nodded.

"Oh, no…I didn't see anything. I never looked in the hole."

If Achilles would've been closer and could've understood English, his ears would've perked up like mine did. I didn't know if the peeping hole had anything to do with Elizabeth's murder, but it was certainly a possibility—especially now that Ty mentioned it. Someone could've been watching her, she could've caught them, and then things could've gotten ugly. If this scenario turned out to be true, Ty was my killer.

"And what hole are you talking about?"

"Um, um…" Ty stammered, as though he realized he'd already said too much. "I didn't make a hole in the wall."

"I know you didn't—it was the old janitor." I studied his face for a second. "When did you first notice the hole?"

"I don't know anything about a hole."

"Look, it's okay if you saw the hole. We all know you didn't make it, so you can't be responsible for what happens with it. Okay? You can't be in trouble for seeing the hole." I paused, then nodded. "Now, can you tell me when you first saw the hole?"

He was quiet for a long moment and I thought he was going to evade my question. But he didn't. "I saw it one day when I first started working there."

"How long have you been there?"

"I started last year."

"Did you ever look through that hole? You know, maybe out of curiosity?" I was hoping he would say no, but I was not so lucky.

"Not all the time. I only looked when I thought I heard people talking to me through the wall." He shifted his eyes and it was clear he was uncomfortable. "Sometimes I hear voices that aren't there and I start thinking something's wrong with my ears. Well, when the wall would talk, I'd look in the hole and see people. That's when I knew it was okay."

I was very familiar with Ty's struggle with mental illness and felt bad for him. "So, you would hear people talking through the wall and you would look to see if they were talking to you?"

"I guess so."

I took a step closer to Ty. "Look, this is very important—did you hear Miss Liz talking to you from the hole on Tuesday?"

"I…I don't know if I should say. I don't want to get in trouble."

"Did you do something wrong?" I asked slowly. "Did you do something to hurt Miss Liz?"

He shook his head violently. "Oh, no, I would never hurt Miss Liz. She's nice to me."

I felt a little better that Ty was referring to Elizabeth in the present tense. Before I could say another word, he whirled around and disappeared inside his camper, leaving the door open behind him. I craned my neck to see what he was doing, but he'd gone too far into the camper. Within seconds, he returned and was cradling a book in both hands.

"She gave me this book to read, and it's my favorite one so far." He lifted the book and I saw that it was an aged copy of WHITE FANG by Jack London. I smiled, remembering how much I loved that book as a kid. I was tempted to ask him to borrow it, but I wouldn't likely have time to read anything for pleasure anytime soon.

"That was really nice of her; it's a great book." I took the novel and turned it over, loving the feel of it in my hands. When I looked up again, I nodded for emphasis. "I believe you when you say you would never hurt her, but now I need your help—Miss Liz needs your help."

"But I don't know how I can help her."

"Just tell me what you heard and saw that day at the school."

Ty hesitated. "I don't want to get in trouble. I can't go back to the hospital. It's…I just can't."

"As long as you didn't hurt her, you won't be in trouble—I promise." I put a hand on his shoulder to reassure him. "Everything you say here will stay here. I just need to know what happened."

Ty took a seat on the metal steps to the camper and rested his elbows on his knees. "I was picking up the mop bucket when I heard some noise through the hole in the closet wall. It was a woman's voice, but it wasn't Miss Liz. I didn't pay attention to it, but then I heard a man's voice, too. I thought it was strange that a man and woman were in the bathroom at the same time."

Ty paused to take a breath and I thought he would stop talking, but he finally continued.

"I did look in the hole, but only to see what was going on—I wasn't trying to see any private parts."

"It's okay, Ty, just tell me what happened."

"I couldn't see anybody, but I could hear them talking and giggling. It sounded like they were doing something bad. The woman was making weird sounds and it sounded like sex." Ty's face turned red from embarrassment. "Since I couldn't see anything, I turned away from the hole, but then I heard someone scream and it sounded like Miss Liz."

"So, she was in the bathroom?"

"I think so. I heard her scream and then I heard the other woman yell. The man started talking and he sounded angry about something." He rubbed his face. "I heard Miss Liz telling the man that he was going to be in trouble, but then she screamed again and that was all I heard. I…I got scared and left."

"Did you recognize the man's voice?"

Ty shook his head. "He was angry, so it was hard to tell who it was. The only voice I really recognized was Miss Liz'."

"You said she screamed. Did it sound like she was in trouble, or did it sound like she was angry?"

"She was in trouble. Or maybe she was angry. I can't be sure."

"It's okay." I pondered what he'd just told me. It was consistent with the phone message Elizabeth had sent to her husband, telling him she had seen something she shouldn't have, but what was it? What had she stumbled into? Had she caught the man in an act of adultery? Did he then kill her to silence her? Did she interrupt a rape? What about drugs—had she walked into the middle of a drug transaction? And what if Ty was the man in the bathroom? It wouldn't be the first time a suspect had confessed in third person. Of course, Ty seemed certain that the first woman was giggling and he thought he heard what sounded like sex, so drugs and rape might be out of the question.

"Ty, you mentioned that you got scared and left," I said slowly. "Did you see Miss Liz as you were leaving?"

"I didn't see anyone. I went out the side door and walked through the football field and headed straight home. I didn't pass *Go* and I didn't collect two hundred dollars."

I laughed at his joke, then sobered up. "Did you see any shoes on the football field? A pair of women's shoes, perhaps?"

"No. There was nothing on the football field when I walked through it. I cut the grass two days before Tuesday and it still looked clean."

"Do you think anyone knew you were there? In the school, I mean."

He shook his head. "I was quiet."

"Did you hear any more screaming or see anyone running in the area?"

He shook his head. "I went straight home. I didn't see anyone. I think everyone had already evacuated, because the streets looked like they do in The Walking Dead."

"What about a tornado? Did you see a tornado?"

He was thoughtful. "I think I remember hearing sirens when the sky got really dark. I get confused sometimes, especially when a lot of things are going on around me. I just can't be sure if I saw a tornado."

I nodded slowly, wondering who in the hell the man and woman could've been. And why would Elizabeth scream at the man? It couldn't have been her husband, because he'd been in the Gulf of Mexico at the time. What if she was also having an affair with the man and she caught him with another woman? She did step out on Steve before, and it was possible she'd strayed again. If that was the case, things could've gotten out of hand between her and the man and he could've chased her out into the field and then killed her somewhere along the way.

I knew I would have to contact Kevin Shelton again and find out if he knew about any extramarital affairs taking place between two of his teachers. Of course, as the boss, I expected he'd be the last to know. If two teachers *were* screwing around, there's a good chance no one would know about it except the people closest to them. And before I could find the people closest to *them*, I'd have to figure out who *they* were.

I'd looked at the school's faculty list earlier and there were four male teachers listed. Kevin said he and his wife had evacuated Monday night, so he wasn't in town on Tuesday and wouldn't possess any firsthand knowledge about the whereabouts of his other teachers. Hell, as far as he had known, Elizabeth had evacuated, and we now knew that wasn't correct.

I'd also have to consult the re-entry list from Baylor and crosscheck the faculty list against it. Either the man or woman in that bathroom had to possess a key to the school, or they would've entered with Elizabeth. There was also the possibility they broke into the place. Perhaps Elizabeth caught them burglarizing the school and they killed her for it. I'd worked a number of cases in the city of La Mort where homeowners had interrupted burglars and been killed for it—

As quickly as the thought came to me, I dismissed it, remembering there hadn't been any signs of forced entry. *Damn, I could've really used that surveillance footage!*

"Where is Miss Liz?" Ty finally asked, interrupting my thoughts. "Will I be able to help her? Did I give you some good information?"

"The voices you heard—could they have been kids?"

"I guess so. I couldn't tell how old they were by the way they sounded." He stared right in my eyes, as though thinking I was avoiding his question. "Where's Miss Liz?"

I wanted to tell him that Elizabeth was dead, but I didn't want to cause him any emotional problems. Of course, finding out from the newspaper would be worse, so I squatted in front of him.

"Ty, Miss Liz had an accident."

His face was blank. "An accident? Will she be okay?"

I frowned. "No, Ty. I'm sorry, but she's dead."

CHAPTER 26

I spent about thirty minutes with Ty, trying to console him. Finally, I walked him to his mother's house and woke her up. When I told her what was going on—leaving out the part about the hole in the wall at school—she quickly ushered Ty inside and waved for me to join them. There were candles positioned on the table and on several of the counters in the kitchen, and they cast an eerie glow about the room.

"Thank you so much, detective," she said. "You've always been so kind to my boy."

"He's my buddy," I said. "That's what buddies do."

After telling Ty to sit at the table, Mrs. Richardson fired up the gas stove. She bustled about the room, making tea and fixing sandwiches. She asked if I wanted some.

"No, ma'am, I've got to get going."

She promptly put down the loaf of bread and jar of mayonnaise, walked me to the door. Once we were out of earshot of Ty, she whispered, "He loved Liz so much. She was so nice to him and would give him books to read. I hope you catch the person who hurt her."

I told her I'd do my best and was turning to leave when she called out to me. "Wait, do you think Ty is in danger? I mean, if he was in the school when it happened, couldn't they have known? Couldn't they be looking for him, too?"

While Ty had been certain no one knew he was there, I couldn't rule it out.

"Do you have a landline?" I asked.

"You mean a house phone?"

"Yeah."

She nodded.

"While I don't think anyone will be looking for Ty, just make sure to keep your doors locked and call 911 if you hear or see anything suspicious." I shot a thumb over my shoulder. "I'll have an officer make regular passes through here, and I'll make some passes myself."

That seemed to reassure her and she thanked me again before I left. I conferred with Achilles about the case as I drove straight to the police department, but he didn't offer much in the way of advice. After allowing him to run around under the building for a while, I made my way upstairs. Things were quiet inside and I found Beth Gandy, our nighttime dispatcher, sitting in the dispatcher's station. Her eyes grew excited when she saw Achilles and she immediately went to him.

"Hey, Beth, when did you roll back into town?" I lifted my head and tested the air with my nose. It smelled like chicken and sausage gumbo, and I suddenly realized how hungry I was.

"Jeez, what happened to your face?" Beth asked, looking up from where she was rubbing Achilles' head. She stood and leaned close, apparently noticing the patch of my hair that stuck out a little farther than normal. She reached up and touched the bump on my head. "Did Susan finally get tired of your crap and pop you one?"

We both laughed and I explained what had happened with the bump and the scrapes. She frowned when I was done.

"I heard about Elizabeth Bankston, but they didn't tell me you almost got killed trying to get her out of the tree." She rubbed Achilles' head idly, and he loved every second of it. "I knew Elizabeth. It's quite a shame."

"How well did you know her?"

"I just knew her because she taught Troy in seventh grade. I liked her as a teacher, but we weren't friends or anything."

I looked around and sighed. "A lot has happened since you've been gone."

"Yeah, so I heard. Susan told me about the baby." Tears formed in her eyes and I knew she was thinking about her son Troy. She quickly brushed away the tears and bit down hard. "That was so sad. The only good thing about that whole situation is that God took the mom and dad with the baby so they wouldn't have to suffer for the rest of their lives."

My brow furrowed as I wondered if God was really the one who had taken them away. If she would've asked me, I would've blamed it all on the devil, but I wasn't much of a religious person. However, I could relate to Beth's sentiment. She and I were both suffering and would continue to suffer for the rest of our lives.

"Speaking of Susan, where is she?"

Beth indicated toward the hall that led to Susan's office. "She ate and then went to bed. She wasn't very talkative. I think she's still upset."

I wanted to check on Susan, but I didn't want to disturb her sleep. It was always better if I slipped into bed after she'd been sleeping for an hour or so. Otherwise, I'd just wake her up and she wouldn't be able to go back to sleep. She'd worked hard and had had a rough day, so she needed her sleep.

I asked Beth again when it was that she'd rolled into town.

"I got here a few hours ago."

"I smell food." I indicated with my head toward the lunch room. "Who's cooking?"

"Melvin decided to make a pot of gumbo, and Claire whipped up some potato salad."

My stomach was grumbling now and I didn't wait a second longer. Achilles and I made our way to the lunch room and found Melvin, Claire, Delilah, and Amy sitting at the table.

"Oh, damn, we ate it all," Melvin said, trying to stifle a grin. "I figured you'd be working that case all night and wouldn't be stopping to eat."

"No, Daddy, there's got some more food left!" Delilah said in her broken English. She'd made three last month and was as precious a little girl as I'd ever seen.

"You saved me some food?" I asked.

She shook her little head. "No, but Daddy did."

I tousled her hair and then fed Achilles his food before grabbing a bowl for myself. Once I had my food, I found a seat at the table, took a bite, and savored it for a long moment before swallowing. I didn't know if it was because I was so hungry or if it was true, but at that moment I thought it was the best gumbo I'd ever tasted—and I let Melvin know it.

"Thanks, but it was Delilah who cooked it."

I turned to Delilah and gave her a high five. "Good job, little chef!"

"What's a shelf, Daddy?" She turned toward Melvin and waited with her face scrunched up curiously while he explained the difference between a shelf and a chef. Her eyes then opened wide. "Yippy! I'm a chef! I can cook stuff!"

I ate in silence while I watched Delilah run around the room. She was curious about everything—especially Achilles—and she asked tons of questions. She reminded me of Abigail, who would run around like that when she was three. My heart ached as I thought of that fateful day five years ago when Abigail was six. I was afraid I'd start crying, so I tried not to dwell on it. Instead, I forced my mind to work through the evidence in Elizabeth Bankston's murder case.

There wasn't much, that's for sure. All two of the original suspects—Jude and Liam—were elsewhere at the time of the offense. Since clearing them, I hadn't been able to develop new suspects. Although the information Ty provided was promising, they hadn't led to the killer's identity. All I knew for certain was that Elizabeth was in the bathroom with a man and a woman, but who they were was anybody's guess. Of course, there was the possibility that Ty was either lying or mistaken.

Melvin and Claire were gone by the time I'd finished eating. They'd taken Delilah to bed and left me and Achilles alone with Amy, who was sitting across the table from me writing reports.

Her blonde hair was pulled back in a pony tail and her uniform was disheveled. I glanced down at my own clothes, grunted to myself. We all looked like we'd been through hell and back—twice. Amy caught me staring and looked up.

"What's going on with you?" she asked. "You haven't said a word since you started eating."

"I was hungry." I pushed my plate away. "Who's working tonight?"

"Baylor's patrolling right now and Takecia's working the checkpoint. Melvin and I will be going out in a few hours, and then we'll all go back to assessing the damage when daylight comes." She rested her elbows on the table. "We covered the worst-hit areas, so everything should be downhill from here on out."

We were both quiet for a long moment, and then I told her I was worried I wouldn't solve this case.

"Oh, you'll solve it." She nodded with a confidence I wished I shared. "You always do."

"I hope you're right." I cleaned up my dishes and then walked to the dispatcher's station, where Beth was reading a book. I glanced around the room. "Did Baylor turn in the re-entry logs from the checkpoint?"

"He sure did." Beth leaned forward on her desk and pulled out an envelope. It had my name on it. "He made copies for you."

I thanked her and took the envelope back to the lunch room. I would've preferred to work in Susan's office, but I didn't want to disturb her. Achilles stretched out on the floor at my feet, seemingly bored. Amy had finished her reports and headed for the shower, so I had the room to myself. After grabbing another can of Coke, I spread the logs on the table and accessed the school faculty list on my phone.

"Time to find out which one of you cheaters were in that school Tuesday," I said out loud, comparing the first name on the re-entry log to the long faculty list. "Even if it takes all night, I'm going to find you."

Achilles' ears perked up for a second when I spoke, but then he went right back to sleep.

CHAPTER 27

Friday, September 22

I worked into the morning comparing the re-entry logs against the faculty list. I stopped once to feed Achilles again, another time to take him for a walk to do his business, and another time for me to fix another plate of food.

It was almost three o'clock when I reached the end of the re-entry logs. I scowled, turned all of the pages over looking for more names.

"Something's wrong," I muttered.

"What's wrong?" asked Melvin.

I looked up as he and Amy walked into the lunch room. They each wore a fresh uniform, but they looked tired.

"I didn't find a single faculty member from the school on the re-entry log." I picked up my satellite phone and pulled out the card Susan had given me earlier that listed everyone's SAT phone numbers. "They all evacuated, so there should be at least a few of their names on it."

"Maybe none of them made it back yet." Amy suggested. "I know a lot of people are waiting for the power to come back on before they head back home."

She did have a point, but I called Baylor anyway. When he answered, I asked him if it was possible someone might've slipped through the checkpoint without being seen.

"Hell, no," he said. "We stopped every single car that came through and got the names of every occupant in every vehicle."

"Are you sure no one got through without being documented?"

"If they did, they were a ghost, because we stopped everything we saw."

I ended the call and stared blankly at the stack of re-entry logs. After a moment, I rifled through them and checked the evening hours again. There, big as life, was Beth Gandy's name. I then checked the morning hours, going down the list name by name. I checked and rechecked the nine o'clock hour.

"What a no-good, lying bastard!" I pounded my fist on the table and leaned back in my chair, stared up at Melvin and Amy. "Kevin Shelton lied about leaving town."

Amy had been making a sandwich and she paused with a knife in one hand and a can of potted meat in the other. "Who's Kevin?"

"He's the principal of Mechant Loup Middle School." The more I thought about it, the more it started to make sense. "He told me he and his wife had evacuated and that they returned home yesterday morning at around nine, but he's not on the list."

"Maybe they slipped through without being noticed," Melvin offered. "It wouldn't be the first time something like that happened."

"Baylor's positive no one slipped through."

Melvin and Amy traded looks. When they turned back to me, Amy spoke first. "Are you saying it's possible a principal killed Elizabeth? That the principal of the middle school is a suspect?"

"I wouldn't have thought it, but he lied about evacuating. If he didn't evacuate, that means he had opportunity to kill Elizabeth. And if he didn't kill Elizabeth, why lie about evacuating?"

"Just because he lied about evacuating doesn't mean he's a murderer, though," Melvin said. "Right?"

"If you lie small, you'll lie big." I told them about what Ty had witnessed and also about the missing hard drive from the surveillance system. "Kevin was already in the school when I got there, and he could've easily removed the hard drive. Hell, it has to be him. There was no one else around."

"What'll you do now?" Amy asked. "Are you going to arrest him? If you're wrong, that'll ruin his career."

"No, I'm not going to arrest him—yet." I shook my head for emphasis. "I need to build a case against him, and the first thing I need to do is prove he never left Mechant Loup."

"How will you do that?" Melvin asked.

"I'm going to find his wife and talk to her." I stood and glanced at the clock, feeling better about the direction of the case. "But first I'm going to get a few hours of sleep."

I took Achilles outside one last time and groaned when I saw that it was raining. The window on my cruiser was still broken and the interior would get drenched in the morning if it was still raining. Working quickly, I retrieved a garbage bag and some duct tape from the office and set about securing the opening. When I was done, I stepped back and admired my handiwork.

"What do you think, big man?" I asked Achilles. "Will it hold?"

His bark echoed loudly against the concrete underside of the police department. I couldn't be sure if it was a bark of approval, but I wasn't changing it. My best guess was that he was mad because he wouldn't be able to stick his head out of the window anymore.

"Okay, let's get to bed." I led him up into the building and told him to stay with Beth while I went to the bathroom and got ready for bed. Once I was done, we made our way down the hall and into Susan's office. I winced when he padded across the room toward his bed and his nails made scratching noises on the hardwood floor. I held my breath until he was finally lying down, hoping he hadn't disturbed Susan's sleep. I relaxed when I heard her steady breathing. She was actually snoring just a little, so I knew she had to be tired.

I then undressed and eased onto my cot. The wood creaked just a little and Susan stopped breathing. I froze in place and cursed under my breath. As I stared up into the darkness, I heard her own cot squeak and then I felt a hand in my face. Fingers pressed against my eyelids and mouth, then I heard Susan's voice beside me.

"Clint, is that you?"

"Yeah, I'm sorry I woke you up."

In an instant, Susan was on top of me, kissing my lips, and telling me how much she loved me. I wasn't sure what had gotten into her, but I just went with it—kissing her back and telling her how much I loved her in return.

Achilles whined from the corner, but, thankfully, he stayed on the pallet of blankets we'd created for him. I'd never made love on a cot, and I didn't want him ruining that opportunity.

CHAPTER 28

Susan and I were half on the cot and half on the floor when we woke up three hours later.

"Damn," I said, rubbing my blurry eyes. "Where'd that come from?"

Susan's face was flushed. "I…I don't know what came over me. I guess it's just that I've been missing you."

"I've been missing you, too." I kissed her and looked around for my jeans. I caught movement from the corner and glanced over at Achilles. His chin was resting on his front paws and he was staring at us with his large drooping eyes. I tossed a sock in his direction. "Oh, cut it out! I've spent more time with you than I have with my wife lately."

Susan laughed and walked over to him wearing nothing but her panties and a loose T-shirt. I had to redirect my attention to the search for my jeans. Otherwise, we'd be late getting our day started.

"It's okay, buddy," Susan said, rubbing his head. "Mommy still loves you."

I was relieved that Susan was feeling better, and I figured she had simply needed some rest. I did notice a lingering sadness to her eyes, though, and I knew the death of the baby was still weighing heavy on her heart. She didn't say anything about it, so I didn't bring it up. I figured if she wanted to talk about it, she would.

After I'd finished getting dressed, I kissed Susan goodbye and walked to the kitchen to get some beignets that Beth had made. I dumped a pile of powdered sugar on my beignets and bit into the first one with a grateful heart. It melted in my mouth and I let out a satisfying groan. As I ate, I handed Achilles some of his favorite snacks and we had breakfast together.

"I wish you would've been here from the start of this thing," I said to Beth as she was cleaning up the kitchen. "To hell with Café Du Monde—Beth Gandy's got it going on!"

She smiled wryly, paused what she was doing to stare up into space. "It was Troy's favorite meal. He loved to eat his beignets with Steen's pure cane syrup."

I frowned, and ate the rest of my food in silence, leaving her to the memories that were apparently swirling around in her head. I was about to pick up my plate when Lindsey rushed into the lunch room.

"Clint, Melvin just called. Elizabeth's husband is at the checkpoint and he's demanding to speak to the detective handling his wife's murder."

I quickly gathered up my stuff and called for Achilles to follow me. We hurried to my Tahoe and I sped out of the driveway, heading straight for the city limits to the north.

When I arrived, I saw Melvin leaning casually against his F-250 talking to a man I'd never seen before. I parked and told Achilles to stay. He plopped his head down and looked up at me as though to say, "I know, asshole…you never let me come out and play."

I walked toward Melvin and the fellow I assumed was Steve, nodded when I got close to them.

"I'm Clint." I stuck my hand out. "We spoke on the phone."

Steve didn't shake my hand. He was about my height, but a bit heavier. His belly hung over the front of his worn jeans and he had missed a button on his shirt.

"What's going on with my wife's case?" He ran his fingers through his greasy hair, and I noticed there was grime under his fingernails.

"Look, why don't you come down to the station and I can give you the full rundown on everything that's been done so far, and—"

"I ain't going to your police station." Steve's hands balled into fists. Out of the corner of my eye, I noticed Melvin push subtly off of his truck and drop his right foot back. One wrong move from Steve and Melvin would drop him.

I raised a hand in an attempt to calm Steve, whose eyes were bloodshot. I knew he couldn't have gotten much sleep and he was probably running on sheer adrenalin and hate for the person who had murdered his wife.

"Okay, let's move over to the side of the road where we can have some privacy." As we walked toward the shoulder of the highway, I gave Melvin a nod to let him know I'd be okay. He didn't look convinced, and I knew he'd be keeping a wary eye on Steve, just waiting to pounce on the man.

Once we were in the shadows of the trees along North Main, I gave him the rundown on what we knew so far. He stared blankly at me until I was done, at which time he said, "Are you telling me you've got nothing? It's been three days since you found my wife and you mean to tell me you've got absolutely nothing?"

I frowned, knowing firsthand how frustrating these cases could be. "Sir, I understand how—"

"Understand?" Steve spat the word, taking a threatening step forward. I didn't flinch. "How the hell could you possibly understand?"

"I've been where you are, only worse."

Steve was confused. "Worse? What do you mean?"

"I lost a wife and a daughter." I took a breath and exhaled, not wanting to get into it with this stranger. "I just want you to know that I understand the anger that's burning inside of you. The helplessness, the guilt—"

"Why in the hell would I feel guilty? I didn't touch my wife."

"You feel guilty because you weren't there to protect her, and now you want to murder the bastard who hurt her."

Steve lowered his head and I could see tears welling up in his eyes. He sank to the ground. "What am I supposed to do now? She's all I've got now."

"If you're a godly man, you can pray that I solve this case soon. If not, you can hope." I squatted beside him. "Meanwhile, you can go check on your in-laws. They need you. You have to be strong for them. Last I saw of them, they were falling apart."

"And I'm not?" He looked up and his eyes were even redder than earlier. "I got myself thrown in jail because I was falling apart."

"Is that why it took you so long to get here?"

He nodded. "My boss finally posted my bail and I got here as soon as I could."

"Is there anything at all you could tell me that might help speed up the process?"

"Like what?"

"Well, did Elizabeth ever suspect any teachers of having affairs at school?"

He shook his head.

"Did she ever say anything about the day-to-day happenings at school?" I was grasping at straws now. "You know how we all have work stories. Did she ever share any that stuck out in your mind as odd?"

"What do you mean?"

"Did she ever talk about two teachers arguing or problems she might've had with some kids? Maybe a parent called the school making threats…things like that."

"Nope, nothing at all."

My shoulders drooped. "Well, let me know if you think of anything. Here's the number to my satellite phone. The cell tower is down, but the landlines still work and your in-laws have a home phone."

"Wait…did you find her phone? She sent me that message and maybe there was more on her phone."

"No. We found her purse, but her phone wasn't inside. Can you describe the phone?"

"It was an iPhone—the latest kind. You know, the big ones that can't fit in your pocket." He was thoughtful. "Oh, yeah, and she had one of those personalized cases she bought online. It was a picture of her and me on the beach. The picture was from a few years ago and it was…it was the last time we went to the beach."

Steve began sniffling, and tears spilled from his eyes again. I wanted to tell him I thought the phone might have been lost when Elizabeth was taken up in the tornado, but I didn't want that image floating around in his head. The less he knew about his wife's final moments, the easier it would be for him to heal—or so I would imagine based on my own experiences.

When Steve stopped crying, I extended my hand. He sighed heavily, and then took it. I helped him to his feet and we walked toward his vehicle together.

"Is that your dog?" he asked, indicating with his head toward Achilles, who sat watching us carefully.

"Yeah, that's Achilles."

"It looks like he wants to jump out of that window and eat me."

"He's protective like that."

"I wish we would've moved like Elizabeth wanted," he said wistfully. "She's been begging me for a big dog—a German shepherd or a Doberman—to keep her safe while I'm offshore, but management at the apartments won't allow it. When they denied her request, she began pestering me to move. She wanted to live on the beach. I think that's why she loved that picture so much. I should've listened to her."

"You can't start second-guessing yourself now." I was speaking from experience. "That won't do any good and it'll only make you more frustrated—"

"Hey, wait a minute, there was something."

I glanced over at him. "What do you mean?"

"You asked if Elizabeth ever talked about her school and any of the teachers, but she never did."

"Right…"

"No, but she did say something about the principal."

I stopped walking and turned to face him. "What'd she say?"

"It was a while back and I didn't think anything of it at the time, but—"

"What the hell did she say?"

Steve leaned back, surprised by the forcefulness of my tone. I didn't apologize.

"It was maybe a year ago; they were in the teacher's lounge all alone and he started talking about his wife. He told her his wife had been diagnosed with early onset dementia. He said she had started being very forgetful and she had become depressed." Steve rubbed his tired eyes, and then continued. "He told Elizabeth his wife had lost interest in doing most of the things they loved to do together, such as dining in fancy restaurants, dancing, and taking weekend trips.

"After going on and on about how his wife was changing and how her illness was affecting *his* life—it sounded to me like he cared more about himself than her—he told Elizabeth that he would get lonely."

"Get lonely?" I asked, echoing him. "Was he trying to hit on her?"

"Yeah, he told her he missed doing all those things with his wife, and he asked her if she liked to dance and dine in fancy restaurants." Steve huffed. "Right away, she knew where he was heading with that conversation, so she shut him down quick."

"What did she say?"

"She told him she was sorry about his wife, but that she didn't feel comfortable with the direction of the conversation and she asked if they could change the subject." He stopped to wipe his eyes. "Elizabeth was always so nice about everything, even when she was mad at you. That's why I find it hard to believe someone would murder her."

I was thoughtful. If what Ty had said was true, the only likely scenario was that Elizabeth walked in on a couple having sex. And now, my most likely male actor would be Kevin, but who was the woman? Had he tried to put the move on another teacher after

Elizabeth rejected him? Did one of those teachers accept his advances? Whoever the woman was, she had to know that Kevin went after Elizabeth. That meant there was a witness out there I needed to find.

A cold chill suddenly reverberated up and down my spine. What if the other woman tried to intercede when Kevin attacked Elizabeth? If so, it was possible Kevin killed her too. That would mean I didn't have another witness out there but, rather, there was another victim.

"How'd Kevin take the rejection?" I asked Steve. "Did he get angry at Elizabeth?"

"Not that I know about." He shrugged. "She never complained about him again, so I figured it was a non-issue."

I asked Steve if he would be staying with Elizabeth's parents, and he said he would. I told him to call if he thought of anything else, and then I jumped into my Tahoe.

"Put on your seatbelt and hold on, big man," I said to Achilles. "We've got a principal to interrogate."

He didn't respond. He seemed disinterested in the case, but his ears perked up when I told him we couldn't interview Kevin's wife because she suffered from early onset dementia.

"She would've been our best hope at catching Kevin in a lie," I explained to my giant German shepherd, "but now we'll have to try and outsmart him."

I glanced around when I realized I was talking out loud, hoping no one had seen my lips moving. Thankfully, there were no cars on the road—other than an occasional emergency vehicle and a returning citizen—and even if someone had seen me, they might've guessed I was using one of those hands-free devices that are so popular nowadays.

The weather was still gloomy and overcast, but the wind had died down considerably, and bucket trucks were starting to move into the area. I frowned when I drove by a house where an elderly man was struggling with a large tree branch that had fallen across his driveway. Without hesitation, I whipped my vehicle around and stopped to help him clear the path to the highway.

Once I was done, I continued my drive to Kevin Shelton's house, which was nearby on North Bayou Tail Lane.

CHAPTER 29

North Bayou Tail was a long and shaded street, lined on either side by a mixture of trees, most of which were pine, oak, or cypress. The Shelton residence was on the right side of the street and the property was butted up against Bayou Tail, making it prime real estate. I let out a whistle when I turned the corner and drove to the end of a private drive named Shelton Place. Achilles' ears perked up, but he settled back down when he realized I wasn't whistling for him.

"Nice place," I muttered.

The house was huge—had to be at least four bedrooms—and it was wrapped in board and batten siding that had been painted gray. The dark green shutters were still closed from the storm prep and I could see several dents in the metal roof, which was the same color as the shutters.

There were two driveways to the residence: one in the back of the house and one in the front yard. The front driveway was oblong and had a crepe myrtle growing in the dirt at its center, and it was along this driveway that I parked.

I glanced at Achilles and started to give the command, but he gave me a look that seemed to say, "Don't bother...I already know you want me to stay."

I rubbed his neck and promised to take him on a boat ride once this case was over and everything was back to normal. I opened my door and started to step out of my Tahoe when a voice called from the opposite side of a long row of large shrubbery. I glanced in that direction but didn't see anyone.

"Over here, detective," called Kevin, waving his hand so I could see it. "I'm fixing my mailbox."

I walked around the edge of the shrubbery and saw him kneeling beside a wooden post. He was trying to hold a large mailbox in place with one hand while working a cordless drill with the other. I stepped forward to lend a hand.

"I'll hold it while you drill," I offered.

"Thanks. I've been fighting with this damn thing for twenty minutes."

I could tell he wasn't much of a handyman by the way he handled the drill, but he eventually secured the box on top of the post. He wiped a bead of sweat from his brow and stood to his feet.

"I know you didn't come here to help with my mailbox, so what can I do for you?"

"I need you to come down to the station so I can get a formal statement from you."

His eyes grew suspicious. "Why does it have to be down at the station? Can't we just talk out here?"

"It'll be more in-depth than our last conversation and I'll want to record it," I explained. "I'll need some detailed insight into all of your teachers and staff. Whoever killed Elizabeth had access to the school, so we'll have to explore them all."

He hesitated, resting an arm on the mailbox. "I would have to find someone to sit with my wife. She has—"

"Early onset dementia." I nodded solemnly. "I know and I'm sorry. Um…" I scrunched my face, as though I were deep in thought. "What about the person who stayed with her while you were at the school yesterday? Who was that?"

"It was my sister." He looked toward the back of the street. "I guess I could see if she wouldn't mind. She might be available."

"That would be great." I looked him right in the eyes. "I really appreciate you working so hard to help me catch the person who murdered your teacher. I'll be sure to let her family know how much help you've been."

He was a good poker player, but I thought I saw his left eye twitch ever so slightly. He nodded quickly and then turned to go inside his house. I waited near my vehicle—keeping an eye on my surroundings and my hand next to my pistol—and he reappeared several minutes later.

"We can go. My sister will be here in a couple of minutes."

I glanced toward the house. "Are you sure? We can wait."

"No, it's okay. She'll be fine alone for a few minutes."

I shrugged and jumped in my vehicle. Kevin headed for the back driveway and within seconds he was driving out in a Porsche. It was an older model, but it was still a Porsche. I didn't know what I expected him to be driving, but that car was nowhere near the top of my list.

I studied Kevin in my rearview mirror as I drove. He rubbed his face quite a lot and he seemed to fidget in his seat. The man was definitely hiding something, and I needed to make him tell me what it was. For a man as smart as he appeared to be, I knew I would need to approach him with logic, but I would also need some sort of convincing evidence to use as leverage.

My only problem was that I had none—nothing, nada—not one single solitary shred of evidence. All I had was a dead woman who was loved by everyone and some circumstantial evidence that was developed from a man who suffered from mental illness...a man who had admitted to peeping through a hole in the bathroom where my victim worked, and who was seemingly the last person to see her alive.

The more I thought about it, the more I realized any reasonable detective would be hauling Ty in for questioning. Not only was he in the school right around the time Elizabeth disappeared, but, as the maintenance man, he knew all the locations of the surveillance cameras, he was most likely familiar with the surveillance equipment, and he could've easily removed the hard disc. But I'd dealt with Ty enough to think I knew he wasn't homicidal. Sure, I could be wrong about him, but I didn't think so.

When we arrived at the police station, I led Kevin to an interview room and then put Achilles in Susan's office, where his water bowl and a snack were waiting for him. I gathered up the re-entry logs, the staff directory, and then flipped the switch on the recorder before settling down in a chair next to Kevin. This was an important interview, and I knew I'd have to take my time with the man. He had too much to lose—a good job, a guaranteed retirement, a beautiful home, his freedom, and his ailing wife—to simply cough up a confession, so I'd have to ease the information out without him noticing it.

I already knew that wouldn't be easy, but as long as I could keep him talking, I figured I could get what I needed to solve this case—provided he was the killer.

CHAPTER 30

"These are re-entry logs," I explained, sliding the logs toward Kevin Shelton. "After a natural disaster, our officers log the names of every citizen who returns to town, and these logs were collected in connection with Hurricane Samson."

Kevin stared blankly at the logs. "What am I supposed to do with them?"

"I'd like you to look them over and identify all of your employees who returned after the storm." I handed him an orange marker. "And just highlight their names when you find them, if you don't mind."

He stared down at the stack of pages, holding the marker in his hand.

"I don't think any of them will be on this list," he said. "I told them to remain where they were until I called and told them it was safe to return to town. I haven't made that call yet."

"Can you just check anyway? Just in case some of them jumped the gun and didn't wait for your call?"

He shrugged and began scrolling down the logs, viewing one page, and then the next, and the next, until he'd examined every one of them. When he'd finished, he shook his head and handed them back to me.

"Like I said, none of them are on the list."

"Did you see any names you recognized?" I asked.

"I think so." He scowled. "I do believe I saw Elizabeth's husband's name. They're the only Bankstons who live around here, so I figured it had to be him when I saw it. I met him once or twice, but I can't remember his first name. Damn, I just saw it…"

He snapped his fingers several times, as though it would help him remember. It seemed to work. "Steve!" he said triumphantly. "Yeah, that's his name...Steve Bankston."

"Did you recognize any other names?"

He shook his head. "Just the one."

I tapped the stack of pages, asked if he located his own name on the lists.

"No, and it wouldn't be there." He pulled out the first sheet and pointed to the time of the first entry. "The logs begin at six-thirty in the morning, and we got back from Arkansas at six."

I remembered him telling me that they'd rolled into town about nine in the morning, but I didn't want to remind him of that conversation just yet. I also didn't tell him that I'd purposefully left off the first page of the logs, which showed the checkpoint began at four o'clock.

"So, did you see the checkpoint that was set up when you first arrived back in town?"

"No, we drove straight through without being challenged." He shrugged, and it was an awkward movement. "I guess we were some of the first to return."

"And what time did y'all get to town?"

"Six...six in the morning."

I rubbed my chin, studied my notepad. "I'm confused."

"Why's that?"

"Didn't you tell me y'all arrived at nine?" I shot a thumb over my shoulder. "Back when we were at the school yesterday?"

"No." He shook his head. "I'm sure I said six."

"Oh, okay. I must've written down the wrong time in my notes. So, where'd y'all go when y'all evacuated?"

"We went to my daughter's house in Arkansas."

"What day did you leave?"

"Monday, about noon."

"What time did you get to your daughter's house?"

"It takes about eight hours to get to her house," Kevin said, "so it must've been around nine. We stopped once for gas and a couple of times for my wife to use the restroom."

"What time did you leave her house to return?"

Kevin was thoughtful as he studied my face. "What's with all the questions? Am I a suspect or something?"

"I don't know, are you?" My eyes bored into Kevin's. He began to fidget in his seat.

"Of course I'm not a suspect." He let out a nervous laugh. "I was out of town when the killing happened. I was just wondering why we were going over all of these questions. I know you have a job to do and I respect your work, but I think your time would be better spent tracking down the actual killer. Like I told you already—twice now—we were in Arkansas. In fact, you called me from the school grounds on Tuesday, as I recall, and we were in Arkansas." He nodded. "I believe I told you I was in Arkansas."

"That you did." I lifted my pen from the table. "What's your daughter's phone number?"

"My daughter's number? Why? She had nothing to do with anything. She's not even from here."

"As a detective, I've got to cover all of my bases. I can't assume anything, so a quick call to your daughter will confirm you were with her and I can clear you as a suspect."

"Oh, sure, I get it." Kevin drummed his fingers on the desk. "Let's see…hmm…I don't remember her number. It's programmed in my phone, but I left my phone home."

I wasn't buying it, but I didn't let on that I thought he was lying. "Look, I could simply contact your cell service provider and get the GPS coordinates from your phone, but that'll take a few days—maybe longer, given the storm. If I can speak with your daughter, it'll clear things up right away and I can do like you said and move on to finding the actual killer."

"Don't you need a warrant for my cell phone records?"

"I do."

"And what probable cause could you possibly have that would convince a judge to sign a warrant for my phone? I haven't done anything wrong, so there's no possible way you could have evidence to support a warrant."

I maintained a blank expression on my face, but it was hard. It was painfully apparent that Kevin knew a thing or two about the criminal justice process, and it would not be easy to rattle him into confessing.

"Well, you're a smart man," I said slowly, "so you know probable cause can be nothing more than a statement from a witness saying they saw you in town at the time of the murder, which would directly contradict your assertion that you were in Arkansas."

Kevin's left eye twitched ever so slightly again, and I realized that was his tell.

"That would be impossible," he said, "because I was in Arkansas."

"Can you explain this?" I calmly pulled out the first page of the re-entry logs and slid it across the table.

He casually glanced at it, then shrugged. "I can't answer why your officers weren't at their assigned stations when my wife and I drove through here. You'll have to question them about that."

"I'm sure there's a reasonable explanation why your name doesn't appear on the logs."

"Certainly."

I leaned my elbows on the desktop. "Did you know of any affairs taking place between any of your teachers?"

"None that I know about. We have a strict policy against fraternization in the school."

"Did you ever violate that policy by making a pass at Elizabeth Bankston?"

"No indeed. I would never violate the sanctity of my marriage— not for Elizabeth, and not for anyone."

"How would you respond if I said that Elizabeth told her husband you came on to her at school one day?"

"That's a lie!" The words spat from his mouth, and I knew I'd struck a nerve. "I've never acted inappropriately with any of my teachers."

"Are you calling Elizabeth a liar?"

"No, I'm calling her husband a liar. He's sort of the jealous type, if you know what I mean. He was always coming by the school checking on her. Sometimes I'd see him outside in his vehicle and I'd think he was waiting for her, but then she would leave in her own vehicle and he would drive away following her. It seemed weird— like he was stalking his own wife." Kevin glanced over his shoulder, as though he wanted to make sure no one was listening to us. "There were times when Elizabeth's husband would get his brother to keep an eye on Elizabeth while he was offshore."

"And how do you know this?"

"Her friend told me. She was worried about Elizabeth and wanted me to know about it. It's possible the brother had something to do with her murder."

"And who's this friend?"

"Linda Garcia."

I remembered seeing her name on the faculty list and I would call her to verify the information, but I felt this was an attempt by Kevin to throw me off his scent. I couldn't think of a scenario wherein Elizabeth's brother-in-law would be in the bathroom of her school with another woman.

"Do you own a gun, Mr. Shelton?"

"I hate the things." He shook his head from side to side. "If I had my say, no one would be able to possess a gun."

"Not even cops?"

"Well, maybe just cops."

"You didn't answer my question."

"No," he said pointedly, "I don't own a gun, and I detest people who do."

I scowled inwardly as I studied the man. Could someone who hated guns use one to murder another person? I would guess not, but what if this was all an act? Kevin was a smart man, so I imagined he wouldn't be above playing a role to get out of trouble. I needed to know more about him and I needed to delve deeper into his thoughts.

I began questioning Kevin about his work as a principal, his family life, and his thoughts on what might've happened Elizabeth. After spending an hour going back and forth with him, I decided it was time to try a baiting question.

"Would it surprise you to learn that Elizabeth sent a video to her husband from her cell phone right before she died?"

He hesitated for a long moment. When he spoke, he tried to sound casual. "Why would it surprise me? People send videos to their spouses all the time."

"But this was a different kind of video." I paused for a moment to hold him in suspense. "This video held evidence that explains the motive for her killing, which helped reveal the killer's identity."

"Well, if that was the case, you would already have the murderer in custody." Kevin straightened in his chair. "Since you don't, I guess you're referring to a hypothetical video."

"How do you know the killer isn't already in custody?" I squinted for emphasis. "That he's not already sitting in this very building?"

"I imagine you wouldn't be wasting my time if you did have the killer in custody."

"Can you prove you weren't in the faculty bathroom of the Mechant Loup Middle School on Tuesday at about one-thirty?"

"I already told you I was at my daughter's house."

"What if that video shows you having sex with another woman and Elizabeth walking in and catching you?"

He turned so red I thought blood would leak from his flesh. He didn't answer.

"Well, what about it? Did you kill Elizabeth because she caught you cheating on your wife?" I leaned closer to Kevin. "What about your lover? Was she in on the murder? Or did you have to also kill her to keep her quiet?"

Kevin's left eye was twitching so much it almost fell off. "I'd like to leave now if I'm not under arrest."

I pushed back my chair and stood up, opening the door for him. "You're free to leave whenever you like, but you should know I'm aware of what happened in that bathroom. You killed Elizabeth and we both know it."

"I…I don't know what you're talking about."

"There's no such thing as a perfect crime, even during a hurricane." My gaze followed him as he stood to his feet and approached the doorway. "Your biggest mistake was raping her before you shot her, which makes it a death penalty case."

"I didn't—" Kevin suddenly clamped his mouth shut and glared at me. The anger he felt was evident on his face. When he opened his mouth again, his voice was hoarse. "I didn't rape or shoot anyone. Now, if you'll excuse me…"

I didn't move, which forced Kevin to squeeze between me and the doorway.

"I'll be seeing much more of you—real soon," I said as he stomped out the door and down the hall, but I wasn't as confident as I sounded. He'd definitely lied about going to Arkansas, and I could prove that from the logs, but did that really mean he was a killer?

CHAPTER 31

Having gotten nowhere with Kevin Shelton, I hurried to my office—which had been vacated earlier by Melvin's wife and daughter—and ran a name inquiry on his daughter. I found a number for her out of Arkansas and quickly called it before Kevin could arrive home and contact her to get their stories straight. After identifying myself to the young woman who answered, I asked if I could speak with her father.

"The storm damaged his school pretty bad," I explained, "and I need to get in touch with him as soon as possible. There's a lot of equipment at risk of being ruined."

"Um, my father isn't here." She sounded befuddled. "I called and spoke with him last night and he said he and my mother were fine, that they didn't have much damage on their house."

"I'm sorry. I thought someone said they evacuated and went to Arkansas to be with their daughter."

"No sir. I haven't seen my parents since Easter."

"Huh." I paused, pretending to be confused. "Does he have another daughter in Arkansas?"

"If he does, he'll be in trouble with my mother." She laughed at her own joke. "But no, I only have one other sibling—a brother who lives in Vermont."

"Well, I'm sorry for bothering you." I jotted down some notes and then called Linda Garcia next. She told me she was holed up in a motel in Leesville, Louisiana. At first, she freaked out when I told her my identity, and she immediately asked if everyone in her family was okay.

Once I explained what it was about, she told me she'd heard

about Elizabeth from another teacher who had heard about it from Kevin. She broke down crying as I questioned her. She verified everything Kevin had said about Elizabeth's husband, and then added, "I wouldn't be surprised if he killed her."

"Impossible," I said idly, wondering if Steve's brother could really be involved. "He was offshore."

"Then I'd put money on his brother." Linda sounded sure of herself. "That guy came into the school a couple of times to speak with Elizabeth—I'm sure it was to spy on her—and he gave me the creeps."

I promised her I'd check him out, then asked, "Do you know of any teachers who are having affairs at the school?"

She hesitated for a bit, and I heard her humming to herself. "I don't think so—at least, not that I know about. I do know that Elizabeth messed around with a guy at a bar one night, and I think that's why Steve doesn't trust her anymore."

"What about Kevin? Has he ever made any inappropriate comments to you?"

"Oh, God no." She chuckled. "Kevin's not like that at all. I don't know if you've ever met him, but he's kind of goofy. He's never been anything but professional with me."

"Has anyone else had any problems with Kevin?"

"If they did, they never told me."

I studied my notes for a minute. "Do you know of anyone who would want Elizabeth dead?"

"Everyone loves her. I can't think of anyone who'd want to hurt her."

We talked for a bit longer and then I ended the call, more frustrated than before. I strode to my office and found a message from Mallory Tuttle letting me know she'd run Jude's name through all of her databases and had found nothing that could help me. At this point, I wasn't surprised by the news, because my sights were set firmly on Kevin Shelton.

Although I didn't expect anything, I called the local hotel and all of the bed and breakfasts in town for the sake of thoroughness. They all reported being empty since the weekend, and none had taken in any customers since then.

Next, I went through the motions of typing up a search warrant for Kevin's phone, house, and office at school, and I actually found a judge who was still in the parish. He said he had remained in northern Chateau with his family throughout the storm. While waiting for him to review the warrant and fax it back to me, I had to hear all about how he was the only judge who'd braved the storm and how he and his family had survived by hunkering down in his fortified gun closet.

"We have enough rations to survive for three weeks," he said, and then I heard him sigh after he finished reading the affidavit. "I don't know, detective, this seems a bit thin."

"As I wrote in my affidavit, other than my victim, he was the only person in town who had a key to the school, he lied about leaving town, and he's made inappropriate comments to the victim in the past."

I could hear a pen drumming the desk in the background. Finally, he spoke. "Okay, I'll sign it, but go careful on this one."

As soon as the search warrant was in my hand, I called Susan and asked for a backup officer to standby while I searched Kevin's house.

"I'll meet you there with Amy," she said. "We're two minutes out."

I waited at the front of North Bayou Tail Lane until I saw Susan's marked police cruiser approaching, and then we proceeded to Kevin's house. He was working out in his yard when we drove up. I could tell he was not happy to see me.

"What now?" he asked, removing some leather gloves and shoving them in the pockets of his loose-fitting sweat pants. "I'm trying to get some yard work done while I have the chance and I don't appreciate all the interruptions."

I handed him a copy of the search warrant as Susan and Amy fanned out behind me. "I have a warrant to search your house, phone, and office."

"For what?"

"Any evidence connecting you to the murder of Elizabeth Bankston."

Kevin's eyes turned to slits. "You're making a big mistake, detective. Do you realize who I am?"

"Do you think I care?"

"Well, you'd better start caring. You can have your fun today, but I assure you, my lawyer and I will be meeting with the mayor first thing Monday morning and you will find yourself out of a job."

Knowing Mayor Pauline Cane as well as I did, I knew that would never happen.

"Well then," I said, "let me get on with it while I still have a job."

"I'll also sue you personally for harassment and defamation." Kevin spat at my feet. "You'll be lucky to have enough money to feed that mutt of yours."

I glanced toward my Tahoe, where Achilles was sitting in the driver seat with his head hanging out of the window. I didn't care what Kevin said about me, but I didn't like him disrespecting my dog.

CHAPTER 32

Two hours later…
Mechant Loup Middle School

I slammed the last drawer closed on the desk in Kevin Shelton's office and settled into his leather chair.

"What are we missing?" I asked Susan, who was rifling through a filing cabinet near the door.

We had searched Kevin's house up and down and then tore up his office here at school, but we hadn't found anything—not Elizabeth's phone, no gun, and no hard drive. We did recover Kevin's cell phone and I was certain it held the key to the case, but he refused to provide the pass code. I had called the state crime lab and the forensic examiner said he wouldn't be able to break into it, but I told him I'd send it to them anyway and then I locked it in my truck.

Susan wiped sweat from her beautiful face and shook her head. "Not a damn thing. Are you sure he's bad?"

I sighed and leaned far back. This was a comfortable chair, and I made a mental note to check out the brand name and type so I could get one for my office. "He's got to be bad. If not, why would he lie about evacuating?"

"Maybe he had something else going on?" Amy offered, stepping into the office. I had asked her to search the library, where Elizabeth taught her classes, just in case I'd missed something my first time through it, but she declared she'd found nothing pertinent to the case.

I glanced to my right and again saw the metal trashcan at the corner of Kevin's desk. There was a white plastic bag in the can that I had searched three times already.

What the hell, I thought, and searched it a fourth time. There were several crumpled up sheets of paper, an empty diet Coke bottle, and a banana peel—just as there had been fifteen minutes ago. I even pulled the bag out to search the bottom of the can again, but there was still nothing inside.

I leaned back in the chair again and sat there looking up at Susan and Amy, hoping one of them would think of something I hadn't thought of yet. They just stared back at me, waiting for me to declare the search complete.

"Well, that's it then. We're done here." I stood to my feet and scowled. "I guess I won't be able to afford dog food for Achilles now."

"I'll feed him," Susan said playfully, "even though he doesn't love me nearly as much as he loves you."

We walked out of Kevin's office and back into the main office. I paused near the counter and scanned the area again. *What am I missing?*

"Come on," Susan said. "We've been over every inch of this place a dozen times already. There's nothing here."

The metal can near the copy machine caught my eye. I had searched that thing several times, too. It didn't have a bag like Kevin's can, so it was easier to see that it was empty—

"Wait a minute!" I yelled the words so loud that Amy jerked in her skin and Susan stopped dead in her tracks.

"You scared the hell out of me," Amy complained.

I pointed to the metal garbage can. "There's no bag in that can."

Susan's face was blank. "And?"

"There's a bag in every other can in this building." I began walking around the room pointing to the other metal cans, then moved to the doorway and pointed to the classroom across the hall. "They all have plastic bags."

"So someone forgot to put a bag in it." Susan shrugged. "Big deal."

"Or the killer threw the hard drive in it and put it out to the trash," I said, not waiting for it to register in their minds.

I immediately marched down the hall and through the exit, heading for the back of the main building. I approached the large blue dumpster that was positioned near the outside air conditioning unit. I grabbed the heavy plastic lid and shoved it into the air. It rotated upward and back, slamming into the back of the dumpster and making a booming noise.

Sure enough, at the center of the giant garbage receptacle was a single white garbage bag. I scrambled up the side of the dumpster and dropped inside. Although it was empty, it still stunk something awful. The rusted metal bottom was coated in a slimy liquid that smelled like warm road kill. I tried not to slip as I approached the bag.

"What's in the *bag*?" Susan asked, doing her best impersonation of Brad Pitt from the movie SEVEN.

"I don't know yet," I muttered, pulling on a pair of latex gloves from my back pocket and hoping it wasn't a severed head. "But I'm willing to bet…"

The bag was heavy—a good sign—and tightly knotted. I had to tear a hole in the side to get it open. I nearly jumped for joy when I saw the hard drive in the bag, but then my heart sank when I saw the condition of the device.

"Damn you, Kevin Shelton!"

"What is it?" Susan asked, peering over the top of the dumpster. "Is it the hard drive?"

I turned the bag up so Susan could see the smashed device and broken pieces of metal at the bottom of the bag. It looked like a hammer had been taken to it.

"He destroyed it," I said, hefting it in one hand. "This was my only hope."

"What about prints and DNA?" Susan asked. "If he threw it away, I'm betting he didn't think it would be found."

"Yeah, if I recover his prints and DNA I can charge him with destruction of state property." I sighed and secured the opening I'd ripped in the bag. I removed one of my gloves and wrapped it around the knot, then handed the bag and contents to Susan so I could climb out of the dumpster.

"Maybe the data can still be recovered," Amy offered from behind Susan. "With luck, he didn't damage the platters."

"The what?" I asked, scrunching my face as I hoisted myself up on the ledge.

"The platters—it's the part of the hard drive that stores the information."

"And how would you know this?" I paused to wait for her answer.

"I studied computers in college before realizing I'd rather break things." Amy shrugged. "Turns out I'm much better at the breaking part."

"Well, it looks like Kevin's good at breaking things, too, because that hard drive is crushed all to hell." I dropped to the ground and grunted when I landed. I thanked Susan and took the bag from her. "I'll log this into evidence and take it up to the crime lab as soon as I get a chance."

Amy and Susan headed for Susan's unit and I headed for mine. I put the bag on the back seat and told Achilles to move over so I could drive. I fired up my engine, but sat there for a long moment, thinking. I knew Kevin destroyed the hard drive, which meant there was something on it that implicated him in a crime, but was it murder?

I had combed every inch of this school, but hadn't found a spent shell casing or a bullet hole or any blood. If the murder hadn't happened here, why would he destroy the hard drive? I could only come up with one logical explanation: the motive for Elizabeth's murder was on that hard drive.

Armed with this new information, I wanted another crack at Kevin. My only hope was that he hadn't lawyered up yet. I shoved the gearshift in *Drive* and sped out of the parking lot. If he killed Elizabeth, he must've had a gun, but why hadn't I found it? Had he discarded it in the trash like he'd discarded the hard drive? I'd checked the trash at his house, but hadn't found anything of evidence. What if he'd thrown it in someone else's garbage? Or Bayou Tail? Without some hint of its location, it would be nearly impossible to find.

I hadn't made it far from the school when my radio scratched to life and Lindsey called for me. When I picked up the mic and told her to go ahead with her radio traffic, she asked if I could respond to a report of a found item.

"The location is off of Cypress Highway, north of East Coconut Lane," Lindsey explained. "Please contact a Mr. Spencer Boudreaux. He found a cell phone while cutting his grass. Be advised all other units are busy."

"Hold on, Achilles!" I hollered, whipping my vehicle around. "They might have found Elizabeth's cell phone!"

CHAPTER 33

We hadn't seen the sun in a few days and it was darker than it should've been when I pulled up to Spencer Boudreaux's gray one-story home. The front yard was littered with branches and roofing shingles. Two men—about twenty years old—had accessed the roof via an aluminum folding ladder and were trying to drape a blue tarp over the damaged area. The wind, while not as strong as earlier, was still giving them fits. An elderly man dressed in black jeans, a black shirt, and a black ball cap was giving instructions from the ground.

Debris crunched under my tires as I pulled into the driveway. The three men stopped what they were doing and turned to stare. The old man removed his ball cap and rubbed his gray hair.

"Hurry up and get that hole covered before it starts raining again," he hollered up at the two young men. "I'll see what this is."

He walked around the front of my Tahoe and reached the driver's side just as I was stepping out.

"Nice dog you've got there," he said, leaning forward to see Achilles better. "Is it a black wolf?"

"It's a German shepherd."

"Damn fine German shepherd."

I nodded my thanks, stuck out my hand, and introduced myself. "Did you call the police department?" I asked.

"Yeah." He waved for me to follow him and he led the way to the edge of the highway and then north along his property. "I was cutting my grass up along the ditch and I hit something with my lawn mower. It was loud and I thought it was a root at first, but then I saw some pieces of silver metal strewn all over the yard."

Boudreaux stopped when we reached the push mower and he

pointed to a chunk of twisted metal and broken plastic in the wet grass. I groaned outwardly when I saw a small piece of plastic displaying Steve Bankston's face.

"What is it?" the man asked. "Do you recognize the phone?"

I squatted beside the damaged phone and lifted a small piece from the ground, holding it by its cracked edges. The pieces were probably too small to process for fingerprints and the operating system had been destroyed, so there was no chance of recovering anything from it.

"I do recognize it," was all I said. I walked to my vehicle and grabbed an evidence bag. After shoving some latex gloves in my back pocket, I pulled another pair over my hands and walked back across the yard. Once the pieces of the phone and cover had been recovered, I secured them in my crime scene box. I was about to thank Spencer Boudreaux and then leave, when a thought occurred to me.

I'd noticed an empty milk jug, several bottles, and a hubcap in the ditch along the Boudreaux property. I turned toward the house, where Spencer had gone back to barking orders at the two younger men.

"Mr. Boudreaux," I called, pointing toward the ditch, "do people often throw their garbage in the ditch?"

"All the damn time."

"Mind if take my dog and continue searching your property?"

"Be my guest."

I opened the driver door and called for Achilles to heel and we headed for the spot where I'd recovered the cell phone. With him strolling by my side—his tongue dangling happily from his open mouth—I began walking along the eastern edge of the ditch first. I must've covered two miles, stopping often to push tall patches of broadleaf weeds aside so I could see through to the ground, but I didn't find a pistol. Achilles and I then crossed to the western side of the ditch and we began making our way back toward Spencer Boudreaux's house.

It was almost dark when we made it back to my truck. Spencer and his helpers were no longer outside and the lawn mower had been picked up. I drove north along Cypress Highway and parked where we had stopped the earlier search. Grabbing my spotlight, we continued searching each edge of the ditch. Although the wind was still blowing, it didn't keep the mosquitoes away and we were getting eaten up by the tiny bloodsuckers.

I received a call from Susan around eight to ask if everything was okay. We had worked our way about six miles north of Spencer Boudreaux's house by that time.

"The last radio traffic we received from you was when you went out to recover the found item," she said, her voice sounding a little terse. "I was worried about you."

"Sorry, but I've been busy. Achilles and I are searching the shoulder of Cypress Highway, making our way toward Bayou View Apartments." I wiped sweat from my brow and swatted at a mosquito that drilled into my neck. "When the killer drove to Elizabeth's apartment, he threw her phone out the window and it got hit by a lawn mower. I'm thinking the gun might've been thrown out the window, too."

Susan was quiet on the other end of the phone for a few seconds. Finally, she asked, "Why not just leave the phone and the gun in the trunk of Elizabeth's car with the purse?"

"The killer didn't leave the gun and phone where we could find it because he knew it could lead us right to him." I nodded as I said it out loud, knowing I had to be right. "That's why he discarded those items. I need to find this gun, Sue. It's our last hope."

"Is the phone salvageable?"

"It's completely smashed—just like the hard drive." I glanced over my shoulder when I heard Achilles crash through the thick weeds in the ditch. "Where are you going, boy?"

I was standing on the western edge of the ditch, walking the shoulder of Cypress Highway, and Achilles had jumped to the eastern side of the ditch. He disappeared in the tall grass and then stopped moving. I aimed my light in his direction.

"Let me call you back, Sue," I said. "Achilles found something. It might be a water moccasin."

I ended the call and waded through the grass, which was chest high. "Where are you, big man?"

Even with my powerful LED light, I couldn't see Achilles through the dark shadows of the grass. It wasn't until I was almost on top of him that I made out his strong back through the weeds.

"Hey, boy, whatcha got there?"

Achilles was sniffing aggressively at the bottom of the ditch and I had to give him a tug before he would respond to my commands to back off. My heart leapt in my chest when I saw what he was sniffing. There, in the soft mud of the ditch, rested a silver revolver.

"Sit!" I ordered, not wanting him to mess with the revolver anymore.

Using the camera feature on my cell phone, I took a few

pictures—over-all views, mid-range, and close-ups—and then donned a pair of gloves. My hands shook slightly as I reached for the revolver. It had pressed into the soft mud upon landing there, but for the most part, it had been protected from the elements by the thick weeds surrounding it. I knew I never would've seen it had it not been for Achilles sniffing it out.

I rained verbal praises down on him as I held the revolver in one hand and my flashlight in the other. When the light hit it, I saw that it was a Ruger GP100. I carefully opened the cylinder—keeping it lined up exactly as I'd found it—and noted that there were five live rounds and one spent casing in the six chambers. I held the rounds in place with my gloved hand and tilted the revolver so I could see down the bore.

"This is it!" My voice was so loud and unexpected that Achilles' head jerked around to see what all the fuss was about. Just inside the muzzle and along the crown were specks of dried blood and flesh. "This is the gun that killed Elizabeth."

I was excited and my heart was beating fast, especially when I checked for the serial number and saw that it was intact. This was the break I'd been waiting for. All that was needed now was to send a request to the ATF's National Tracing Center and then submit the gun to the crime lab.

The trace would tell me the name of the original purchaser, and that would give me a starting point in my quest to identify the person who had possession of the gun. Once the gun was at the crime lab, the DNA analysts would be able to compare the blood and flesh from the bore and muzzle of the pistol against the known DNA samples from Elizabeth's autopsy. If they matched, I could prove with certainty that this was the pistol that killed my victim.

"Let's get out of here, boy," I said to Achilles. "We've got some work to do."

CHAPTER 34

It was early in the morning when Susan and I woke up to the sound of Achilles barking. I checked the time. It was almost seven. I groaned, wanting to tap him on the head like a snooze button so I could get a little more sleep, but I knew it wouldn't work.

"He wants to go out and potty," Susan muttered from the cot next to me. "That's his bark for having to pee."

I threw my bare feet off the edge of my cot and stretched long and hard. When I stood, Achilles' tail began wagging furiously as he stood anxiously by the door. I snatched a shirt from the back of Susan's desk chair and shrugged into it as I opened the door.

Once we were outside, I began walking down the street with him while checking my phone to see if I'd heard from Tracy Dinger, who was one of the firearms examiners at the La Mort crime lab. I'd called her cell phone last night to find out if she could pull a favor and have the revolver processed for DNA, but I hadn't heard back from her yet. I wasn't sure what was going on in the city since the storm. Maybe the crime lab had been blown away or maybe something bad had happened to Tracy. I grunted. It wouldn't be the first time a law enforcement officer had lost his or her life during a hurricane.

Achilles sidled up to me and pushed his cold nose against my hand. I rubbed his head idly and decided to call Tracy again. This time she answered.

"Hey, Clint, how's it going down in the deep south? I heard y'all took a direct hit."

"We're alive. What about the city?"

"It passed to the east of us, so we made out okay. We've got a few hundred downed power lines, thousands out of electricity, dozens of damaged buildings, some street flooding, but no deaths. Other than the damage and a bit of looting, we're fine."

Not wanting to waste much time, I got straight to the point. "Did you get my message? I've got a murder weapon I need processed for DNA. It's important and I didn't know who to call."

"All of your cases are important," she mumbled. When I didn't comment, she continued. "I did get a message from you, but I couldn't hear it well because it was scratchy. Our cell service is starting to come back, but it's far from reliable at the moment. So, what's the story with the weapon?"

I gave her the abridged version of the murder investigation and about how I'd found the weapon. "There's blowback in the bore and I need to know if the DNA on it belongs to my victim."

"No suspects?"

"I'm waiting for the trace results to come back from the ATF. I think I know who did it, but I'll be sure once I have the original purchaser's name."

"It's Saturday and we've just been hit by a monster hurricane," Tracy said, "so I doubt I'll be able to find someone willing to come out today."

"I'll owe you…"

"You already owe me." She paused for a few long seconds. "How soon can you get here?"

"An hour or two, depending on traffic."

"Okay," she said. "I've got a colleague who might be willing to begin working it up immediately. It won't be ready until the middle of the week, but if you deliver the weapon and the known sample today, I'll get the ball rolling for you."

I thanked her, and Achilles and I turned to head back to the police department. Many of the shops along Washington Avenue had their doors open and we could hear banging and sawing coming from inside the buildings. I smiled in admiration. One thing I'd learned about this place since moving here: after a disaster, the folks in town didn't waste time waiting for others to come in and assist them. They immediately began putting things back together. Neighbors helped neighbors and everyone looked out for each other.

Of course, like anywhere, there was a certain percentage of the populace that tried to capitalize on disasters by looting and trying to scheme unsuspecting victims. We tried to always remain vigilant when it came to fighting crime, but there was a heightened sense of awareness during and after natural disasters.

"What about it, Achilles?" I asked as we approached the police department. He glanced at me when I mentioned his name. "Want to come with me to La Mort?"

"Why are you going to La Mort?" Susan asked from her perch atop the steps. I had shown her the gun and phone last night when I had returned to the office, and she'd agreed that it had to be the murder weapon. "Are you bringing the murder weapon to the lab?"

"Yeah." I looked up at her and was surprised to see she was already dressed in her uniform. "Where are you going so early in the morning?"

She began clambering down the steps, her boots landing heavily on the concrete, and I headed up. We met at the halfway point.

"I've got to meet with the mayor and provide an update of the recovery efforts." She shot a thumb toward the sky, which was still overcast. "The ass end of the storm hasn't completely passed yet and they're already wondering how soon we can be open for business."

A steady breeze was still blowing, with a few strong gusts every now and then, so the workers from the power company were going about their job cautiously. I understood the town was losing money each day we weren't open, but we couldn't start letting strangers in until our citizens were settled, and we couldn't rush the power company. Their employees had dangerous jobs, and the rest of us just needed to be patient.

"Well, good luck with the meeting." I squeezed her hand and hurried past her. "I've got to get dressed and head out of here."

CHAPTER 35

One hour later…

I was still fifteen minutes from the crime lab when Tracy called to say her friend in the DNA section had agreed to process my evidence. I gave a triumphant yell and Achilles, who had been lying on the seat beside me, lifted his head briefly. When he realized I wasn't going to give him something fun to do, he lowered his head and closed his eyes. He was bored.

I didn't blame him. I was bored, too. There were virtually no cars in my lane of traffic on the interstate, but the opposite side was flowing steadily. At one point, a convoy of bucket trucks had passed by, heading toward the south, and I could've sworn I'd seen a Canadian flag painted on the doors of a dozen of them. The others were from various parts of the country, with all of them joining forces to come assist with the recovery effort.

My heart swelled with pride for having been born an American, and I was also very appreciative that our neighbors to the north were joining in to help out. While our town had been spared heavy destruction, I'd heard on the radio that some of the parishes and towns east of us had been nearly wiped out, and I was sure that's where most of the bucket trucks were headed.

Along the route to La Mort, I noticed that more than a dozen trees had been blown down and more than a few billboards had been completely destroyed—one had been twisted like a pretzel and then deposited on the shoulder of the highway. At least the highway was passable, and for that I was grateful.

Within a few minutes, I took the exit to the crime lab and then made my way through city streets until I arrived in the parking lot. I called Tracy and she met me at the entrance, where I parked along the sidewalk and left my door open.

"Here"—she handed me a chain of custody form—"sign on the X and I'll get these to the DNA section."

I signed her chain of custody form and then handed her the box of evidence and a lab submittal form. She ran her finger down the form, nodded when she verified everything was correct.

"So, you want the tissue and blood from the muzzle and bore compared to the known sample of Elizabeth Bankston, right?"

"Yep," I said. "You've got my number; please call as soon as you know something."

"Will do." She smiled and waved as I walked to my Tahoe and sped off, heading for town.

The drive back to town took a little longer, thanks to the large volume of residents and volunteers heading in the same direction. Achilles wasn't impressed with the drive, and I could tell he was ready to be back home roaming around the yard and exploring the cane fields. He had disappeared in those fields more than once, and I often wished he could talk when he came back, because I was sure he'd been off on some crazy adventure and I wanted to hear all about it.

It was ten thirty when we pulled back under the police department. I was grateful it hadn't rained, because I didn't know how well my plastic window would perform in bad weather. I let Achilles out of my cruiser and waited while he peed on every car in the parking lot. Once he was empty, we lumbered up the steps and into my office. I began organizing my notes so I could start on my report when I was interrupted.

"Clint!" Lindsey called from the dispatcher's station. "You got a fax from the ATF."

My left hip crashed violently into my desk as I jumped to my feet and rushed out the door. "Please tell me they were able to trace it!"

"They were able to trace it," Lindsey said flatly, as I cleared the doorway into her station.

"Really?" I reached for the document atop the fax machine, trying to read the whole thing at once.

"How should I know?" Lindsey asked. "I didn't look at it—I was only saying what you told me to say."

I grunted as I read, then stopped when I saw the name of the original purchaser.

"Damn," I said slowly, stopping to scratch my head. "That's not who I expected."

"Who is it?" Lindsey asked eagerly. "Who does the gun belong to?"

I heard her question, but ignored it. I walked down the hall and into my office, where I gathered up my file and snatched my keys from the desk. "It's almost that time, big man," I said as Achilles followed me out the door and into my Tahoe. "We're about to put the cuffs on this case."

I knew I needed the DNA results to confirm that the gun in question was the actual murder weapon, but I had enough to start rattling some cages. After all, I was almost 100% certain the results would link the revolver to Elizabeth's murder, so I should be able to bluff the suspect into confessing. And it didn't take long to reach the suspect's house.

"Stay," I said to Achilles when I parked in the driveway of the familiar residence. "I'll only be a minute."

I rapped loudly on the outer wall, and it only took seconds for the curtain on the door to be brushed aside. I saw Beverly Wells' face on the other side of the smudged glass. She smiled when she recognized me.

"My dad's not here," she said when she opened the door. "He went to my grandpa's house down the street."

"Is Liam with him?"

She nodded. "Is he in trouble?"

"I don't know," I said slowly, staring off in the direction she'd pointed. "Maybe."

"Well, I don't know what he's being accused of, but I'm sure he's probably guilty." She shook her head slowly. "That kid will never change. He's given my mom and dad fits since he was four."

"What's your grandpa's address?"

When she gave it to me, I turned and hurried to my Tahoe. I found the address with no problem and was soon standing with Liam and Smitty in the front yard of the grandpa's house.

"I need to speak with Liam again about Elizabeth Bankston's murder," I said to Smitty. "And this time it's serious. I've got real evidence now."

"What kind of evidence?" Smitty's gaze wandered toward his son. "Boy, you'd better hope he's wrong about this."

"I'm not," I said with confidence. "The gun that killed Elizabeth was a Ruger GP100 .357 magnum—and it was registered to you, Mr. Wells."

CHAPTER 36

"But my gun was stolen from my car," Smitty said when he and I were seated alone in the conference room at the police department, "so why do you think Liam did it?"

"Well, you have to admit it would be quite a coincidence for someone to steal your gun two years ago and then use it last week to kill a teacher Liam hated." I studied Smitty closely. "I believe your son stole the gun and kept it hidden until Tuesday, when he used it to shoot Elizabeth Bankston."

Smitty scowled, and I knew I was getting through to him. "I just can't believe Liam would ever kill anyone. I know he likes to act tough, but he's a soft kid. I catch him crying sometimes when we watch sad movies. His mom makes fun of him for it, but he always denies it and leaves the room pissed off."

"That doesn't mean he's not a killer." I rested my elbows on the table, leaned forward. "Look, I need him to tell me everything he knows about that gun."

"But I really don't think he stole it, detective."

I pulled the burglary report from my file folder and slid it across the table. I'd located it earlier when I ran Smitty's name in our database. "Look at the date you filed the report."

Smitty glanced at it, and then shrugged. "So? What of it?"

"You reported the burglary on the fifth of January, which was a Monday," I said, "but you told the officer you noticed it missing on the fourth. Why did you wait a day to report it?"

He was thoughtful. "I...I really don't remember. Maybe I was waiting until a weekday?"

I pulled out a flash drive and shoved it into one of the USB ports on the desktop computer. Once I'd accessed the folders, I located a file titled *Statement of Smitty Wells*, and then played it. Smitty's head drooped as he heard his own words explaining why he waited to call the police.

"You told the officer you didn't call right away because you thought Liam had taken the pistol and you wanted to talk to him first." I stopped the recording. "You said he'd done it once before and you'd gotten him to admit to taking it. You said he'd taken it to show a friend and you found the gun in his closet tucked into one of his shoes."

"I do remember saying that now," he acknowledged, "but Liam swore he hadn't taken it this time, and I believed him."

"Why would you believe him?" I wanted to know. "He'd taken it before, so what makes you think he hadn't done it this time?"

"He admitted to it the first time, so I figured if he'd done it again, he would've admitted to it like the other time. Besides, I searched his room high and low but didn't find it."

That did make sense, but my money was on Liam stealing it. "Well, I need to go in there and talk to him, and I need to get the truth out of him—whatever it is. I have to give you some time alone with him, and I hope you convince him to do the right thing and tell the truth."

Smitty sighed heavily, stood to his feet. "I'll talk to him, but I don't think he took my gun and I certainly don't think he shot anyone with it."

I led him to the interview room, where Liam was sitting at the desk, his leg bouncing nervously.

"Can I leave?" Liam asked, jumping from him seat.

"Sit back down," Smitty ordered his son. "We've got some things to talk about."

I closed the door and walked away, intending to allow them fifteen minutes alone. I made my way to the lunch room and fixed a bologna sandwich with mustard and Doritos. I dropped to the table and was halfway through my food when Susan walked in.

"I still don't know how you can eat that garbage." She scrunched her face. "Why do you put your chips on the sandwich?"

"It's better that way." I took a sip of Coke. "How's your day going?"

"Busy." She took the seat across from me. "We're stretched thin. Baylor's standing-by in the parking lot of Mechant Groceries while the National Guard hands out water and other supplies. Melvin and Takecia took the boat to check on the residents living on the water.

And Amy has been running from complaint to complaint trying to keep up."

"Want a sandwich?" I asked, taking the last bite of mine.

"Nah, I've got to get back on the road. I'm helping Amy answer calls." She stood and stretched, and then stared down at me, her brown eyes tired. "So, I heard you traced the gun to Smitty Wells."

"Yeah, I'm thinking it had to be Liam who killed her."

"If so, how do you explain what Ty saw?"

"I can't."

"And how does Kevin factor into the case now?"

"I don't know." I gathered up my trash and sat there for a long moment, thoughtful. "Ty's either right or wrong—it can't be both—but I can't believe it's a coincidence that the murder weapon is linked to Liam. He has to be connected to Kevin some kind of way—"

"Detective," Smitty Wells suddenly called from the doorway of the interview room, "Liam's willing to talk to you."

Without telling Susan goodbye, I jumped to my feet and dropped my trash in the garbage can. I was down the hall and in the interview room in a flash. I finished filling out the rights form I'd begun earlier and asked Liam if he was willing to make a statement.

"Yes sir, I'll tell you what I know."

I pushed the signed forms aside. "Okay, tell me how you came to be in possession of your dad's revolver?"

"I wasn't. I don't know what happened. All I know is one of my friends slept over that weekend and he might've taken it. We're not friends anymore, and I think that might be why."

"Well, then," I said, raising my voice a little, "how would you explain your DNA being on the gun?"

Liam blinked. "I…I don't know."

"Isn't it true your DNA is on the gun because you stole it to kill your teacher?"

"No sir!"

"Absent an explanation from you, I have to think that's exactly why you stole it. Do you know that if you're convicted of murder you could spend the rest of your life in prison? That means you'd die in there."

"But I didn't kill anyone!" Liam's eyes were clouding over. "I'm being set up!"

"Well, you definitely stole the gun." I crossed my arms in front of my chest. "If you won't admit it, I've got to believe it's because you murdered her with it."

"No! I swear to God!"

"Look, if you—"

"Don't you dare bring God into this," Smitty said heatedly, interrupting me. "If you took the damn gun, just say you did it. Otherwise, this man is going to think you murdered that poor teacher. Don't you understand that, boy? If you don't start telling the truth, I'll ask the detective to step outside and give me five minutes alone with you, and you don't want that."

Liam's lower lip was trembling now. He nodded as he swallowed hard, and I could tell he feared his father more than he feared life in prison. "Yes sir, I…I took your gun."

"Don't look at me," Smitty said, his face red with anger, "look at Detective Wolf."

"It was a long time ago…" Liam hesitated, glanced fearfully at his dad before looking back in my direction. "So, it's hard to remember everything—"

"Don't you even start with that nonsense," Smitty warned. "Tell the damn truth and stop wasting my time."

"Yes sir." He shifted in his seat. "Like I was saying, it was a long time ago, so it's hard to remember exactly what day it was, but I know it was a Friday night. I…um…one of my friends and me were hanging out around the house and he wanted to see my dad's guns. My dad was inside, so I couldn't show him the automatic because it was in my parents' room. We waited until later in the evening when my dad went to bed and I took him outside to the car, where my dad kept his wheel gun."

I didn't correct Liam when he called the semi-automatic pistol an "automatic", because it didn't really matter. There were lots of folks who misidentified semi-autos for automatics, and now wasn't the time for a firearms lesson—it was time to hear his confession. I was, however, impressed that he called the revolver a "wheel-gun". I'd picked up that term as a kid reading western novels, and I wondered where Liam might've learned that description.

"What happened next?" I asked when Liam paused.

"I opened the glove box and the gun was inside. He had it in a black holster and he had another holster with two of those fast loading things." Liam looked at his dad again, as though to apologize with his eyes, before going on with his story. "I took it, but I meant to put it back. We were just going to shoot it in the woods the next day and I didn't think my dad would go in his car until Monday, so I had plenty of time to put it back."

"Did y'all shoot it on Saturday?"

"Yeah, we went to the woods on the east side and shot some bullets my friend got from his dad. He had brought some nines and some .357s." Liam lowered his head. "As luck would have it, Dad got called out to work Sunday morning while we were still sleeping and before I had time to put the gun back. Mom woke us up on Sunday morning and told me my friend had to go home and she said I wasn't allowed to leave the house until Dad got back from work. She said he was mad about something."

"I *was* mad," Smitty acknowledged. "I thought he took it at first, but I believed him when he said he hadn't. I see now I was wrong. I should've trusted my gut."

Liam chewed on his lower lip while his dad was speaking. I told him to go on once Smitty was finished.

"When Dad got home, he questioned me about the gun and I got scared so I lied."

"Why wouldn't you just tell him you showed your buddy the gun? I'm sure he wouldn't be so mad about that."

"I showed his gun to one of my other friends once before and he told me he'd beat my ass with a belt if I ever did it again." He avoided eye contact with his dad. "I was scared, so that's why I lied."

Smitty nodded. "I did tell him that."

I leaned forward, resting my elbows on the desk. "Where's the gun now, Liam?"

"I don't know."

"When's the last time you saw it?" I asked.

"Um, it was last school year." He shifted nervously in his chair. "I might have taken it to school."

"You did *what*?" I thought Smitty was going to knock Liam out of his chair. "You took my gun to *school*? Are you crazy?"

I had appreciated Smitty's help getting his son to open up, but I was growing tired of his interruptions. I held up a hand.

"Do you mind letting him go on with his story?" I asked. "I need him to tell me everything he knows, and I need it quick."

"You heard the detective." Smitty waved his hand in disgust. "Go on and tell him what he needs to know."

"An eighth grader was bullying me last year and he threatened to bring a knife to school, so I brought the six-shooter. I showed two of my buddies and one of them ratted on me. It was taken away and that's the last I saw of it."

"Who ratted on you?"

"I'm not sure."

"Who'd they tell?"

"I'm not sure, but a teacher came rushing over and told everyone to back away from me and get into a classroom. She told me to please have mercy and not to hurt anyone." He grunted. "She acted like I was going to start shooting, because she then ran off and locked herself in the classroom with her students."

A thought suddenly occurred to me. "Are you saying you brought a gun to Mechant Loup Middle School?"

"I mean, it stayed in my backpack. I never took it out."

"You said you showed your buddies."

"I unzipped my bag and let them peek inside, but I never took it out."

"And this happened last year? Right here in town?"

He nodded.

"Why didn't we know about this?" I asked incredulously, looking from him to his dad. "Why didn't anyone call the police department? Why weren't you arrested for this?"

"I don't know if anyone called the police, but I wasn't arrested—that much I know for sure. I mean, it's not like I pointed it at anybody." His expression was blank, as though he didn't realize how serious it was to bring a gun to school. "I really don't know why they didn't call the police. I guess it was because I never pulled it out."

"The school didn't even call my wife or me to tell us our son brought a gun to school." Smitty shook his head as he stared at me. "I'm as surprised as you are—and pissed off."

Liam shivered. "I'm sorry, Dad. I know it was a mistake now, but that was last year. I didn't know better back then."

"Oh, you knew better, Liam Joseph." Smitty crossed his arms and glared at his son. "I'll deal with you when we get home."

"What happened next?" I asked. "After the teacher locked herself in the classroom?"

"Well, Principal Shelton came running over and he told me to drop my backpack, so I did. He took the backpack and he grabbed my arm and dragged me to the office. Once we were there, he took the gun and we talked for a while. He told me I could get into real trouble, but then he told me everything was going to be okay and that I needed to keep it confidential." He shrugged. "I don't know what happened, but when he stepped out of the office I heard him tell his secretary to let everyone know that everything was okay. He told her to spread the word that it was a toy gun and it was all a false alarm."

"A toy gun?" I echoed. "Principal Shelton lied to his secretary?"

"Yes sir."

"Why would he do that?"

Liam shrugged again. "I really don't know. He just told me not to say anything about it to anyone."

I drummed my pen on the desk, deep in thought. What in the hell had Kevin Shelton been up to? Had he viewed that incident as an opportunity to get his hands on a throw-away gun? If Liam was telling the truth, then Kevin killed Elizabeth Bankston with his dad's gun. But there was still the possibility that Liam was lying and he was the one who killed Elizabeth. Liam's voice was deep enough that Ty Richardson might have mistaken him for a man. In any event, I needed to speak with Kevin immediately, while also keeping Liam on ice.

"Mr. Wells," I said, standing to my feet, "I need you and Liam to wait here while I conduct an interview."

"Am I in trouble?" Liam asked. "Am I going to jail?"

"That remains to be determined." I gathered up my file and headed for the door. "If y'all need anything—a bathroom break, something to eat or drink—just knock on the door and someone will come."

CHAPTER 37

One hour later…
Mechant Loup Police Department, Interview Room Two

"Detective, this is bordering on harassment," Kevin Shelton said in a strained voice as he stood with his back to me. "If you don't release me immediately, I'm going to call my lawyer."

I removed his handcuffs and pointed toward a chair. He dropped heavily into it. I walked to the other side of the desk and tossed the cuffs into a drawer. I took my seat and watched him rub the feeling back into his wrists.

"I warned you that I'd be seeing a lot more of you." I waved my hand around the room. "Promise made, promise kept."

"You still haven't told me why you illegally detained me."

"I did, but you weren't listening." I pulled a copy of the arrest warrant from my file. I had faxed the affidavit to the same judge who'd signed the search warrant, and he believed I was getting warmer in my search for the killer. "You were too busy yelling at me and threatening to sue my ass off."

"What the hell is this?" Kevin stared at the warrant, but his eyes were red and I was sure they were blurry with anger.

"You're under arrest for accessory after the fact to a student carrying a firearm on school property and to possession of a stolen firearm."

"This is ludicrous! I did no such thing!"

"I have a witness statement and DNA evidence that'll prove otherwise. You caught Liam Wells carrying a firearm on school property about one year ago, yet you did nothing. You confiscated the firearm and released him." I leaned back in my chair. "That firearm was stolen and it remained in your possession until last Tuesday, when you used it to kill Elizabeth Bankston—"

"That's bullshit!" Kevin smashed his fist loudly on the desk. "That's all a lie!"

"Ah," I said slowly, "that's the Kevin I've been looking for—the *real* Kevin, the one who lost his temper and murdered Elizabeth in cold blood.

"Now, as I was saying," I continued, "you used the stolen gun you confiscated from Liam Wells to kill Elizabeth Bankston, and then you discarded the gun when you drove her car back to her house. I know you weren't alone, because someone had to drive you back to the school to retrieve your own vehicle, so I'm guessing your lover went with you."

Kevin's head was hanging low now. So low, in fact, that it was almost resting in his lap.

"We recovered the gun and it's being processed as we speak for DNA and fingerprints. When it comes back with your prints and DNA on it, as well as Elizabeth's DNA in the barrel, I'll be obtaining a warrant for murder. We also recovered Elizabeth's phone, and you'll be happy to know we're sending it to the lab in an attempt to retrieve that video I spoke about earlier." I paused and watched the man's body break into an uncontrollable tremble. "I see I've got your attention now."

"But…but I didn't kill anyone."

"Then tell me who did."

A long moment went by when neither of us said anything. I allowed the silence to hang heavy in the room, knowing it would become uncomfortable for him. Finally, he cleared his throat.

"Can I have some water first?" He lifted his face and I saw that his eyes were bloodshot. "And then I'll tell you everything you want to know."

Not trusting him enough to leave him alone, I picked up the phone on the desk and dialed Lindsey's extension, asked if someone could bring him a glass of water. Five minutes later—and it was five more minutes of complete silence—Amy Cooke stuck her head in the door. She was carrying a plastic bottle of water and motioned for me to step out into the hallway.

"What's up?" I asked after I'd given the water to Kevin and met her right outside the door.

"Lindsey said that Mr. Wells asked to use the bathroom, so I let him go. When we got back to the interview room, I saw Liam on the desk phone. I asked him who he'd called, but he said he was just messing around on the phone."

"Did you check it?" I asked, mildly curious.

Amy nodded. "I hit the redial button, but it only dialed up three numbers."

"He could've hit random numbers after the call," I said, thoughtful. I couldn't think of any reason he might have for calling someone to destroy evidence or for any other nefarious reason, so I shrugged and thanked Amy.

"I'm willing to talk and admit to my part in everything," Kevin said when I entered the room, "but I won't name names."

"You're willing to admit to killing Elizabeth?"

"If I did, it would be a lie, because I didn't kill her."

Right, I thought sarcastically. Instead of arguing, I simply said, "Go on."

"I was at the school that day—on Tuesday—and I was with another woman." He licked his dry lips. "We were having a rendezvous in the staff bathroom when Elizabeth walked in and caught us. I didn't know anyone was in the school and it kind of freaked me out—it scared me. At first, I thought someone had broken in and I reacted defensively. You know, to protect the school. After all, I'd ordered everyone to evacuate, so I didn't think any of the staff would be at the school. I figured it had to be an intruder."

Kevin paused, as though trying to summon the strength to continue. "Um, well, Elizabeth began making accusations and I tried to calm her down, but she wouldn't listen. She became hysterical. She was freaking out and I might have accidentally pushed her in an attempt to get her to calm down." He wiped sweat from his upper lip. "I was afraid she'd hurt herself."

"You accidentally pushed her?" I asked, raising an eyebrow.

"Yeah, it was all an accident." He hesitated for another long moment. "That's when my lover ran out of the bathroom. She must've gone to my office, because the next time I saw her she had the revolver I'd confiscated from Liam. I don't know the sequence of events during that whole time, but I know a tornado hit near the school and she told me Elizabeth hadn't made it.

"We were both upset about Elizabeth and didn't know what to do. She told me we had to get rid of the gun and we also had to get rid of Elizabeth's car. She didn't tell me why, she just said we had to do it. So, she gathered up all of Elizabeth's things and locked them in the trunk of the car."

He stopped talking and I had to encourage him to continue.

"Well, I drove my car and she drove Elizabeth's car and we brought it to Elizabeth's apartment. She put Elizabeth's car keys in the apartment and locked up the car, then I drove her back to the school. I haven't seen her since and I didn't know what happened to Elizabeth until you told me she was murdered. Up until that point, I thought she'd been killed by the tornado."

"Wait a minute." I held up a hand. "You left a few things out."

"Sorry, but I already said I'm not giving up her name."

"Fair enough, but what did she do with the gun and Elizabeth's phone?"

"Oh, yeah, that." Kevin nodded. "When we were driving back from the apartment, she handed me the gun and phone and told me to throw them as far as I could out the window, so I did. I threw them out along Cypress Highway in a big ditch that was overgrown with giant weeds."

"Why'd you destroy the hard drive?" I studied him closely as I asked the question. "And when did you do it?"

He sighed. "I did it Thursday, after you left to get the generator. I didn't realize someone would be working a murder case in the middle of a hurricane, so I didn't think to destroy it on Tuesday."

"So, you now admit you knew your lover murdered Elizabeth?"

Kevin blinked several times and his face lost a shade of pink. "I…I didn't…that's not what I said."

"Why won't you give up the name of the woman who killed Elizabeth?" I pressed. "I can't make any promises, but you might be able to make a deal with the district attorney's office. I could call them and you could talk to them—"

"That's never going to happen." Kevin set his jaw in dogged determination. "I will never rat on her."

I sighed. "Did anyone else have a hand in Elizabeth's murder? Like Steve or his brother? Hell, you don't have to name them, just let me know if more people were involved."

"No, no one else was involved." Kevin shook his head for emphasis. "It was only her—the woman I was having an affair with. And I swear to God I didn't know she was capable of doing something that horrible. I'm now scared that she'll hurt me if I rat on her. In fact, that's the reason I went along with helping her bring back the car and clean up the scene—I thought she was going to kill me next."

After asking a few more probing questions, I sat there going over his story in my head. He certainly didn't seem like the self-sacrificial type—he didn't have the stones for that kind of move—and I couldn't think of a single reason why he would *not* give up his lover.

"Kevin, I hate to tell you this, but I don't believe your story. The only reason I can think of for you not giving up your lover's name is because she doesn't exist." I leaned forward on my elbows. "Isn't it true that you made sexual advances toward Elizabeth and she turned you down?"

I was fishing for more, but I wasn't sure I'd get it. He seemed determined to keep his lover's name a secret.

"That's absolutely false. I've never said or done anything inappropriate with any of my teachers, and for the last time, I didn't kill Elizabeth. Regardless of what you think, I know for a fact there *was* a woman present and she *is* the one who killed Elizabeth, but this"—he thumped his chest with a fist—"is as close as you're going to get to finding her. I also know for a fact that I cannot be compelled to cooperate with an investigation, so I'll be on my way now."

He said the last part with a sort of arrogance that annoyed me, and I was even more determined now to identify his lover, because I was certain she would point the finger at him and give me the evidence I needed to put him away for life.

"Rejection is hard for a man like you to take, isn't it?" I asked.

"What's that supposed to mean?" His face was purple with anger. "What are you trying to say?"

"It means whatever you want it to mean." I nodded knowingly. "Yeah, I'm sure it stung when she turned you down, and that's why you killed her."

"That's not what happened." He crossed his arms in front of his chest. "I already told you what happened and I won't say another word about it until I speak with my lawyer."

I wanted to tell him he'd already said enough to put him away, but I didn't. Instead, I stood him up, spun him around, and ratcheted the cuffs on his wrists. I then guided him through the door and toward the holding cells.

"Wait a minute," Kevin said, trying to pull away. "I asked for my lawyer. You can't do this! I demand to see my lawyer immediately!"

"Once you exercise your right to an attorney, all questioning must cease," I explained, "so there will be no more questions. However, you'll be held here until we're ready to transport you to the Chateau Parish Detention Center. At that point, a judge will set a bond and the jail will allow you a phone call. You can call your lawyer, your daughter, your priest—hell, anyone you want to call—but you'd best call someone who has enough money to bail you out."

"Why am I going to jail? I told you I didn't kill anyone. This is ludicrous!"

"What's ludicrous is that you really believe you'll walk free for everything you've done." I pushed him forward. "In addition to the warrants I've already shown you, you're under arrest for accessory after the fact to second degree murder, and that's based solely on your own story. Once I find the woman you were cheating with, I'll have enough to put you away for life."

"You'll never find her." Kevin sneered. "And you'll never be able to prove I had anything to do with any of this. I'm a well-respected principal of the best middle school in the tri-parish area. My reputation is impeccable."

The locking mechanism made a loud clanking noise after I placed Kevin in his cell and turned the key. Although he had sounded confident, he sure shivered when he heard that noise.

CHAPTER 38

It was mid-afternoon and I was walking back to the interview room to finish up with Liam and his dad when Susan met me in the hallway. She was holding an evidence bag.

"This bag was on your desk," she said, "and it keeps ringing. I could hear it all the way from my office."

I scowled. The bag contained Kevin Shelton's cell phone that I needed to bring to the crime lab.

"Who could be calling him?" I mused aloud, then sucked in a mouthful of air. "What if it's his lover?"

"It looks like a landline, but it doesn't register a name."

I took the evidence bag from Susan and leaned against the wall as I dug out the phone. An idea occurred to me. Sure, the phone was locked and Kevin had refused to give me his pass code, but that wouldn't prevent me from answering it or seeing who was calling him.

"I can run the number if you want," Susan offered. "Maybe we'll get lucky and it'll come back to someone."

I nodded and pressed the home button on Kevin's phone. The screen lit up, showing that there had been eleven missed calls from the same number. Based on the three-digit prefix, I knew it was a local landline. I was tempted to call the number, but that might spook the caller. I gave the number to Susan and she hurried off. With luck, she would come back with a name, and we could go out and get this mystery caller. It had to be Kevin's lover, and she must've heard he was at the police department.

I was still contemplating what to do when the phone rang loudly in my hands. I jerked off the wall and nearly dropped it. A quick glance told me what I needed to know—it was the same number.

Acting on instinct, I walked away from the interview room and slid my thumb to the right across the screen. My heart thumped in my chest. I put the phone to my ear. Not wanting to scare away the caller, I just held it there for a second.

"Hello?" It was a female's voice. "Kevin?"

I knew I didn't sound like Kevin, so in my softest voice possible, I grunted a little.

"Hey, it's me. Can you talk?"

I grunted again, turning abruptly when I heard Susan's boot approaching.

"Is it your wife? Is she around?"

"Huh," I said softly, signaling with my hand for Susan to be quiet as she approached the end of the hallway.

"You're acting weird, Kevin." The female huffed on the other end. "Look, you'd better say something quick or I'm hanging up."

"It's me." I tried to distort my voice as best as possible. "My wife is coming—"

Clunk!

"Damn it!" I said. "She hung up on me and there's no way she's calling back."

"I know who that caller is and I know why Kevin covered for Liam." She held up a printout. "It's the kid's mom."

I gasped when I saw that the phone was registered to Smitty and Anne Wells. I remembered Anne being overly friendly, but she hadn't looked like the type of woman who would stray from her marriage. Of course, one could never tell by looking at another individual. A cheating wife could look as innocent as a nun and a faithful wife could look like a street walker. The outer shell didn't matter. What was important was the stuff that was on the inside.

"I guess I'd better pay Mrs. Wells a visit," I said, returning the phone to the evidence bag.

"I'm coming with you."

"Nah, I don't want to spook her, so I think it's best if I go alone."

"She's a murder suspect!" Susan shook her head in protest. "There's no way I'm letting you go in there by yourself."

"A missed phone call isn't enough to get a warrant, and it's not evidence that she murdered anyone. Hell, she could be just another one of Kevin's women on the side and might have nothing to do with the case." I scratched my head. "Even if it is her, she doesn't suspect anything, so there shouldn't be any problems."

"Doesn't suspect anything?" Susan's voice was almost shrill.

"Your Kevin impersonation was horrible! Look, she potentially executed someone in cold blood, so you've got to let me tag along."

"But I've got the murder weapon. What's she going to do now—beat me with a stick?"

Susan objected some more and we debated the issue for several long minutes. Finally, we reached a compromise. I would drive in alone and she would be waiting toward the front of the street, while Amy would be waiting toward the back. I would leave my radio keyed up so they could hear everything that was going on.

"Are you sure you can spare Amy?" I asked. "I know things are still hectic around town and you said she's been busy."

"She caught a break. We haven't had another call in about twenty minutes. Besides, it shouldn't take long, right?"

I nodded and, sighing in resignation, followed Susan toward the front door. We stopped only long enough to ask Lindsey to keep an eye on the interview room. "Don't let Liam out of the room," I said. "If they need something, call one of us off the road first."

Lindsey swallowed hard and nodded. "Is it safe for me to be in here?"

"The doors are locked," I assured her. "There's no way they're getting out."

Having not moved back home yet and not wanting to leave Achilles alone with Lindsey, I called for him to jump in the front seat of my Tahoe. Once Susan and Amy had pulled out of the parking lot behind me, I headed east on Washington. We hadn't made it to Back Street when Lindsey's voice came over the police radio, calling frantically for Susan.

"Chief, there's been a building collapse south of town at a shrimp shed," she radioed. "Three people are trapped under the rubble. They need help ASAP!"

I glanced in my rearview mirror and made eye contact with Susan in the reflection. Her face was troubled and I knew she was conflicted. I pulled to the shoulder and waved for her to go. She set her jaw and gunned her engine, racing past me with Amy hot on her bumper. She radioed back and told Lindsey she and Amy were en route.

I pulled onto the highway and kept driving south, trying to decide if I should abandon my murder case and keep following Susan and Amy. With Melvin and Takecia on the water and Baylor tied up with the National Guard, they would be the only officers responding to the disaster. But then I had Smitty and Liam Wells waiting at the office.

Sometimes I miss the good ole days, I thought, reflecting back to my time as a La Mort detective, *when there were ten cops on every corner.*

I was just driving past Pine Street when I saw a fire rescue truck approaching from behind. There were at least three firemen in the vehicle and I pulled off the road to allow them through. I heard more sirens sounding from across town, and I caught a glimpse of an ambulance whipping down a cross street several blocks away.

Satisfied that the response to the shrimp shed was adequate, I turned around and made my way back to Pine. I knew Susan would not be happy with me going it alone and I knew it would've been better to have backup available, but sometimes cops had to do what they had to do to get the job done. Besides, I didn't have time to wait and I wasn't planning on fighting Anne Wells.

CHAPTER 39

The plastic bag that covered my broken passenger window flapped loudly as I drove down Pine Street. Achilles cocked his head to the side and stared. I glanced over and saw that a strip of duct tape had peeled off and was dancing in the breeze. We hadn't seen the sun since Tuesday, but the clouds were not as dark anymore and the wind not as violent.

As soon as this case was over and things settled down a little, I would have to get that window fixed. But, at this moment, I needed to make contact with Anne Wells and hopefully convince her to accompany me to the police station and confess to her crimes.

I parked on the street in front of the Wells' home and shut off the engine. Keeping an eye on the front of the house, I told Achilles to stay in the cruiser and then I slipped from my seat. The place seemed quiet and I wondered if anyone was home. As I made my approach to the front of the house, I wondered if Anne had suspected something when she'd made the call to Kevin's phone earlier. What if she'd high-tailed it out of town?

I quickly dismissed the thought. Kevin didn't even know his own daughter's phone number, so it was quite possible he didn't know Anne's number either. If not, it was quite possible he hadn't told her his phone had been confiscated.

When I'd made it to the front door, I reached out and tested the knob. It was locked. I thought about knocking, but decided to check the perimeter of the house first. I knew I could've received permission from Smitty to search the residence, but I didn't want him knowing what I'd learned just yet. I wanted his wife to cooperate with the investigation, which meant I needed to catch her by surprise.

I began making my way around the left side of the house toward the back, when I heard a door slam shut. Curious, I hurried toward the back corner and was about to round it when a figure instantly appeared and ran smack dab into me. As we collided, the figure bounced off of my left shoulder and tumbled past me. I spun around and faced the front of the house, where the figure was scrambling to its feet.

I recognized immediately that the person was too small to be Anne. It was only after she was facing me that I realized it was Liam's sister Beverly—the good one.

I was about to open my mouth to speak when I saw the gun in her hand. It was Smitty's Ruger P85 nine millimeter pistol and it was pointed directly at me.

"Whoa, there, young lady," I said, lifting my hands slowly, "what's this all about?"

The girl might've been a high school student, but she appeared mature—as though her innocence had been stolen at too young an age—and her eyes carried more hate than I'd noticed when I'd first met her.

"You know what this is about," she said calmly. "You answered Kevin's phone earlier and tried to trap me into saying things about him."

"Wait a minute." I was confused. "That was you calling Principal Kevin Shelton?"

Beverly's thick lips curled upward. "You know it was."

Befuddled, I asked, "Why on earth would you be calling him?"

"Why do you call your wife?"

"Because she's my wife," I said flatly. "Again, why on earth would you be calling Kevin Shelton? You're not his wife."

"No, but I'm his girlfriend."

I nearly vomited. This girl was, at most, fifteen years of age. Kevin was older than her dad, and Kevin's daughter was older than she was. I took a step back and tried to steady myself. The thought of him dating her—or any underage girl—was revolting and maddening, and it was enough to make my head spin. I hated people who harmed children in any way, and I suddenly hated Kevin Shelton.

"So, that's why he never gave you up," I said. "Had he done so, he would've implicated himself in the worst type of crime imaginable—even worse than murder."

"Love isn't criminal." Beverly had the muzzle of the pistol leveled at my stomach, and something in her voice made me think she was very capable of shooting me. As though I didn't need any further proof, she said, "Do you want to know what happened to the last person who tried to come between us?"

"I'd love to know." I was stalling now, waiting for an opportunity to draw my own pistol. "Was it Mrs. Bankston?"

I expected a denial, but she sneered and said, "That bitch thought she was better than me. She looked down on me because I was younger, but who's laughing now?"

I decided to play along. "I got the same impression from a few of the other teachers—that she was a bitch."

"Yeah, she rubbed people wrong."

"What did she say when she caught you and Kevin in the bathroom?"

A hint of hesitation. "You know about that?"

"I know everything that happened that day. Kevin sang like a bird, providing every detail except your name." I started to slowly lower my right hand. "But I'd like to hear it from your perspective, because the angle I got painted you in a bad light. And I don't believe you're bad like that. Of course, that's only if you're okay with telling me your story."

"Of course I'm okay with telling my story."

"Are you willing to tell me how you killed Elizabeth Bankston?"

"Sure." Keeping the gun leveled on me, she began to speak. "Kevin and I have been seeing each other since last year, back when I was in eighth grade. It all began one day after school when I was waiting for a ride—"

"Please spare me the sordid details," I said. "Just get on about how y'all killed Elizabeth."

Beverly's eyes narrowed, but she continued. "Kevin told me he'd instructed everyone to evacuate, so he figured we would have the school to ourselves. We were in the faculty lounge and moved to the bathroom, where we started to get frisky. Well, we heard some noise and before we could do anything, Elizabeth walked into the bathroom and caught us."

She shook her head. "I never did like Liz because she always thought she was better than everyone else, and she really pissed me off that day. She began yelling at Kevin and cursing him out. She threatened to go to the police. He began begging her, asking for a second chance. He told her he would break up with me and he promised he'd never see me again. When that didn't work, things got physical and he pushed her. That really freaked her out and she became hysterical."

"How'd you feel about him saying he would break up with you?"

"It did piss me off, especially when he called it a mistake, but then I figured he was only saying that to buy time. I realized he wanted me to handle the situation." She shifted her feet, but the pistol didn't waver. "I knew he had taken my dad's gun away from Liam last year and he kept it in his desk drawer, so I ran out of the bathroom and got it."

"Wait," I interrupted, "how'd you know about your dad's gun?"

"Kevin told me about it when it happened, and so did Liam."

"Did Liam know about you and Kevin?"

She nodded.

"That's why Kevin didn't make a police report about the gun." I pursed my lips. "He knew if Liam got arrested he would rat on y'all."

"Liam would never rat on anyone, but Kevin felt it would attract unnecessary attention." She tossed her head to the side. "Oh, and Liam called a minute ago and told me everything you asked him. He's loyal like that."

So, the little prick was making a phone call after all, I thought.

"Why would he call you?"

"He wanted me to know you were closing in on Kevin, so I could distance myself from him."

"Let's get back to Tuesday. What happened next?"

"When I got back to the bathroom, Elizabeth was backed into a corner and she was still arguing with Kevin. That's when I pointed the gun at her." There was delight in Beverly's eyes as she explained how Elizabeth reacted. "She changed her tune when she saw the gun, that's for sure. She started begging me not to shoot her and she promised she wouldn't say anything."

Beverly scoffed, said, "I swear, people will say anything to keep from being shot."

"What happened next?"

"Well, Elizabeth was really scared now, so she started fighting. She kicked Kevin in the groin and then pushed him into me. That's the only reason she was able to make it out of the school. She was gone by the time I got outside, but she'd lost one of her shoes and I was able to figure out which direction she went.

"I caught up to her in the football field and tackled her to the ground." Beverly grunted. "She's pretty tough and she can run—I'll give her that. She kicked me and got away, but she lost her other shoe and she was forced to slow down when she hit the hard surface of the road."

Beverly paused when the hum of a car engine approached. I stole a glance over my shoulder, hoping it was Susan, but it wasn't. The car just zipped on by, the driver not paying any attention to his surroundings.

"Did you eventually catch up to her?" I asked, trying to keep her talking. Her finger was wrapping tightly around the trigger, and I knew it could go off at any moment.

"Oh, yeah, I caught her. She was trying to knock on doors, but everyone was gone. She was talking on the phone to someone when I finally tackled her near a house on Library Way." Beverly smirked. "It was a ghost town, so I knew I could do whatever I wanted to and get away with it. She was kneeling down, staring up at me and begging me to spare her life."

There was a dreamy look in Beverly's eyes, as though she were reliving the moment and enjoying it.

"I put the gun to her head and was contemplating whether or not to pull the trigger." Beverly nodded slowly. "I knew this was my decision—I held the power to spare her life or take it—and it felt good. I made her give me her phone and she told me she had tried to call her husband but he didn't answer. I still wasn't sure what I would do with her, but then she pointed up at the sky behind me.

"At first, I thought it was a trick, but then it got cold all of a sudden and some hail began falling. When I turned to see what she was pointing at, a tornado came out of the sky and touched down right behind us, maybe a hundred yards away."

Beverly paused and I waited for a long moment. When she didn't continue, I asked, "Is that when you shot her?"

"I was still looking up at the tornado and she grabbed my hand. I had no choice—I had to shoot her at that point." Beverly shuddered. "It was so scary! I started running as fast as I could."

"So, shooting someone is scary?" I felt a little better that she expressed some displeasure about committing murder, and I figured I'd be able to talk her down.

"What?" Beverly's face twisted in contempt. "No! That tornado was scary. I thought it would get me. I had to run as fast as I could to get out of its way. I looked back once and saw it take Liz up in the air. That's when I knew I would be okay, because everyone would think the tornado killed her."

Damn, you're evil! I thought, but didn't say it. Instead, I asked what happened next. She repeated much of what Kevin had said, filling in a few more details as she went along.

"I knew we had to get rid of the gun and the phone, and we had to bring all of her stuff to her house so no one would link it to the school." She frowned. "I can't believe her body ended up right at the school. It's as though the tornado testified against us. I really thought it would drop her across the bayou."

"I don't understand why you would murder her for telling on Kevin," I said as she closed out her story. "It seems a bit extreme."

"It's not extreme at all. She was threatening my way of life—my future."

"What's that mean?" My right hand was low enough now that I could probably reach my pistol before she could pull the trigger. "How could she possibly be threatening your future? It's not like Kevin would ever leave his wife and marry you."

"No, but he was going to pay for my college." She waved her left hand in the air. "Look at this place…my mom and dad can't afford to send me to college. Kevin was giving me an allowance every week and he was putting money in a college fund for me. If he gets arrested, I'll lose everything. And I'm not about to turn out like my parents. No sir, I'm going to be a lawyer."

As I listened, I was taken aback by how willing and casual she was about admitting to the murder, and I knew she couldn't realize the severity of the situation. My facial expression must've given away my thoughts, because she smirked again.

"What's the matter?" she asked. "Are you surprised that I want to be a lawyer?"

"No, I'm surprised you think you'll be anything but an inmate for the rest of your life. It's over, kid."

"Over? How's it over?" A smile played across her mouth, and it was a wicked one. "It's not like you'll ever repeat what I'm telling you."

"How's that?"

"Because I'm gonna kill you."

She said it so matter-of-factly that a chill reverberated up and down my spine. I was astutely familiar with the Bible verse in Mathews where Jesus said if you live by the sword you'll die by the sword, and I'd always expected my end would be a violent one. However, I never dreamed it would be at the hand of a teenager.

"Do you know the penalty for murdering a cop?"

"It's nothing if I don't get caught."

"Oh, you're already caught." I shot a thumb toward the left. "You see that officer over there?"

She took the bait and turned her head, gasped when she realized no one was there. I instantly drew my pistol and aimed it right for her chest.

"Drop the gun now or I'll drop you!" I ordered in a loud and authoritative voice.

Beverly shrieked when she saw my pistol. Without blinking, she pulled the trigger and shot me right in the stomach.

CHAPTER 40

I'd never been hit by one of Susan's mule kicks, but I imagined this is what it felt like to get kicked by a professional mixed martial arts fighter. I sank to my knees, the wind having been ripped violently from my lungs. I wheezed and fought for air. Somehow, through the pain and struggle for air, I kept my pistol leveled at Beverly Wells.

"Drop...drop your gun," I finally managed to say after several attempts. My voice was strained and raspy, and my vision blurry.

Beverly stared curiously at me and took a step closer. She lifted her pistol and took aim at my head.

"I want you to beg like Liz begged," she said. "Go on...do it."

I steadied my shaking right hand with the left one, trying to focus on the front sight of my pistol. My right index finger was on the trigger, but it wasn't working. I tried to apply pressure—to will the finger to move—but it wouldn't budge.

Like a bucket of ice cold water, it suddenly hit me—I couldn't shoot this young girl! I'd spent years mentally preparing myself to take the lives of bad people in order to save good people. Part of that training had included the ugly reality that I might have to take the life of a child to save another child's life, and I was mentally and emotionally prepared to do just that if called upon. However, I'd never considered having to kill a child to save my own life, and I now realized I couldn't do it. Given the choice, I'd rather risk my own life and spare the life of a child.

"What the hell's wrong with you?" Beverly asked when I lowered my pistol. She lowered her own gun and cocked her head to the side. "Are you suicidal?"

"Stop...stop before it's too late," I said through clenched teeth. The pain in my stomach radiated up through my chest. I could breathe a little better now, but the pain was crippling.

"It's already too late." Beverly stepped forward and lifted her pistol, her jaw set and her eyes mere slits.

I didn't look away. Instead, I brought myself high on my knees and stared right into her eyes, bracing myself for the impact of the bullet. Right when I thought the shot would come, I felt something hard brush against my right shoulder and I toppled over. Beverly's face twisted into shock.

I caught myself with my left hand and looked up to see Achilles lunging at Beverly. She tried to back away, but she was no match for his blinding speed. He latched onto her right wrist with his bear-trap jaws and began jerking her arm from side to side. She screamed in pain as her shoulder appeared to be wrenched from its socket. Her face was cloaked in terror. Although she'd just tried to murder me, I was overcome with compassion.

"Achilles!" I said loudly. "Off!"

He didn't listen and I had to scream the command several more times. Finally, my voice broke through and there was a brief moment when everything just stopped. Achilles was frozen in place, Beverly's arm dangling from his jowls. Beverly stood motionless—her face ashen and her jaw trembling—staring in fear at Achilles. I was propped up on one knee, my breath coming in ragged gasps. Beverly's pistol was on the ground at her feet and mine was dangling in my right hand.

"Off!" I said again, directing my comment to Achilles.

He reluctantly opened his jaws and backed away. He wanted to continue his attack, but he was obedient and he trusted me.

Beverly collapsed in a heap on the ground and began crying. I couldn't help but feel sorry for the young girl. Although she'd been so vicious a minute earlier, she now seemed like a typical teenager who was hurt and in need of assistance. Had it not been for Kevin taking advantage of her, she would never have been in this predicament. I couldn't wait to have another conversation with him.

Achilles turned away from Beverly and strode to my side. I was up on both knees now and rubbed his neck with my left hand, while keeping my eyes on Beverly. She was still crying loudly, but I detected a shift in her tone. I realized in an instant that her left hand was reaching for the pistol.

"No!" I shouted, but it was too late. She was bringing the pistol to bear on Achilles, who was sitting quietly now, his tongue hanging from his panting mouth. I didn't have time to push him out of the way and I didn't have time to get between them. She was too quick. I only had one option, and it was the Beretta 92FS semi-automatic pistol in my right hand.

Without hesitation, I lifted my pistol and shot Beverly Wells twice in the chest. I watched in horror as her expression turned to shock and a large red stain spread across the front of her shirt. This young girl, who could've just as easily been my own daughter, collapsed to the ground and rolled to her back.

I dropped my own gun and scrambled toward her, begging her not to die. Achilles was confused and didn't know what to do. I told him to sit and he obeyed. When I reached Beverly, I ripped off my shirt and rolled it into a ball and applied pressure to her bullet wounds.

"Hang on, kid," I said, my voice betraying my trepidation. "Please don't die!"

She reached out with her good hand, begging me for help. "Please, I don't want to die!"

"You won't," I promised. "Just hang on."

Blood seeped through my shirt and onto my hand. There was too much of it and I knew I was losing her. "Come on, Beverly, stay with me!"

But it was no use. The light slowly left her eyes. I shook her, but she didn't respond. I quickly shoved two fingers to her neck. There was no pulse. I grabbed my radio from my back pocket and called desperately for an ambulance, then immediately began CPR.

I don't know how long I did CPR before a scream sounded from down the street. I turned in that direction and saw Anne Wells running from the direction of the kids' grandpa's house. Her face was twisted in terror and she was pumping her legs as fast as they would go.

Achilles had whipped around when she screamed and he was studying her with bad intentions. Afraid that he would view her actions as an attack on me, I hollered at him to sit and stay. He did as he was told, but his eyes were fixed like lasers on Anne as she rounded the corner by the driveway and raced into the yard.

"What happened?" she asked, screaming the question.

I saw the realization hit her as her gaze took in the scene: me, wearing nothing but my pants and a ballistic vest with a bullet lodged in the front of it, Beverly lying on the ground with two bullet holes in her chest, and two pistols on the ground at our feet.

Anne clutched her throat with pale hands. "Dear Lord, you killed my baby girl!"

Her shock soon turned to anger and the scene erupted in chaos as she launched an attack of fists and elbows, all of them aimed at my face. I didn't even try to fend off her attack, feeling like I deserved it. Even if I wanted to block her strikes, I couldn't because I was too busy trying to keep Achilles from eating her.

Although I knew she was a grieving mother and I was willing to take my medicine, Achilles was having none of it. He lunged and snapped at her repeatedly while I got socked in the face multiple times. I managed to hold him at bay for the most part, but she screamed in pain several times and I knew he had gotten a bite or two in.

After what seemed like hours, screeching tires and blaring sirens pulled into the yard. I caught sight of Amy rushing over and jerking Anne roughly away from me. I called out for her to be gentle, that the woman didn't know what she was doing. Susan brushed by me and dropped to her knees near Beverly, quickly assessed the young girl's condition. I knew it was too late when she didn't even begin CPR.

As Amy dragged a handcuffed and angry Anne to her patrol car, Susan stood and stared wide-eyed around the scene.

"What in God's name happened out here, Clint?" she asked.

I stared down at Beverly's young and lifeless body and tears came to my eyes. I'd lost my daughter at the hands of another, and now Smitty and Anne Wells had lost their daughter at my hands. I knew the circumstances were vastly different, but it didn't make me feel any better about myself.

"Hell happened here, Sue," I said in a choked voice. "Pure hell."

CHAPTER 41

One week later…

I was sitting on the backyard swing at home with Achilles when I heard a door slam from the driveway. I knew it was Susan getting off of work, and she knew I'd be in the back yard, so I just sat there waiting for her to join us. After killing Beverly Wells, I'd decided to take a few days away from work to clear my mind and to let the investigation into the shooting unfold.

Achilles jumped from the swing and rushed to the gate, where he plopped to his butt and waited for Susan to appear. But when I heard the side door to the house slam shut, I realized she'd gone inside first.

"It's okay, big man," I said, turning to watch two squirrels chase each other around a tree, "she'll be out here before you know it."

I guess he didn't believe me, because he returned to the swing and jumped up beside me. I reached over and rubbed his neck. For the umpteenth time, I thanked him for saving my life. As usual when I spoke to him, he had this befuddled expression on his face as though he didn't think it had been such a big deal. It was one of the reasons I loved him—he was humble.

I pulled my cell phone from my pocket and checked to see if I'd received any new messages. I hadn't. Rather than sitting around doing nothing during my time away from work, I'd decided to go around town helping fellow townsfolk with the cleanup effort. Not only was I doing a good service, but it helped to get my mind off of young Beverly Wells. I found that working with my hands was the best way to clear my mind. Instead of thinking about my problems, I focused all of my thoughts and energy into the job in front of me.

Today, that job had entailed tearing down an old shed for a young couple who had a newborn baby. The father had been forced to return to work as soon as the electricity had been restored to the town, and he hadn't had time to deal with the destroyed shed. The wife was still laid up from giving birth to a ten-pound baby boy and she couldn't do anything about the wreckage.

"What happened to your arm?" Susan asked when she finally joined Achilles and me in the back yard. She lifted my wrist and gingerly rubbed the long cut on the back of my forearm. "Did you even clean it off?"

While the bruise on my head from the flying tree branch and the cuts on my face from my exploding truck window were beginning to heal, I'd earned a new round of injuries from today's work.

"I washed most of the blood off," I said, "but that's about it."

"Come inside so I can clean you off." Like a stern mother who was tired of her son hurting himself, she pulled me into the house and down the hall to the bathroom. Once I was sitting on the counter and she was standing in front of me with a bottle of peroxide, she said, "Tell me about your day."

"Did the lab results come in?" I asked, ignoring her question. I'd received word that the lab report from the blowback in the Ruger GP100 revolver was in.

"Damn, you're all business all the time, aren't you?" Susan told me the results did come in and they proved that Elizabeth Bankston had, indeed, been shot with Smitty Wells' stolen gun. "Also, the lab wasn't able to recover anything from the damaged hard drive and I got the sheriff's office report from the shooting."

"Oh, yeah?" I tried to act nonchalant about it, but my insides were having fits. I didn't know if the sheriff's office detectives who had handled the shooting investigation or the district attorney's office would have a problem with me shooting a human to protect my dog's life or not, and that had caused me some anxious moments. "What did they conclude?"

"They called it a righteous shooting; that you acted in self-defense."

I expelled the air I'd been inadvertently holding. "Really?"

"Yep."

I breathed a long sigh of relief, but asked about their reasoning just to be sure.

"They concluded that Beverly had already shot you once, so when she swung the gun in your direction, you had no way of knowing if she was going to shoot you or Achilles." Susan poured peroxide directly onto my wound, using a towel to catch the runoff. "The district attorney's office said they'll bring it to a grand jury, but they don't have a problem with what you did."

"Has Kevin Shelton bonded out of jail yet?" I had booked Kevin on charges of felony carnal knowledge of a juvenile and accessory after the fact to second degree murder. With any luck, the man would never get out of jail again.

"No," Susan said. "His wife went to stay with her sister and they're refusing to put up any money for his bail."

That pleased me, but something in Susan's expression gave me pause. "What's going on?" I asked. "You look troubled by something."

"We got a threatening phone call at the office today." She frowned. "It came in right as I was leaving."

When she didn't continue, I asked, "Who was it and what did they say?"

"The number was blocked. They said you're going to pay dearly for killing Beverly Wells. They said you'll pay with your life." She clenched her fists. "When I find out who it is—"

"I'm not worried about any threats." I cocked my head to the side, much the same as Achilles did when I talked to him. "There's something else you're not telling me."

Susan licked her lips and reached a hand in the back pocket of her shorts. She hadn't wasted any time getting out of her uniform, and I'd taken notice.

"Well?" I asked when she paused with her hand behind her back. "What is it?"

She moved her hand to the front and held up a white plastic object that was about four inches long. I studied the object, noting that there was a pee stick on one end and two tiny windows on the side facing me. In one of the windows there was a symbol. I leaned closer to see. It was a "+" sign.

"No way!" I jumped to my feet, sending the peroxide bottle flying across the room. "You're pregnant?"

"Yep!" She was beaming now. "We're going to have a baby!"

I wrapped her in my arms and squeezed tight. As we held each other, I considered the threat on my life, and remembered the Bible verse about living and dying by the sword. I knew I would probably end up on the wrong end of a bullet someday while doing my job. Hell, it was the nature of the beast. I lived by the gun, so then, I would probably die by the gun.

"I just hope it doesn't happen for at least twenty-five or thirty years," I said silently, "because I'd love to live long enough to see my kids graduate from college and go off on their own."

BJ Bourg

BJ Bourg is an award-winning mystery writer and former professional boxer who hails from the swamps of Louisiana. Dubbed the "real deal" by other mystery writers, he has spent his entire adult life solving crimes as a patrol cop, detective sergeant, and chief investigator for a district attorney's office. Not only does he know his way around crime scenes, interrogations, and courtrooms, but he also served as a police sniper commander (earning the title of "Top Shooter" at an FBI sniper school) and a police academy instructor.

BJ is a four-time traditionally-published novelist (his debut novel, JAMES 516, won the 2016 EPIC eBook Award for Best Mystery) and dozens of his articles and stories have been published in national magazines such as Woman's World, Boys' Life, and Writer's Digest. He is a regular contributor to two of the nation's leading law enforcement magazines, Law and Order and Tactical Response, and he has taught at conferences for law enforcement officers, tactical police officers, and writers. Above all else, he is a father and husband, and the highlight of his life is spending time with his beautiful wife and wonderful children.

http://www.bjbourg.com